DECEIVED

A Sam McClellan Tale

LAURA S. WHARTON

Deceived
A Sam McClellan Tale
© 2015 by Laura S. Wharton

All Rights Reserved. No part of this book may be used or reproduced in any manner whatsoever without the expressed written permission of the author. The characters and event portrayed in this book are fictitious. Any similarity to real persons, living or dead, is coincidental and not intended by the author.

Address all inquiries to:
Broad Creek Press
253 Farmbrook Road
Mt. Airy, NC 27030

Wharton, Laura S.
Deceived/by Laura S. Wharton
Mt. Airy, NC: Broad Creek Press, 2015

813.54
p. cm – (Deceived)
Summary: With the help of sassy sidekick Molly Monroe and other well-rounded characters, Detective Sam McClellan uncovers a vast drug network which winds its way through the resort beach towns of North Carolina.

Print Book ISBN: 978-0-9904662-4-6
[1. Thriller—Fiction. 2. Adventure—Fiction. 3. North Carolina—Fiction. 4. Sailing—Fiction.]
Printed in the United States of America

DEDICATION

For John and Darlene.
Truth is often stranger than fiction.

—LSW

OTHER NOVELS BY LAURA S. WHARTON

Award-winning novels for Young Adults and Adults:

Stung! A Sam McClellan Tale
In Julia's Garden, A Lily McGuire Mystery
Leaving Lukens
The Pirate's Bastard

Award-winning mysteries for Children:

Mystery at the Lake House #1: Monsters Below
Mystery at the Lake House #2: The Mermaid's Tale
Mystery at the Lake House #3: The Secret of the Compass
Mystery at the Phoenix Festival
The Wizard's Quest

All titles are available as print and e-books.
To learn more about Laura's other books,
visit www.LauraWhartonBooks.com

CHAPTER ONE

"My partner Lee was lighting another cigarette. I saw the glow when I came out of the store with these Fritos," said Sam McClellan. He waved the crushed bag in the cop's face as the man wrote down Sam's account of the incident. "God, how I hated his stinking up my car." Sam blinked back glistening tears in the nearly abandoned Circle K's glaring lights. This particular gas station was just outside Wilmington, North Carolina, near the town of Navassa.

"What happened next, Sam?" The Navassa officer waited patiently for Sam to tell his story as a flurry of activity surrounded Sam's black Chevy Blazer, its passenger door hanging from one hinge thanks to an over-zealous rescue attempt. Crime scene investigators buzzed about like flies as they collected evidence: samples of shattered glass, samples of blood on the dark seat, and a hunk of matted hair and mangled flesh dangling from the steering wheel. Sam knew that from here on out, it was just procedure. Different police force, same rules.

"We were on our way back from dropping a bunch of kids off at their homes. Lee's car wouldn't hold them all after a day of bowling, so I volunteered to help get them home. The kids were friends of Lee's, I guess. I didn't ask. He just needed a ride for all of them, so I obliged. After that, we stopped here to grab a snack before I drove him back to the bowling alley to get his car. Then, I dunno. All of a sudden, I heard the explosion of gunfire, and Lee's head was…gone. Just like that." He snapped his fingers for effect. "I raced out here, but I was too late."

"Do you have any idea who would want him gone?" the officer asked without looking up from his notebook. Sam didn't like the tone of this guy's voice. Sam didn't know his name, didn't even bother to look at his nametag above his pocket. He just knew he hated this particular cop for his show of disrespect toward a fellow officer, even if he was from a different town.

"No." Sam made no attempt to hide his disgust.

"Did you see the shooter's car?"

"I was focused on Lee, so I didn't see anything," Sam muttered. "But I heard it. A souped-up muscle car. It idled real rough." He'd file that sound away in his brain. He didn't have a choice: the sound still rang in his ears, and Sam knew he'd never forget it.

The officer scribbled some other notes before telling Sam to stick around.

"Like I've got any place to go," quipped Sam, wondering whether the officer now trotting away toward the police car could feel the daggers Sam was mentally hurling into his back. Noticing the bag of Fritos still gripped in his hand, Sam threw it to the ground in disgust.

Finding a curb to wait at, Sam fought back the tears he felt welling up behind his eyes. He'd known Lee Elliott since their police training camp days. When they both wound up on the same force, in the sleepy seaside town of Carolina Beach just up the road from the more frenetic Wrightsville Beach, it was natural they became partners. They had hung out on their off-duty hours and enjoyed tinkering around on their sailboats. Sam snorted when remembering how Lee had helped him hook up a new propane stove amid jokes of things that go *boom* on boats, and Sam was grateful Lee was there for him through a rough patch in his life. Sam had few friends, and the last one he had was dead. Now he had to face Jenny. What was he going to tell her?

By the time the tow truck came, Sam was wired on his third cup of black coffee. He accepted a ride as far as the marina where he docked his live-aboard sailboat. As soon as the patrol car, which gave him a ride to the marina, left the parking lot, Sam did too. He practiced what he would say to Jenny as he walked to the beachfront home she had shared with Lee. No matter what he whispered, though, nothing sounded like the right thing to say. He supposed nothing ever would.

CHAPTER TWO

Jenny won't be expecting me, Sam thought, *but she might worry that Lee didn't call in to let her know he was on his way.* It was about eight blocks to the beach condo. Sam knew the route well, but he stopped short one block away from Jenny's home when he saw two unmarked police cars already in the driveway. One was from the Carolina Beach office. Sam didn't recognize the other.

Sam made his way toward the condo through another's backyard and snugged up close to the beachfront screened porch, thinking that's where Jenny would most likely be this evening, but he heard Jenny sobbing in the living room, caught up in one officer's explanation of what he thought had happened and congratulating her on her husband's bravery. Adjacent to the screen door was a window to a small den; through the window, Sam could see somebody was rifling through the desk and closet.

"What the...?" Sam caught his voice before a sound escaped his lips. Making his way back to the front of the condo, Sam knocked before entering.

"Hi, Jenny!" he called as he entered the condo's main room. "I came as soon as I could." Sam walked directly to Jenny and hugged her tightly. When he released her, she sat robotically on the sofa.

"Word travels fast," he said to Andy Keller, a fellow Carolina Beach officer, who stood to leave.

"Yeah, I picked it up on the scanner, Sam. Got over here as soon as I could." He made his way to the door. "Glad to see you're okay, man. Never know about the crazies anymore."

"Have you heard anything? Why?" Sam's question was unanswered.

"Don't know," Andy said. "Chief's going to want answers, though. You want me to give you a ride to the marina?"

"No," Sam said. "I'll sit with Jenny a while." Sam listened for movement in the den, but he heard none.

"It's okay, Sam," Jenny said haltingly. "I've called my neighbor to come be with me, so you go with him."

"Call if you need me," Sam said, his eyes searching Jenny's for evidence of shock.

"I will…I think I'd really just like to be alone now, though."

Sam hugged her, then got up to leave. He made an excuse of needing a glass of water so he could peek into the den. All he saw was a window left wide open. He went in to close it, and to search for clues, but he found none. Looking at the rest of the room, nothing seemed out of place. *What was Lee into that would cause this kind of a ruckus?*

"Come on, Sam," said Andy when he returned to the living room. "I'll give you a ride." Sam mulled over why there could have been another policeman at Jenny's, but he decided not to broach the subject with Andy—just yet. Call it shock, call it mistrust. Sam wasn't willing to consider what the nagging voice in the back of his mind was telling him, though.

When Andy dropped him off at the marina, Sam made his way down the floating ramp to his dock at a fast clip to his boat—his home. His live aboard boat looked like it had been tossed and pummeled by a rogue wave: the hatch boards had been ripped off of their hinges, his propane stove on the stern railing was upside down, and each of the cockpit cushions Sam had just finished re-covering in a smart Persian green Sumbrella fabric were slashed to ribbons.

Down below, things looked worse. The salon settee table was torn from the bulkhead, all of his books were off their shelves, and the finely-cut teak fiddles that had so neatly held them in place were splinters. Every bit of food Sam had stored in box compartments under both bunks was strewn around the galley and salon, and the PVC pipes under the galley sink were slashed.

"They were thorough," Sam said to no one as he started to pick up the mess in the salon. "Wonder what *they* think I have?"

By the time he found his clock in a pile on the salon floor, he saw it was four o'clock in the morning. He pushed the books off the V-berth and fell into a fitful sleep.

CHAPTER THREE

Three hours passed. Sam's cell phone woke him.

"Come on in, Sam. We need to talk."

Rumpled, Sam started on the three-block walk to police station. Any other time, such a walk in the moist sea air would have been almost pleasant, the marina's halyards clanging like wind chimes. This early morning walk was labored.

A blast of cold air slammed Sam in the face when he opened the door to the overly air-conditioned building for a hastily called morning meeting with the Chief of Police, Dan Singleton.

"Sam, I've looked over the reports and talked with the officers. We still don't see the leads. The media folks are all over this one. They want a suspect, and so do we. Do you have any idea what this was about?"

"We weren't onto anything, Chief. Just the regular stuff, nothing major."

"Word is that Lee was caught up in some sort of love triangle gone bad. Know anything about that?"

"Lee? No way! He and Jenny were tight." Sam rubbed his unshaven angular jaw and leaned back in the wooden chair, rocking it back on its legs to the point of danger. "I can't believe there'd be anything to that. Is that what the guys think?"

"Nah; we're thinking it's a random act of violence. We're gonna get the killer, regardless of the scenario. I just wanted to know as much as I could before getting started. I got a call into the Wilmington office, too. They'll want to help, if they can."

Dan stood up and reached for his coat. Even though he was shorter than Sam's 6'2" lean frame, his bulk made him appear bigger.

"Have to go address the team now. There will be a service for Lee later this week. If you need to, take a few days off. You look like you could use some rest." The chief stepped briskly out of the cool of his office and disappeared down the hall to the conference room.

"I don't need rest," Sam muttered. "I need answers."

Walking slowly to the conference room, Sam felt the grip of grief around his neck. He braced himself for the meeting to come by leaning against the doorjamb. Not wanting the attention he was sure would follow, he preferred to stay to the back of the small pale-blue tactics room now crowded with fellow officers. Stoic, they listened as their chief cited how a valiant officer had fallen—one of the brothers who sought to fight crime on the streets of Carolina Beach—for no apparent reason.

"Lee Elliott was a good man, a good husband, and a good officer. He stood for what was right, and he tried to make things better for the people he met. We all knew

Lee as a diligent cop, but what some of you may not know about Lee is that in the years he's been here, he's gotten involved with the community through charity work. In his off hours, he gave talks at some of the high schools to help keep kids off drugs. He regularly attended church, and he enjoyed taking teens out on his boat to show them there was more to life than just hanging out, looking for trouble. His efforts helped to keep our town safe. That's why his death is such a punch in the face. Not only have we lost one of our own, but the community has lost a treasure." Dan measured his words for effect.

"If anyone has information about why this happened, we need to know now so we can nab the killer," Dan stated plainly. He sat down heavily and took a sip from a glass of water at the head of the table. "Meeting adjourned," he said quietly.

The officers left the room solemnly. Some did not make eye contact with Sam, while others stopped momentarily to rest a hand on his sagging shoulders. No words were needed now.

Sam left the building without purpose. His boat was a wreck, his car was impounded, and his best friend was dead. "What did Lee have that somebody wanted?" he pondered.

Before long, he found himself a block away from Jenny's. He crossed over to the beach and slowly stepped through the soft sand closest to the diminishing dunes. Every time a storm ripped through here, the beach lost a little more ground to the ocean. Often, while Lee and Sam had enjoyed the view of tourists roasting like pecans on the beach just steps away from his screened porch, Lee had said that fragile ecosystems like these barrier islands seemed to be magnets for three things: hurricanes, developers, and nuts. "All the nuts roll downhill to the coast," Lee had joked.

Sam happened to think he was right. As the sun peeked over the ocean's dark gray edge, Sam saw a few tourists already lining the beach with their obnoxiously bright coolers, towels, and umbrellas. May was warming up fast. It wouldn't be long before the road was bumper-to-bumper with traffic and the beach was filled with visitors who all wished *they* were locals. *Little do they know,* Sam thought.

Jenny was sitting on the porch, one leg slung over the arm of the wide wicker chair and the other planted on the floor. Sam waved as he approached her.

Jenny unenthusiastically waved back, then absent-mindedly ran her fingers through her short curly blond hair. Coming closer, Sam noticed a thin line of rubber laying across her legs. On the floor was a pie cutter-like tool.

"Hey, Jen, just wanted to see how you were doing today," Sam called through the door. "What are you doing?"

"Lee had a long list of honey-do's around here, so I thought I might as well get to them this morning, seeing as how I need something to do to keep my mind off of… things." She got up and unlatched the screen door to let him in. "The only problem is I don't know how to do half of what's on his list. Take this, for instance." She pointed at the top of the door where a screen was partially blown out. "Am I supposed to pull the whole door off its hinges and take it apart, or can I fix it while it's on there? That's why these things were on his list, not mine." She collapsed in the chair again and started sobbing, her eyes already puffy and red.

Sam focused on the door so as not to join in her distress. He gently took the rubber strip out of her clutch and began to repair the door while she cried. Once it was done, he pulled up a white plastic chair and sat down beside her.

"Jen, there are no words I can tell you right now that will make things better. Lee was a good man and a good friend. I miss him too." Sam gently placed his hand on Jenny's shoulder, and she put hers on top of his hand.

"Thanks, Sam. When Andy came last night, he said you couldn't come by. But you and Lee were together. Do you know what happened?" She was hopeful.

"No, I really haven't had a chance to look into things yet, but I promise you I will find out who did this, Jen." He hesitated before continuing. "Jen, when I walked up to your condo last night, I thought I heard somebody in your den looking for something in the desk drawer. I couldn't see who it was in the darkness. Had you asked Andy to get something for you?"

Jenny looked puzzled. "I…don't think so. Andy was with me."

Not wanting to alarm Jenny, Sam changed his tack. "I must have been seeing things."

"Why did this happen, Sam?" Jenny asked pointedly, as if hearing the news of her husband's death for the first time.

"That's the thing. Lee and I weren't working on anything major, so I thought maybe he had told you about something he had going on."

Jenny shook her head and wiped at her eyes with the sleeve of her bright yellow T-shirt. "We had a policy around here about him not telling me how his day was. I really didn't want to know anything more than when he was coming home." Jenny looked down at her hands, then up at the fixed screen door. "We were talking about fixing this place up to see what we could get for it, so he sometimes kept a list of what he was going to do to bring a higher price." Jenny paused, then continued. "We were thinking maybe it was time for a house, with a yard. We were thinking, you know, about starting a family." Sam knew, all right. Lee had talked with him frequently about what it would be like to raise a child on the beach. It might be fun, sure, but Lee was fearful of a toddler running out of the screened door and into the ocean before Jenny or Lee could get to the child. Sam and Lee had been part of one too many rescue efforts to know those sorts of accidents happened all the time.

Jenny got up and walked to the screen door. She ran her hands over the smoothed edge of screen that just moments before was rough. "Thank you for fixing that,

Sam. I do appreciate it." She walked into the condo, and Sam followed.

It took a minute for his eyes to adjust to the darkness and to see that Jenny had crossed the living room and disappeared into the den.

"It doesn't look like anyone's been in here, Sam. Are you sure you saw somebody?"

Sam entered the den. There was nothing out of place, nothing disturbed. "Yeah, I know what I saw. Do you see anything that looks…weird?"

"No, Sam. Everything looks the way it did yesterday afternoon when I was in here doing the bookkeeping." She opened the top desk drawer and pulled out a folder full of bills to be paid. In the drawers below were files filled with statements and paid invoices. "There's not anything in here worth getting shot over, Sam; I can tell you that. Lee earned just barely enough for us to live on while I worked on my paintings, but he insisted I keep at it. He encouraged me to pursue what I loved, and so I tried to make things easier for him by tending to tasks he didn't like to do…like paying the bills."

"What about his to-do list? Where do you think he put that last?" Sam watched Jenny move to the closet in a smaller room, her studio. He watched as she looked in the closet filled with tools.

"This closet was his workshop," she smiled. "We thought the next house should have a bigger garage so he could have some real woodworking equipment. We love living on the beach…." She caught herself, stopped, and started again. "I love living on the beach, but now, I don't think I can stay in this place without him." She paused and then rooted around on the makeshift shelves on cinderblocks that held Lee's tools, tennis balls, and racquet, and some spare parts for their boat. "He kept his list of stuff to do for the boat in here, and a second one of projects he wanted to complete on our condo. Here's the boat book," Jenny produced a small green journal with a photo of their 1989 thirty-foot Catalina *Stormy Monday* on it. Flipping through tattered pages, she tossed it to Sam.

"What will you do with *Stormy*, Jen?" Sam asked as he reviewed the maintenance log for the boat's engine, glanced a few pages further to see the fuel and radio logs, and then closed the book.

"I really hadn't thought about it yet. There's too much to think about. I just wish…." She turned back to the closet shelves, now digging furiously through Lee's duffle bag, then his toolbox. "Here. Here's the condo list." Jenny held up a small, royal blue spiral-bound notepad, and handed it to Sam.

Sam immediately recognized it. He'd seen it dozens of times before, peeping out of Lee's shirt pocket when they went to the local hardware store to get supplies for various projects.

Most of the pages were filled with scratched off projects. Sam remembered helping Lee with many of them: rebuilding the small steps and deck with the outside shower; installing privacy partitions around the shower to keep the wind, sand, and curious eyes off Jenny (she liked to shower outside after swimming each day in the ocean); regrouting the tiles in the master bathroom's shower. Lee was meticulous about keeping all receipts for supplies, and they were stapled to each of the separate project pages.

"Do you think there's something there, Sam?"

She looks tired, Sam thought. "I don't know. Would you mind if I held on to it for a few days?"

"Take it. Take the boat book, too. Oh, the boat! Sam, I completely forgot about it. Would you mind checking on it? I haven't been there in a few weeks. We were going to get it ready for the season this coming weekend, but I don't have the heart to go see *Stormy* now."

Sam nodded.

Jenny felt around the inside of the closet door for the keys to the padlock on the boat's hatch boards. "Thanks, Sam; I appreciate it." She gulped and tears welled up in her eyes again. Sam pulled Jenny to him in a bear hug. It was the only thing he could think to do. "I'll be here if you need me." He patted her on the back gently until she stopped crying. "Call me if you need anything, Jen. I'm only a few blocks away, so I can be here in no time flat."

She nodded, and they walked silently to the back door. "Thanks for coming, Sam. Would you do me one favor?"

"Anything."

"Find whoever made me a widow."

Sam nodded and closed the screen door quietly behind him. Jenny's words echoed in his ears all the way back to the marina.

Sam walked past his slip and six more boats to *Stormy Monday*, her deep blue hull gleaming in the mid-morning sun. The hatch boards were locked in place. Sam opened them and saw that the boat's interior was straight, just the way Lee would have left it after a day of sailing. Everything was put away where it was supposed to be, and Sam envied the boat's tidiness. He sighed, then climbed up the companionway steps and replaced the hatch boards and lock.

Stepping back aboard his own boat, Sam threw the two little notepads on a shelf over the galley sink and changed his clothes. He opened all the hatches, popped in an old cassette tape of Elmore James, and got to work putting his boat back in order. As he worked, he tried to recount every call he and Lee had investigated over the past year, but he could think of nothing that would get Lee killed or his boat tossed. But then what were "they" looking for? Who were "they"? Why wasn't Lee's boat tossed, instead of his?

Once he got the salon and galley back in place, he made himself a turkey sandwich, grabbed a Foster's from the top-loading refrigerator, and reviewed the two notebooks. Maybe one held a clue.

CHAPTER FOUR

For the next few days, Sam reviewed every page of the boat book, searching for irregular comments about engine repairs, notations in the radio log, or errant comments in cruising notes. Lee was a safety-conscientious sailor and routinely maintained all systems aboard *Stormy Monday*. He had upgraded the battery banks to handle a new refrigerator, added small solar panels to keep a charge on the batteries when he and Jenny anchored out on their weekend cruises, and took exceptional notes in his engineer-like block printing of all boating-related activities. "Anal retentive," Lee used to claim about his habit of writing everything down, but there was nothing unexpected or irrelevant in the boat book.

"Anybody home?" a voice called out from the dock.

Startled, Sam quickly put the books on the settee beside him and threw a dish towel over them. "Yeah. Oh, hi, Chuck." Sam waved him aboard as he climbed up the companionway stairs. "You want a beer?"

The boat rocked as Chuck Owens clamored over the safety lines and under the cockpit's covering bimini. "No thanks, man; I'm still on duty. I just stopped by to check on you. I don't know how you can possibly live aboard, Sam; you got to be a damn contortionist just to get on the boat!" Chuck's 280-pound bulk made the otherwise spacious cockpit seem small as he plopped down on one of the cushions. Noting the torn cloth, he let out a low whistle. "Wow, you must have some kinda cat on board."

"Yeah, a large cat with attitude," Sam sneered, sitting opposite Chuck, stretching his long legs across to the molded seat on the cockpit's other side. Not interested in volunteering information, he steered the conversation. "Any thoughts on what happened?"

"No, Sam. Dan's got half the department on it, so you can rest easy that there will be an answer. We all want to know. Have you been to see Jenny yet?"

"Yeah, and I've checked on her some over the last few days. She's trying to stay busy, Chuck. She appreciated that Andy stopped by that night. Sorry I couldn't be there myself. I just wasn't ready to face her," Sam hedged a bit.

"Understood, brother. Understood."

"She's in shock, I think. She said the service is going to be tomorrow, you know. It's just so hard to think that Lee's…gone. You know he was a straight shooter. Nothing going on that Jenny knew of, and nothing I didn't know about, either. Lee was just a good cop and a good husband. Now without him, Jenny is facing selling that condo. I suspect she'll find work to keep her busy, but it would be such a shame for her to have to give up her painting."

"She any good?" Chuck quizzed.

"I like her work. Mostly boat and beach scenes, the kind that tourists like to take home."

"You know, my wife Lisa could probably arrange something, maybe a show, since she owns the Blue Moon Gallery."

"That'd be great. Let me know if I can help."

"No, Sam, I'll take care of it. You take a few days off and rest. Maybe think about getting rid of the big cat, too." Chuck winked as he stepped gingerly under the bimini and over the life lines, holding on to whatever he could grab to steady himself as he wobbled onto the dock.

"I'll be waiting for you in the marina's parking lot at ten tomorrow morning, Sam. Call if you need anything between now and then."

"Will do," Sam called back. Sam liked Chuck. He seemed like a good cop, but at this point, Sam thought it wise not to trust anyone explicitly.

Sam headed below again to the notepad of condo projects. After a few pages, he was sure there was nothing there that didn't belong. As he tossed the notepad back on the table, though, it flipped over and the back cover opened up to reveal some numbers written on the back of the last page. The slanted, loopy handwriting wasn't Lee's.

"2118717," Sam whispered. He reached for his cell phone and dialed 211-8717. An annoying three-tone sound followed by a mechanical voice told him he had reached a number that was not in service, and that he should try again. Then he searched the notepad from the back, flipping pages forward. A few pages from the back was a single word hastily scribbled: "seacock."

"That should have been in the boat journal," Sam thought as he continued flipping through the rest of the pad, but he found nothing else. After rooting around a drawer for a plastic baggie and heavy duty duct tape, Sam removed the companionway stairs from their position and placed them on the salon floor halfway into the V-berth so he could get to the engine compartment. Once the bulkhead-mounted light was on, he crawled into the tight space and taped the notebooks in the sealed baggie on a three-inch wide shelf directly above the starboard water tank. This shelf usually held his tools or an extra lamp when he worked on the engine, its flanged lip keeping most anything from falling into the black bilge below. Sam backed out of the engine room, turned off the light, closed the door, and repositioned the companionway stairs.

Sitting in the cockpit, Sam looked around at his boat. "Deck needs to be repainted. Toe rails need to be caulked and sanded. And the rub rail needs to be replaced. Sheesh." He thought about going to the hardware store to buy a bucket of paint. The sky changed from its deep, clear Carolina blue of spring to a hazy peachy-pink of evening while Sam sat contemplating boat projects and seacocks. Lee hadn't mentioned this as a task on *Stormy Monday*, but then again, he hadn't mentioned the loopy numbers or the person who wrote them. They looked like a woman's handwriting.

Tomorrow would be the service for Lee. Sam thought about the day ahead and headed below to spit-shine his shoes. "Not for anybody else, Lee, would I do this," he muttered as he dug out the rarely used shoeshine kit from a locker's depths.

CHAPTER FIVE

The following day dawned shrouded in mist. "Appropriate," Sam thought, as he got into Chuck's waiting car. Sam's own car was still impounded, and he figured it might be released to him today, though he felt it would be best to drive it to the nearest used car lot and unload it. Sam was not ordinarily a superstitious man, but driving a car tinged with Lee's death was not his idea of good karma.

"Morning, Sam. What a day this is going to be." Chuck was monotone as he looked straight ahead, still seated behind the wheel of his Ford Taurus.

"I hear ya," was all Sam could say.

They drove in silence until they reached the Blue Moon Gallery. Sam saw Chuck's wife, Lisa, waving furiously with one hand as she locked the front door with the other.

"Hello, Sam." Lisa hugged Sam as he held open the car's door for her. "This is all so sad. I was just telling Chuck the other day that I looked forward to his retirement. This is such a dangerous job; I fear for him every single day." Lisa seemed to be the champion of the motor-mouth speedway as she illuminated Sam and Chuck on the potential hazards of their line of work. Her mouth only came to a stop when they reached the church.

Sam saw the beach's entire police force, plus a few uniforms he knew were from Wilmington and Southport. He spotted Jenny being escorted by Andy Keller into a small "chapel" room that appeared to be full to capacity between its pale green walls. Sam watched as Jenny clutched Andy's arm for support as if a strong gust of wind might blow her through the open windows at any minute.

Lee's parents sat in the front row, and his brother, Larry, was there to offer support to his mother. Larry and Lee had never gotten along, Sam knew, and on the few occasions he had met Larry, Sam didn't care too much for Larry's bad attitude either. It seemed Larry felt entitled to more than his share of life, yet he wasn't willing to do much to get it. Having spent years overseas with a big corporation gave him an attitude that he was somehow better than his only brother. On the rare occasions when he came to town, he gloated about his big house in New Jersey, and his trophy wife (who could never be bothered with coming to North Carolina to visit), and his shiny black Jaguar.

But when the corporation went belly up, he served time for embezzling corporate funds. Once he got out, he was no less humbled and let everyone he met know that the world "owed" him even more. He lost his big house, his fine car, and his trophy wife all in a matter of months. So he now sponged off of his parents, living in a small, one-room "cottage" on their property. He expected his mother to cook for him, and he didn't lift a finger to help out around the house. He was sure the "next deal" would put him back on top of the world. Of course, it never came.

Sam recognized a few others who filed in solemnly: in addition to the police force, town officials, and support staff for the city of Carolina Beach, there was Edgar Reese, the owner of the Crow's Nest Diner, Lee's favorite place to grab lunch.

And here was Jenny's best friend, Sally Hinton, with whom Jenny had tried to set Sam up several times. *Sure,* thought Sam, *she's hot—nice figure, but she's like a cheerleader on a mega-dose of caffeine.* Today was a case in point: Sally nearly mowed down three people to get to Jenny, embracing her and coddling her as Jenny rigidly sat down on a small pew right near the front of the room.

The line of people entering the chapel was long, filled with more friends and members of Lee's church. Lee had been well-liked, Sam judged, by the number of folks who entered through the door.

Everyone who could get to a pew was seated, and the rest stood along the back of the room. Sam sat in the row behind Jenny, and he placed a hand on her stiff shoulder as the service began.

The minister was polite and practiced as he greeted his guests and wished everyone peace. He soon relinquished the short podium to one after another speaker, each of whom had something to say about Lee Elliott. The phrases "good man" and "pillar" were often recited.

After the fourth person got up to speak, Sam felt nauseous. He held on for the ride as long as he could. Mercifully, it ended with Jenny being presented Lee's badge, a flag, and a small mock-brass container of ashes, all that was left of Lee.

Sam leaned over to help Jenny up, but Sally shot him a mother-bear look that almost included teeth, so Sam backed off and made his way out of the building.

The morning clouds were starting to burn off. People milled around outside with their own thoughts. Edgar offered a reception of sorts at his diner, and many funeral participants looked relieved to have someplace to go. Those police on duty declined, and the rest drove willingly after Edgar.

"Sam, do you want a ride to the Crow's Nest?" Andy called over his shoulder as he helped Jenny into his unmarked car. Sally was already in the backseat, and Sam could see her soothing Jenny as soon as she got in.

"No, thanks. I don't have the stomach for any more of this today." Sam waved him off.

Sam watched as the parking lot emptied, one car after another. Some of the people who had known Lee, and thus Sam by default, stopped to offer condolences to Sam before leaving. Sam braved a smile, but it was the last thing he felt like doing. He shook hands and nodded, tuning out the voices so that the words melted together into a single hum.

"Lee was killed because of this."

Sam felt it before he saw her, a slip of paper being pressed hard into his hand by the tall woman clothed in a stylish black suit, low-dipping hat, dark hose, and high heels.

He snapped to attention at her words, and he held her hand two seconds longer than any of the hands he'd shook of those who had come before her.

"What did you say?" Sam whispered as she quickly hugged him, as so many of the well-wishers had that morning. As he breathed in her smell of jasmine, he noticed a loose strand of black hair at the nape of her neck. He shoved the paper into his pocket, leaving his hand there so as not to call attention to the movement as he hugged her with the other arm.

She just pulled away and smiled, her deep burgundy lips parting slightly to reveal perfectly straight bright teeth. She turned and walked swiftly to her little red Miata convertible while fishing her keys out at the same time. Her sassy, swinging walk was unforgettable as she deftly maneuvered over the sidewalk, down the curb, and across the parking lot.

Sam wanted to go after her, but the line persisted. He was hugged and had his hand shaken for several minutes more as he watched the woman drive away.

Chuck and Lisa were last in line, hanging back a bit until the crowd subsided. "You need a lift back to that boat of yours?" Chuck asked. "Or do you want to come with us to the Crow's Nest? We probably won't stay that long, just long enough to get some lunch."

Feeling the note snuggly in his pocket, Sam declined. "Actually, I would prefer to go pick up my Blazer. Can you drop me by impound?"

"It isn't ready," the chief spoke up from behind Sam. "We need a little more time with it to fix the window for you, Sam. You'll have to get another set of wheels. Why don't you ride back to the station with me? I'm heading back there now, and I have a car that would work for you for a few days until yours is ready."

Lisa slipped her arm into Sam's. "We will bring him. I want more time with Sam," Lisa gushed. "We are both so sorry about Lee, Sam. I only met him at the office functions, but he seemed like a great guy." She cozied up to Sam as they walked toward the Owens' tan Ford Taurus wagon, telling him how she had insisted that she would never drive a "mommy van," but she needed the room for hauling her finds purchased at art and craft shows she frequented up and down the coast.

"Chuck tells me that Lee's wife is an artist. I don't think I've met her, but I would be glad to see her work. I'm planning to call her in a few weeks, you know, after all this…well, after she's had a little time to adjust. If she's willing, we could add her work to the gallery's selection and I could start representing her. You know, I have quite a following of locals and out-of-towners who make my gallery the first place they visit when they come to town or when they need something special."

Lisa continued her monologue all the way to the station, telling Sam more than he wanted to know about how the fine art and craft shows she visited impacted her sales over the years, and how her efforts in the gallery inspired local art collectors to look beyond what was normally considered art to encompass functional pieces of furnishings and décor. She, of course, had studied art history in college, she droned on, but when she and Chuck learned she was going to have twins, well, she just had to drop out of her art courses and focus quickly on business management courses before the babies came. She didn't regret taking the courses, but she wished she had stayed with her art. This gallery was a way she could be near the things she loved but could never afford, she said. Now that their sons were away in college, she was able to turn her attention to the gallery's collection, and she was eager to develop more of a following.

As Sam stepped out of the car, he saw Lisa waving vigorously as if she had found a new customer and lifelong friend. He imagined Chuck smirking at the idea of priceless works of art aboard Sam's boat.

Sam entered the station, signed the requisite paperwork, and walked out with a set of keys to the dark green Nissan Altima. Not exactly his style, but at least he had wheels. Sam drove to the marina and slid out of his uniform as soon as he entered the aft cabin.

He popped open the overhead hatches for some fresh air, feeling immediate relief in the stuffy cabin. Fishing for some shorts in one of the drawers, Sam took pleasure in the array of cabinets that banked both sides of the small space. He had gone to great lengths in tearing out the bunk that ran the width of the boat and designing a center-line bunk with cabinets, shelves, and drawers on either side of it. It took months to measure, cut, and install, but once it was done, Sam was pleased at his progress of making the old boat more functional and livable. He even crafted the bunk's base so that a section of it could be raised to access the rudder unit and stuffing box beneath it. And rather than the typical four-inch closed cell foam found on most boats' bunks, he added a custom-fitted, watertight full spring mattress found on larger, far more expensive yachts.

My carpentry skills aren't great, Sam thought as he pulled a green T-shirt from a drawer, *but they are certainly better than average. Besides, it's been a good project to focus on so I don't think about the divorce.*

The 1973 thirty-six-foot Morgan Out Island ketch had been beat up when Sam and Angel had bought it, but after three years of upgrading and renovating, the boat looked really good.

That's when Sam started messing around with a pretty young thing he met at the marina one afternoon while he was sanding his teak cockpit grates. He was only interested in flirting and a short break from his work, but the little brunette with a smaller bikini made it hard to stay focused on his task. At the time, Sam was fighting off the dread of turning forty. The lithe nymph thought nothing of stepping aboard uninvited. She made him feel like he was sixteen again, young and agile, eager to impress. After a full day of sailing and an unexplainable night anchored in a quiet stretch of the waterway behind Figure Eight Island, Sam knew Angel would not forgive him this time, no matter how much he begged.

"Last time I forgave you, Sam," Angel had said quietly as she packed a duffle bag for him. "This time, I can't. You will just do it again and again. Just because you still look like you're twenty doesn't mean you have to act that way whenever some little chickie winks at you. You have a problem, Sam. You need to deal with it. I don't."

She was right. And she was gone.

Not long after Sam moved aboard their boat, Angel sold their small house near Monkey Junction and moved to California to be closer to their only son Frank who was stationed in San Francisco.

Four years passed before Sam could get motivated to go sailing or even haul the boat for a much-needed bottom job. Now *Angel* was finally close to shipshape again. He'd meant to change the name on the stern, but he had never got around to it. "Maybe this year," he had told Lee.

Sam dug deep into his uniform's pants pocket and pulled out the carefully folded note. The loopy handwriting matched that of the note scribbled in the back of Lee's notepad.

It read, "Lee found out what was going on. He tried to help, and he got killed. They need to be stopped, but I don't know where Lee put the key. I'll be on the last ferry to Southport today." The note was not signed.

Key? Where? And to what?

After putting the note with the notebooks in the engine compartment, Sam slipped on his Teva sandals and locked the hatches. He drove to Jenny's to see about Lee's keychain, but she wasn't there. Looking at his watch, he saw that the day was zipping by and he hadn't eaten anything yet.

He headed to Bungie's Deli where he ordered a mile-high sub with everything on it and a cold tea. As Sam sat outside under the blue-striped umbrella, Andy drove up in his unmarked car. He was still dressed in his uniform.

"Hey, Sam. Sorry you missed the lunch. Edgar put on a real nice spread for us. I think he's going to miss one of his best customers." Andy sat down opposite Sam on the cement bench.

"Chuck tells me you are going to take a few days off. If you decide to go sailing and want some crew, let me know. I haven't taken my boat out in a while, so I would love to go if you're going. I'll see if I can get an afternoon off to join you."

"Thanks, Andy. I'll call you if I go out. Right now, I'm more interested in what happened."

"I hear ya, man. It's a tragedy. But Chief's got a few ideas, and he's working on this case. I spoke with him briefly after the service today and he's got that look in his eyes."

"What look is that, An'?" Sam asked with a mouthful of sub.

"That look he gets when he is burning inside about a case. I've seen it before. It means he won't quit until he finds the answers."

"Hmm." Sam nodded his head, his mouth too full to speak.

"Well, I think I'll get one of them teas. Give me a call if you want crew, hear?"

"Sure thing, Andy." Sam raised a hand in a single wave and shoved another bite in. He watched Andy order a drink and leave in his car.

Then Sam headed back to Jenny's.

CHAPTER SIX

Jenny was still in her black dress when she opened the front door for Sam. Without a word, she walked to the beachside screened porch and resumed sitting, staring into the ocean's midday glare.

Sam followed like a chastened puppy, afraid to break the silence, but eager to ask about Lee's keys. He sat down on the wicker ottoman at her feet and took a deep breath before speaking.

"Jen, I wonder if I could borrow Lee's keys."

"Keys? They're in the clamshell on the dresser. Help yourself. But what do you need them for? I already gave you the key to *Stormy Monday*." Not once did she look away from the ocean's glassy horizon.

"I just thought I would drive his car so you wouldn't have to. It's important to run that Mustang's engine every couple of days, you know."

"That's what Lee always said, too. Sure, you know where it is. Excuse me if I don't join you." With that, Jenny looked right through Sam and stepped out on the beach.

Sam watched her walk toward the water's edge, then turn north. Her walk was slow and steady now, not like this morning at the service, Sam noticed. He headed to Lee and Jenny's bedroom and found the keys in the wide shell on top of the dresser.

Doing as he said he would, he opened the garage door and slid into the driver's seat of the classic 1968 Acapulco Blue fastback. This vintage model was a four-speed with a V8 engine. The polished chrome-styled steel on the wheel rims gleamed, and the blue interior looked like something out of a showroom. Even though he was not the Mustang buff Lee was, Sam knew Lee's car was worth about $25,000 in its current condition. He had helped Lee many nights, taking apart some aspect of that car and putting it back together again. Sam smiled at the dream of owning it, but he shrugged it off when he thought of his salary.

Sam fingered the keys hanging from the ring while the engine purred. No unusual keys, just a house key, a key to Jenny's maroon Jeep, and the one in the ignition.

Sam pulled out of the driveway and drove toward the highway to warm up the car's innards. *Poor Jenny. One more thing to deal with,* Sam thought. But at least this car was a collector's item. It would sell fast, unlike Lee's boat.

Stormy Monday. Sam thought about the note mentioning "seacock." After about an hour on the road, Sam returned to the condo. He turned off the car, quickly felt inside the empty glove compartment and trunk, and then returned the keys to their place on the dresser.

Back at the dock, Sam stopped by *Angel* long enough to grab that key. *Stormy* was well tied in her slip just a few slips down from his boat. Sam noted the extra spring lines Lee had put out.

"Must make a note to do that for my boat before the next strong wind," Sam thought. He stepped aboard her stern and into the cockpit. Lee's handiwork was apparent everywhere; mounted drink holders, mesh bags for lines and winch handles, and canvas winch and binnacle covers were all well-protected by the hard dodger he had formed and constructed a few summers ago. On top of the dodger were mounted two solar panels. Under the dodger, Lee had fashioned sleek dry boxes for *Stormy*'s instruments and electrical hook-ups for the electronic gear stored off the boat during winter months. After unlocking the companionway hatch boards, Sam entered the salon. Unlike *Angel*'s center-cockpit, *Stormy*'s cockpit was aft. This layout had its advantages, including only one hatch to fumble with during foul weather while sailing. Below, the L-shaped galley was to port opposite a small navigation station whose seat doubled as the top of a quarter berth, extending the boat's width. Lee had fashioned a back rest at the nav station as well as some removable partitions that sectioned off the quarter berth into manageable storage for coolers, extra lines, anchors, and dry goods—a novel idea. Lee was trying to figure out a way to patent his design before approaching the folks at Catalina, the boat's manufacturer.

Stormy's salon had a dinette to port and a long bunk to starboard with shelves over it, holding countless CDs and paperbacks. Forward was a head to port and a deep hanging locker, which had been converted for the HVAC system, a blessing on sticky nights at dock, for which North Carolina is famous. Forward was a small but adequate V-berth stacked high with the cockpit cushions Jenny had covered.

Seeing them reminded Sam of the weekends when Jenny and he had taken turns on her sewing machine, making new covers for their respective boats. Though Jenny's were covered with a splashy bright fish pattern, they were similar to his in size and design. Sam wondered whether he would be able to repair his slashed cushions, but he guessed he'd have to start again.

Convinced that everything was the way it was supposed to be on a boat not yet prepared for the approaching sailing season, Sam moved aft to look at the engine compartment. First, he checked the hoses, then the belts on the engine. Next, he opened the seacock in the engine compartment. There were no apparent leaks. He checked the engine's oil, getting just a little on his fingers to test its viscosity, and finally the engine's water level, which needed to be topped off a bit. Once everything checked out below, Sam went topside, checked that the throttle was in neutral, and turned the key in the ignition. After a few turns, the engine came to life. Sam dashed aft and looked over the rail to see what the engine might be spewing out. Ejecting water was a signal that the engine's mix of oil and fuel was correct.

While Sam ran the engine to let it get warm, he stepped below to the galley to wash the oil off his hands. He reached for the water pump switch on the switch panel and turned the faucet's knob. Grayish green water sputtered out hesitantly, then grew into a steady, clear stream.

The sink filled halfway before Sam remembered what he had forgotten to do: open the seacock under the sink so the water could drain. He quickly turned off the water, grabbed a paper towel, and looked under the sink. He tried to move the brass handle from its horizontal position, but no amount of pushing or pulling budged it. The seacock's handle was frozen solidly in place. Sam wasn't anticipating a handyman special on Lee's boat, but he had to open the seacock to drain the water.

Returning momentarily to his own boat to fetch his tools, Sam overheard the screaming owner of the large motor yacht in the slip next to Lee's. Glancing toward the high cockpit of the forty-two-foot Hatteras, Sam saw the backside of the large man. His thick, hairy neck peeking out from his multi-colored golf-shirt collar was the color of a lobster just plucked from boiling water. The man cursed into the cell phone nearly hidden in his fat fist. Sam tried hard not to listen, but it wasn't easy to miss the gist of the one-sided conversation. "What do you mean they found it? Look; your ass is on the line for this one. We've got too much riding on it, and somebody is going to pay!" the chunky man yelled. Sam reboarded

Lee's boat and headed down below to get to work on the seacock, but he took two seconds to pop open the starboard portholes so he could hear more of the yelling, just for sport.

This particular "boater" was the bane of the marina. He thought nothing of waking the entrance as he brought his boat in, and he had ripped up more than one piling getting into his slip over the last few months. He claimed he was a yacht broker to everyone in the marina, though there was little evidence that he did any actual work either on or off his boat.

When the fat man was on board sporadically, everybody knew he was there by the volume of his voice and the show of "prospective buyers" aboard, not a few of whom wore high heels and extremely short skirts. And whenever this overweight "captain" did take his yacht out, every other boater in the marina, and probably on nearby waters, cringed. Sam mused that this guy's expertise must be in selling because it sure wasn't in boating. Maybe he only had to sell a few a year to keep up with his own boat's expenses and the yard crew that took care of it for him. Sam didn't know his name, but this guy was entertaining, to say the least.

Applying WD-40 and elbow grease, Sam was able to loosen the seacock's handle a bit. He decided to see whether the seacock was fouled, so he kept a tethered six-inch long wooden peg at the ready to plug the seacock when he took it apart. Carefully loosening all of the mounting bolts around the handle, he yanked the fitting off quickly and prepared to plug the hole so water wouldn't gush in. But there was no water gushing. Not even a trickle.

Training his flashlight on the interior, he saw a secondary block had been cut just large enough to fill the hole.

"What's this?" Sam wondered, reaching for the wooden circle. A small handle was fitted on the top, just large enough to grip with a pair of pliers. Again, Sam stood ready to stop a rush of water with the long tapered plug, but as he extracted this circular block, there was no water.

Attached with some form of epoxy to the underside of the round wooden peg was a small waterproof dry bag. And further still in the seacock was another smaller plug, also with a tiny d-ring for a handle.

"Lee was thorough," Sam smiled. He pulled at this smaller plug and at last was pleased to see water rushing in so he could stop it with the long tapered plug. He deftly reinstalled the seacock mounting and handle, tightened all the bolts, and cleaned up the watery mess that the quick job left. Sam hid the blocks of wood in the locker of the port settee and stuffed the dry bag into his pocket. He would study it as soon as he got back aboard *Angel*.

Turning off *Stormy Monday*'s engine, Sam could hear with greater accuracy the ranting of the man on the Hatteras as his deep voice rose in pitch. Surely, the entire marina could hear him.

"I don't care who was at fault. That was my haul, and I want it back. You're supposed to be handling things, not me. If you've got to hire divers, then do it! I'm coming down there."

With that, the hefty man stormed from the cockpit and was out of sight. The air was still now that his shouting was over. It was as if birds breathed a collective sigh of relief and started chirping again, and a flock of small purple martins flew about the docks, working on their nest-building skills once more.

The quiet gave Sam a moment to think. What time was it? Looking at his watch, Sam realized he'd be pushed to catch the last ferry of the day, so he hurriedly closed the ports and secured Lee's boat. He had just stepped over *Angel*'s lifeline into the cockpit when the fat man pounded up the dock toward the parking lot, his weight leaving a small wake of its own with every step.

Sam ducked below and grabbed a pair of well-worn jeans and a copper-colored sweatshirt. It was starting to cool off a little, and a ferry ride could add to the chill. He took the little dry bag from Lee's hiding place under the galley sink with him, figuring that no one was the wiser that he had it, whatever *it* was. He'd have to look at it later.

CHAPTER SEVEN

Sam's was the last car to board the Fort Fisher-to-Southport ferry. He was waved aboard by a crew member dressed from head to toe in khakis who motioned him to stop while shoving a hunk of wood under his rear tire. Once the ferry was underway, Sam got out of his car and moved about the open platform ferry, all the while looking for a red Miata. It wasn't aboard.

Maybe she missed the boat, Sam thought, *or perhaps brought a different car.* Casually walking to the upper deck and peering into the fishbowl-like passengers' cabin, Sam didn't see anyone who looked like the woman who had hugged him at this morning's service.

"Maybe my boat's getting tossed again," he thought, feeling the small dry bag in his jeans pocket.

Leaning over the railing of the upper deck, Sam saw a woman standing next to a battered blue bicycle. A ball cap hid her hair, but when she walked to the rear of the ferry, Sam was sure it was her. She was sassy even in shorts and a baggy white cable knit sweater.

Sam slowly made his way against the people walking up the stairs and meandered between parked cars until he was within five feet of her. He leaned on the railing, looking at the brackish waters of the Cape Fear River rushing by. *The ride won't take that long, so if she intends to talk, she had better get started*, Sam thought.

Sam kicked the side of the solid metal panels meant to keep cars on and waves off. The thud-thud sound had its desired impact.

She glanced at him, then inched closer until their elbows nearly touched on the top of the railing. She too leaned over and stared at the water.

Sam kept his eyes on the water, but he glanced at her every few seconds. He guessed her to be in her late twenties, nearly half his age. He guessed she was pretty, though her oversized sunglasses hid her eyes, and the too-large black ball cap hid her hair with only a few long strands finding their way out of the hole in the back of it. In canvas sneakers, she was about 5'6". And she was not smiling this afternoon.

"Thanks for coming," she started in little more than a whisper. "I didn't know Lee very well, but he spoke highly of you and told me he was going to tell you about me. I didn't know who else to trust. Did he have a chance to tell you what happened?"

Sam looked intently at the water, not sure what she meant. "Lee didn't tell me anything."

"I am sure he would have if he'd had a chance. He was a good guy."

"What was it that he didn't get to tell me, uh, what did you say your name was?"

"Oh, sorry. Deloris, but everyone calls me Del. I guess you can, too." Del sighed and pushed her hat up a bit, revealing a tan furrowed forehead. "Lee sort of stumbled onto a really bad scene, and I think the further he looked into it, the worse it got. My boyfriend Tommy got killed over it. Tommy wasn't too bright sometimes, but he took really good care of me and Emily, our little girl. I wanted to nail the guys who left Emily without her daddy, so I found out through the grapevine about Lee, how he was this good cop on a mission to help others. I wasn't sure how to approach him, so I had one of my friends find him. She said he was trying to help kids stay off the streets by taking them sailing or something like that, and her boy, Sharick, was getting a lot out of it. Sailing was keeping him out of trouble. So one day when Reneeta dropped Sharick off for a day of sailing, I had her slip him a note telling him about Tommy and the trouble he had caught. Well, Lee was on it in a hurry. We met a couple of times, and he took down everything I knew about Tommy, his friends, and the boats."

"The boats?"

"Yeah, drug boats. They bring the stuff in, right here to Southport. It's a mean business. Tommy was just a little fish. He was trying to go straight for Emily and me, but his boss wouldn't let him. Tommy told me he had one more run to do, and then we would be moving to Florida where he could do something else. We talked about running a dive shop or something like that.

"Anyway, on this last run of his, his boat got boarded by a gang and Tommy got killed. Two of his crew were down below in the galley when they heard an approaching boat coming at high speed, so they hid. They both have records, and I guess they thought it was the Coast Guard. Anyway, they heard it all happen, but they didn't see anything. The boat was holed, and it sank."

"What about the crew? What happened to them?"

"As the boat was sinking, they slipped into the water and swam to Bald Head Island. I bet those fancy-pants property owners over there didn't know what to make of them two washing up on their pristine shores. They rode home on the contractors' boat the next day, and no one was the wiser. When Tommy didn't come home, I tracked them down and hounded them until they told me what had happened. Then I contacted Lee."

Sam took it all in. "What about the cargo? What happened to it?"

"That's the thing. There wasn't any, according to the two guys who were with Tommy. They were on their way out to meet one of the shrimpers. Tommy had an old beat-up Grady White. It wasn't much to look at, but it sure could move."

"You mentioned a key in your note this morning. I'm assuming you wrote the note, didn't you?"

Del nodded her head. "That's right. I wrote that note."

"What did the key open?"

"Oh, it wasn't that kind of key. Lee was making what he called a matrix, a key to a chart or something like that.

He was putting together all the pieces of the puzzle, he said, and the matrix helped him keep the players straight. I figured if I could get it back, maybe I could see what it all meant and find out who killed Tommy and maybe Lee. Tommy sometimes mentioned the number on the scrap of paper I gave you, so I thought it might be important."

At this, Del looked straight ahead. "Can you help?"

It was a simple question.

"Del, Lee was my friend in addition to being my partner. If what you say is true, then I will find the bastards who killed him and Tommy. You need to focus on Emily. It's probably a good idea for you two to move, if you can. There's not much more you can do here."

Sam turned his back to her, breathing in the moist salt air brushing his face as the ferry moved forward toward Southport's ferry dock. When he turned around again, she was gone. Her bike was still there.

She couldn't have gone too far, he thought, as the ferry slowed and lined up with the boarding ramps on the Southport side of the river. Sam walked briskly to his car, checking between the others for Del. No sign of her. He drove off the ferry, and waited by the vending machines, watching to see whether a lone walker came off, but he didn't see her.

"She must have gotten into a car," he said to himself, searching each passing car hastily, but none contained a driver or passenger resembling Del.

Stumped, Sam drove his borrowed Altima the few miles into the historic deep-water port town of Southport.

CHAPTER EIGHT

It had been a while since he'd been there, but Sam headed toward the waterfront and took a seat in the outside dining section of Provision's Restaurant overlooking the township's smaller of two marinas. The larger marina, Sam knew from experience, was overcrowded and overpriced, but the smaller one had a longer waiting list, plus a tight anchorage for a few snowbirds heading north or south on their annual migrations via the Intracoastal Waterway.

Sam and Angel had anchored here many a night and had rowed in to Provision's for shrimp-burgers and beer. Tonight, the same "island" music blared from hanging speakers in rafters, and the smell of French fries and onion rings wafted throughout the small establishment. The owners were almost as famous as the food because of their generosity to the community when they closed shop every winter and headed south on a migration of their own. Each year, a different destination. A few nights before they left, they cooked all they had in the freezers, popped the kegs, and invited the town to a free dinner. No wonder they had the following they did, Sam noted, as he looked around at the tables that were filling up fast.

Sam ordered a Bass ale and grouper cheeks. His dinner companion was a snowy egret that landed on the rail and watched him intently. Without calling attention to his actions, Sam pulled the dry bag out of his pocket and unfolded the origami-like paper it contained. Just as Deloris had said, it was an incomplete grid with initials written in what Sam recognized to be Lee's handwriting. There were four columns with a few scattered initials in each one: DS, AK, and CO were in the first column, with question marks and lines drawn from each to the second column's only initials: LO. Another set of lines left LO and joined the next column, again with a single entry: JH. The fourth column contained words or names; Sam guessed them to be boat names: *Firefly, Moonglow, Seawitch*. Again, a question mark held court beside each word.

Whatever Lee had been learning, he was putting on the grid. Sam puzzled over it for a few minutes, then folded it tightly and returned it to the dry bag, which went into his pocket.

He watched the evening's tide come in until dark. He saw several shrimp boats coming in to port, their tall riggings coming up as they got closer to Johnson's, which stood only a stone's throw from Provision's.

Sam watched the crowd expand to overflowing on the dock jutting out into the small bay and marina. At low tide, the muck and mud held a faint tinge of sweet in the salty decay. A few of the smaller boats listed in their interior slips sitting on a soft bottom of mud and silt. Sam thought he might like to get out of his marina one day and cruise like the snowbirds he'd seen over the years. They'd anchor out in tranquil spots like this, close enough to a village like Southport and to a small bar like Provision's. Their vessels became part of the scenery, fueling the dreams of every wanderlust-bitten soul and adding to the seaside town's charm for the tourists.

"Picture postcard perfect," Sam cynically thought as a brutally handsome deck jock rowed his buxom redheaded princess up to the dock for supper. Their boat was unscathed, uncluttered, and totally unlike his own. It was these yachties whom wannabes thought of when they breezed through a copy of *Cruising World Magazine*. Yet these sailors were the minority among the cruising community, and certainly only an abstract of the town they bestowed their presence on. They were merely passing through.

Sam finally relinquished his table to the bouncy waitress who zoomed past him as she tended to other customers. She stopped by his seat so frequently to ask, "Is everything all right?" that he knew she wanted to turn that table and that he had overstayed his welcome. He obliged, slipping a tip in a crammed tip jar resting atop a metal counter on the way out.

It was still early, so Sam did what most every other visitor to Southport does. He strolled the waterfront. The largest structure facing the water was Johnson's Fishery, one of the town's mainstays. Sam remembered reading about old man Johnson's death a few years ago. A newspaper article said it was a freak accident that claimed the life of the expert seaman and one of his long-time drinking buddies, Hale Carouth. Sam recalled reading how the two made their way back to the channel of Cape Fear on a moonless night after a day of fishing. A shrimp boat running at full speed cut through the twenty-four-foot sport fishing vessel, and the shrimper claimed he never saw the boat. He said he didn't see any running lights, either.

Sam had heard that shrimpers are notorious for running without their radios on, so it was quite possible that he never heard the warning call from Johnson, if there was one. The whole town turned out for the funeral, though only Hale's body was found among the wreckage. The case was dismissed as a maritime accident, and no charges were filed.

Sam remembered reading that Johnson's son Tripp took over the fishery. Tripp was the first of his family to go to college, and he had some grand ideas about how to improve an already decent business. But as most of the established fishing and shrimping families were used to doing it the way it had been done for generations, they were none too pleased about the changes and new rates. They took their business down the waterway to Calabash and the equivalent of "turf wars" ensued among the local fishermen, forcing Tripp to change his rates to favor the local fishermen again in order to support his other marketing ideas. He opened a bigger retail outlet to the delight of locals and tourists, started an island delivery service ferrying goods to weekly renters and islanders on Bald Head Island and Oak Island, and also wooed out-of-state wholesalers to move his goods through interstate truckers.

To Sam, it looked like the new owner's efforts were paying off. The fishery looked clean and sported a fresh coat of red paint, and on its exterior walls hung brightly painted crabbing buoys and netting, reminiscent of Mystic Harbor.

Too bad the rest of this stretch of the road lags in vision, Sam thought. Beside the face-lifted fishery was a run-down restaurant, the Sea Enchantress, that was often the site of police calls, and the locals who wanted the town to stay local were proud of it. Tourists usually walked on the opposite side of street, making the Enchantress' clientele gleeful. Further up the waterfront was a small boardwalk that straddled the short dune on the river and led to a spit of beach where young couples tried for a little romantic privacy from time to time. From this beach, the roar of the Bald Head Island ferries could be felt. Their wake often made it to shore, rippling waves occasionally washing up surprises.

Lee had once found a small packet of marijuana floating when he and Jenny had walked this beach after an early meal at the other riverfront restaurant at the foot of Howe Street. They stopped to take in the view for a moment, he had said, when the biggest of Bald Head Island's three ferry boats, the *San Souci*, came to the no-wake zone sign where the open part of the Cape Fear River meets the narrower Intracoastal Waterway.

The twin engines roared and slipped, one slowing and the other racing as it failed to make a gear. The captain deftly maneuvered the passenger vessel to slow it down gradually with power from only one engine. By the time it had reached the entrance to the ferry landing down the river a few hundred yards, he had managed to bring the boat to a slow glide and bumped off the pilings to make it turn into the marina. Lee told Sam he heard later that the boat rammed the dock, but it was moving at such a slow speed that damage was minimal. The powerful wake made by the fish-tailing boat pushed up debris onto the beach, and a neat little watertight package landed practically at Lee's feet. He had told Sam that when he opened it, he grinned and took it to his buddy, Chief Richard Gossett of the Southport Police Department. The two had known each other a long time, and Lee said that the chief would take care of things.

Wonder what ever came of it, Sam thought, surveying the river. He made his way back over the sand and continued his walk along the river's edge. He passed by the watchtower, Lois Jane's Inn, and then up to the parade grounds atop a hill overlooking the riverfront and beyond to dredge spoil islands, and to Bald Head. The tree-lined streets of Southport, laid out in a grid pattern, held quirky names like Howe, Dry, I, and Am. The last two were added in jesting remembrance of Prohibition days. But the tidy, picturesque town was the jewel of Brunswick County, and real estate prices reflected this heightened state of awareness. Bald Head Island developers had carved out a new ferry landing rimmed with condos just up the river road near the Fort Fisher-to-Southport ferry landing, and other developers were snatching them up as fast as they could talk the longtime landowners out of their assets and parcel out lots under the grand 200-year-old, live oak trees (the oldest, near the town's library, was claimed to be 800 years old).

Doubling back through narrow streets lined with antique shops, Sam found himself in front of an ice cream shop. The smell of oversized waffle cones wafted through the open doorway, tempting Sam.

"Why not?" he said, half aloud as he entered the small shop lined with sacks of coffee beans on one side and a long freezer and counter affair on the other.

"Death-by-chocolate on a sugar cone," he ordered from the sunburnt fellow behind the counter. Two licks later, he was outside in the cooling night and heading back toward his car.

His stroll was disturbed by a cloud of dust kicked up by a passing semi rig rumbling toward Johnson's Fishery. When Sam got to the parking lot servicing Provision's customers, he noticed the truck had a New York license plate and considered the amount of driving one would have to do to cover territory between Florida and New York, collecting fresh seafood all along the way.

Sam drove slowly through some of the side streets and back out to Howe Street, which was also Highway 211. Southport was a booming town, now sporting a new Sharky's Superstore, much to the chagrin of many of the swank historic district homeowners. They loved that it was close, but they also hated that it was close.

Turning on Highway 87, Sam rolled down his windows and enjoyed the night air as he approached the entrance to the old Brunswicktown ruins and Orton Plantation. He kept meaning to go there, but he never seemed to remember it as a destination when he had time off. He made a mental note to check it out soon. The road from there to Wilmington was desolate, with only an occasional deer surprising a driver racing for the next hourly ferry to Bald Head Island.

Sam had been over there once, but the boat ride was expensive, considering he'd had to rent a golf cart or a bike to get around once on the resort island where no cars were allowed. Sam had been more than a little put off at the snobbery of the waiter and pricey food he found in the resort's restaurant the one time he and Angel had gone. He had hoped to rekindle a dwindling romance between them, but between the high costs, the voracious mosquitoes, and their fighting about money problems, it wasn't a fun day, as he recalled.

Angel had been interested in seeing some of the more isolated beaches known collectively as East Beach, but Sam refused to rent a golf cart. Instead, they walked around the marina to a small beach that faced the river. It really wasn't much to look at, and anyway, Angel had pointed out, they could see it from the ferry's deck.

After going to a little coffee shop and browsing in the gift shop near the bed and breakfast inn called Theodosia's, Angel had wanted to stay the night. But Sam had said they couldn't afford it, and they had fought about money on the walk back to the ferry.

Now that he looked back on it, the $189 a night for a room might have made a difference in their relationship. *Not the money, but the effort,* he thought. Angel didn't really care if they stayed there, but she did want and need some romance, Sam knew. Sam used money as an excuse, though that wasn't the reason. He was selfish, and he knew it. He didn't spend money on *them,* even when he knew it might make a difference.

Sam's thoughts were interrupted by bright headlights in his rearview mirror. The narrow two-lane road had little traffic, so surely the large SUV with rack-mounted lights would pass. But it didn't. It just sped up as it approached Sam. He stomped on the gas to pull away from it. The SUV followed suit, this time ramming the back end of his loaner car. Sam swerved to the edge of the road, then regained control. Once more, the SUV sped up and rammed the left side of the Altima, pushing him off the pavement. But instead of backing off this time, it slammed Sam's car hard in the left rear panel as Sam tried to get back on the pavement. The force set his car spinning out of control, down an embankment, and into a dense row of pine trees lining the road. When the airbag didn't deploy, Sam's head struck the steering wheel and windshield. The last thing he remembered hearing was the sound of screeching tires as the SUV sped away.

CHAPTER NINE

"Dude…are you…like…dead?"

Sam could hear a voice, distant, but throbbing, like it was coming from inside his head. He wanted to sleep, but the voice persisted.

"'Cause if you're dead, I'm thinking I might like to check out your wallet."

Now vaguely aware of a hand moving down his backside to his wallet, Sam felt a tugging and jostling. With all the strength he could muster, he sprang upright and reached with his right hand through the open window for the voice.

The voice shrieked, and Sam latched on to the throat from which it emanated. With a firm hold, he pulled the throat into the car and mashed the button to put up the electric window until it hit the underside of the would-be pickpocket's armpit, capturing an arm, shoulder, and head inside the car. Then Sam let go of the voice's throat. The voice gulped and gasped for air as the window held it tight.

Sam turned on the car's dome light, momentarily blinding his catch. The voice belonged to a dark-haired, pony-tailed woman in her mid-thirties and wearing a soggy, battered Hawaiian print shirt.

"Dude! I didn't mean it! I…I was checking to see if you were all right, man! Really, I didn't mean anything by it," she babbled.

Sam glared at her. She looked harmless enough. Sam looked around for the SUV with the rack lights on top, but he couldn't make out anything in the brilliance of the dome light.

"Why were you trying to run me off the road?" Sam asked calmly.

"I didn't do this to you. You were this way when I found you." She was emphatic.

"What's your name?"

"Monroe."

"*Monroe*," Sam mimicked. "Is that your first or your last name?"

"Last."

"Got a first name, Monroe?"

"Yes, but…but you just call me Monroe."

"What is your first name, Monroe? I would like to know whose hand it is that is reaching into my back pocket."

"Oh, sorry. Like I said, I thought maybe you were dead." Monroe pulled her hand up as far as she could given her current predicament and offered to shake Sam's hand.

Sam didn't acknowledge it. Instead, he climbed slowly over the passenger's seat and out the door. He staggered around the back of the vehicle and to Monroe's back side to frisk her.

"What the…? Hey, you've done that before. You a cop?" Monroe asked nervously. "What are you going to do, dude?"

"Well, for starters, I thought I might see who you are, and what you're up to. You have the right to remain silent."

"But I didn't do anything wrong!" Monroe protested.

"You don't think running someone off the road and leaving him for dead is right, now, do you, *Monroe*?"

"I told you, man, you were already off in the ditch when I found you!" Monroe shouted. "I was just checking to see if you were all right, and if you weren't, well, I was gonna find out who you were, so I could, you know, notify somebody or something."

"Then where did you come from, Monroe? I don't see your car around anywhere," Sam said as he quickly looked around the area.

"I don't have a car right now. I was hitching. Or trying to, anyway. I saw this huge truck with blinding lights on top racing up the road behind me, so I dove into the ditch a few hundred feet back. Then I saw it clobber you, and I figured you were a goner when you went off the road the second time. Hey, can you lower the window or something? My arm is about to fall off here!"

Sam reached for the door handle and jerked the door open. The force of the door hit Monroe on the chest, making her yelp.

"Cripes! You didn't need to do that."

Sam reached into the car and mashed a button, which lowered the window, freeing Monroe.

Monroe stood there, rubbing first her arm, then her head. "Uh, I'll be moving along now." She started backing away from the car and from Sam, but not fast enough.

Sam grabbed her arm and pushed her into the car. "What kind of a truck was it? Did you see the license plate? What color?" Sam rapid-fired his questions.

"I don't know! I told you, the rack lights were blinding. When I dove into the ditch, I didn't see anything! May the fleas of a thousand camels attack the driver in his crotch, and may his arms be too short to scratch!"

"What?" Sam started to laugh, but he hurt. "What did you say?"

"I've placed a curse on the driver," Monroe straightened herself, "on your behalf." Monroe bowed slightly toward Sam, and she smiled a toothy grin. "These things work, see. I learned them from my uncle who traveled all over the world, and he regularly cursed those who betrayed or hurt him, and blessed the ones who helped him. I've found over the years that they work for me, too. Now that driver who tried to run you off the road—and me over, for that matter—will certainly meet with a, well, let's just say an uncomfortable fate." Monroe was quite pleased with herself as she stood there rubbing a sore arm.

"Whatever," Sam said. He pushed Monroe aside and gingerly got back into his car. His head was throbbing, and his chest hurt where it had hit the steering wheel. "Believe what you want." The engine responded after a couple of tries, though the hood was smashed and the front-end dislocated.

"Hey! Aren't you gonna even say thanks?" Monroe feigned her hurt. "The least you could do is offer me a ride."

She ran around the car and pulled on the handle, but Sam had already locked it.

"Dude, you don't mean to leave me out here!" she shouted through the closed window.

"You were out here already! You tried to snatch my wallet, and given the opportunity, you probably would have made off with my car, too!"

"Awww, really, I am sorry about all that. Look: I'll make it up to you. What's your name? I will bestow a blessing on you. Are you a cop?"

"Yes." Sam unlocked the door and let Monroe in. "I am a cop. Where do you live, Monroe?"

"Wilmington. East Fourth Street. I appreciate the ride. I delivered this big-ass boat to an equally big-assed man on Bald Head. He didn't know the first thing about powerboats, and he got this forty-two-foot boat, see. Then he wanted me to party with him at his dock on Bald Head Island. I think he was scared of his new boat or something. Anyway, before I left the dock in Wilmington, the broker told me that he'd send someone for me, but we never connected. So I told the new boat owner maybe he should run me home again, and he said he would. We started out of the marina, but then he got so drunk on the ride up the creek that I was scared to go any farther with the jerk."

"So you probably put a curse on him, too, right?" Sam snickered as he backed out of the trees and ditch and slowly climbed the embankment to the road.

"I sure did. 'May he drink a toast to his liver as he kisses it goodbye, and may a thousand mosquitoes feast on his fat, drunken head.' Oh, and 'May his golf cart batteries run out of juice before he gets back home,'" Monroe added, in delight.

"You're making these up."

"Sure am, and I have a good time doing it, too!" Monroe smiled. "Molly. My first name is Molly." Monroe put out her hand a second time to Sam.

This time, Sam shook it briefly. "Sam McClellan."

"So, Sam, why was that guy trying to run you off the road, anyway?"

"I have a hunch," Sam said half-aloud.

"Care to share? I mean, I feel we are partners or something since he tried to run me over, too."

"I don't think he tried to run you over. I think you just got in the way."

"Yeah? And what's your excuse?"

"I think I am getting in the way, too," Sam stated quietly.

"Um, you wanna talk about this?" Molly offered.

"No."

"Okay. I was just trying to help you out, man. I mean, I know people in this town, and I could, like, put some feelers out for you or something in return for you giving me a ride home tonight. It's a long walk on that road from Southport, especially at night. Those alligators can get mighty hungry."

"Alligators?"

"Yeah, about where you crashed. They live in the pond on the way into Orton Plantation. Me and a bunch of friends used to stop there to see them when we were on our way back to Wilmington. Each time we stopped, there were more of them, and they were monsters!"

"You stopped by there often, did you?"

"Yeah. For a while, I worked on a boat."

"Why not work out of Wilmington?" Sam's head hurt as he squinted against the lights of the occasional oncoming car.

"The money is in Southport. We used to go out on the commercial fishing boats there. The days on the water were long, but the pay was good for a while. In Wilmington, I could be a deckhand on a headboat, but young boys are eager to get your spot, see. So they work for less. I needed more, so I had to go to Southport, where I could move up in rank and pay. Last year, when shrimping got so competitive from the foreigners coming in, well, I gave up on that and started working for a powerboat broker as a delivery captain. The gigs don't happen often, but when they do, they are good money."

"How many boats do you deliver in a month?"

"About three, but there are other opportunities from time to time. I'm a free agent. I work four gigs now and the money's all right. You can let me out up ahead at the corner."

"Don't want me to know where you live or something, Molly?" It was Sam's turn to feign hurt.

"It's not that. I'm going down the street to the bar, the Barbary Coast. This is closer. I don't suppose you've ever been there, but it's like a second home to me."

"I'll bet," Sam said as he pulled to a stop to let Molly hop out.

"Thanks for the ride. Stay out of trouble." Molly opened the door and saluted Sam. Just before she got out, she said, "May the sun shine on you as you track down the ass who tried to kill us, and may you find him when nobody else is around so you can teach him some manners."

Sam nodded and chuckled at Molly's blessing. "Stay out of trouble, Molly Monroe." He pulled away from the corner and headed to his marina in Carolina Beach.

CHAPTER TEN

Carolina Beach is an odd little beach town, Sam thought, as he drove the last few miles toward his marina. During late spring, before the tourists got into a summertime groove, locals swarmed over the town's bars as if it would be the last chance they had. Sam watched them scurry like roaches from bar to bar while he waited at a stoplight. Within a month, Sam knew, the town's character would change from locals just hanging out to families on the boardwalk and college kids with nothing better to do than get drunk. Each night was a party to them, and each day was one big hangover filled with more supposedly clandestine beer on the beach, girl watching and boy watching, and then more partying until their parents from Raleigh came to the beach house for the weekend, or the rental week was over. High-rises were rented out until the middle of September when colleges were back in session, and the younger year-round school kids had their last tracked-out session of the warmer months. By the end of September, the locals breathed a collective sigh of relief, and their world got back to normal.

City officials and those in the hospitality industry relished the increased profits from summer, but locals cursed the nearly four-month-long stretch. Some, who had learned to profit from the mass intrusion, packed up, rented their houses for the summer, and descended upon some other destination where *they* were tourists. Others, like Sam, had to stay put, work through the mess, and generally be a part of it.

That was one of his job's drawbacks, but Sam had wanted to live in a quieter place than Charlotte or Raleigh. He wanted to work in a small town where he could be part of the place as much as he wanted, without getting in the way of major trouble. Unlike some of his co-workers, Sam was not an adrenaline junkie who thrived on fast action. Sam liked to see the younger kids enjoying themselves on the beach and at the amusement park on the boardwalk. It reminded him of his own childhood trips to Dewey Beach and Rehoboth Beach in Maryland. These two quiet sisters of Ocean City were *the* family beaches when he was a kid, and Carolina Beach was similar in size and feel.

When he was twelve, his family moved to Raleigh, and he met Angel. His father worked for the Department of Natural Resources with her father, so the two youngsters were often thrown together at employee functions. In the summer, they sailed on the small lakes around Raleigh with all eyes on them. But back in those days, neither was really interested in the other romantically. Through high school, they dated off and on, a relationship pattern that continued when she was in Meredith College and he tried to stay enrolled at North Carolina State University. The beach was calling him back, so he quit school and rented a small house with a bunch of other drop-outs. His housemates eventually had the sense to go back, but Sam chose a different path. He went through the police academy. Once he graduated, his first station was in Wilmington.

In a quirky twist, he and Angel met again during Wilmington's popular azalea festival, an annual event on the riverfront where hoards of people come to celebrate spring and every street vendor in the region is hoping to sell bird-on-a-stick quality wares. Sam was waiting in line for beer for his date and two buddies when he heard a loud noise and saw a powerboat crash into an already crowded wharf. When he ran to help, he saw Angel on board, with her hand to her bloody head. She had fallen forward and gashed her forehead on the windshield as the bozo driver, who was drunk, tried to dock the boat. Sam rushed her to the hospital where she collected stitches and Sam's stern lecture about accepting rides from drunks…and an invitation to dinner.

From then on, they dated steadily, and finally after nearly a decade apart, they married. Frank was born shortly after they moved to Carolina Beach, where Sam took up his new post.

A carbon-copy of Sam, young Frank loved living at the beach. He grew up in the water, sailing, surfing, and swimming, so it was little surprise that when he was old enough to choose a career, he headed straight for the Coast Guard's recruiting office. What was a surprise was that he gladly accepted a post as far away as he could from home. At first, this move stung Sam. But given their strained relationship prior to Frank's enlistment, Sam eventually let it go. Over the years, with monthly phone calls and an occasional visit to Alaska, Sam and Frank mended their relationship. Sam was proud of his boy.

Angel loved being on the beach, too, and she was content to stay at home when she could. After a few years, she became a bookkeeper for one of the local hotels, and remained there until she left Sam.

Sam wondered whether she was happy in California. Sam didn't feel comfortable asking Frank about her when he called. Frank was *Switzerland* when it came to his parents, and Sam looked forward to seeing him in Norfolk in the fall when Frank arrived at his new duty station.

That is, if Sam could make it through the summer.

Sam's head was still pounding as he made his way down the dock toward his boat. Thankfully, the loudmouthed powerbroker on the Hatteras was quiet. Sam kicked off his shoes, stripped, and flopped onto the aft bunk. Things were getting serious. It was too much of a coincidence—Lee's death, his own boat being tossed, and now an attempt to run him off the road. Unable to sleep, Sam grabbed his pants and rooted in the pocket for the notes Lee had made.

He wanted to talk to Deloris again, but if doing so put her at risk, then he'd have to figure it out on his own.

What were the numbers? Why Lee? What did he know? And why didn't he tell Sam? Sam's head was swimming, still hurting from the crash, but hurting more from the troubling thoughts. Finally, he succumbed to deep sleep.

CHAPTER ELEVEN

Thud!

Sam woke to the noise of a heavy line being thrown down on the hatch over his head. He flew up the companionway stairs in time to see a large female mallard lifting a spare braided spring line in her beak as she tried to make off with it, only to be pulled back forcefully to the boat.

"Shoo!" Sam yelled and swatted at the bird in the pre-dawn light.

Aside from her response of a hiss and quack, all was quiet in the still marina.

"Get!" He came up on deck, expecting the duck to fly off at his presence, but she persisted, tugging the tethered line upward in an attempt to take it.

On the third attempt, the force of the duck's pull worked against her and snapped her down fast onto the deck. The duck sat up, pecked ferociously at the line, and started hissing at it.

Sam laughed at her antics. "You are a persistent little thing, even if your mission is doomed!" He watched the duck for a while as it continued its pecking and hissing.

Finally giving up, the duck waddled over toward the cockpit, and without hesitation, jumped down onto one of the ripped cushions to make herself at home.

"Oh, no, you don't. I will not have you messing up my place. Now get!"

But the duck was unfazed. She looked directly at Sam, quacked once, and nestled her head down on her back to sleep.

"You gotta be kidding me!" Sam tried to wave the duck off the cushion, but she wouldn't budge. She lifted her head up, hissed, and contorted herself again to sleep.

Sam threw his hands up in disgust. "All right, you can stay the night, but you're going in the morning." As he hopped back down the companionway stairs, he called out to the duck as he lay back down on his bunk. "I once had a girlfriend like you. I tried to shoo her away, but she just hissed at me too. She was persistent, too. I remember I told her I wasn't interested in seeing her anymore when Angel and I started getting serious, but she wouldn't take no for an answer. Wonder whatever happened to Kathy? She was pretty. She had long dark hair, and a laugh that was contagious. She was from New York, so she talked funny, but she was cool to hang with for a while. She didn't like Angel, I can tell you that. And she didn't like being dumped, either. I think she thought we were 'the couple' that other kids wanted to be. But in the end, it wasn't meant to be, you know. Angel had my attention pretty quick, and Kathy didn't want to let it go. Kathy. Yep. That suits you. Kathy, I'm telling you now, I don't have room here for you. Tomorrow, you'll just have to shove off. Good night." With that, he rolled over and closed his eyes. It was pointless, this thing called sleep.

CHAPTER TWELVE

After another hour passed without sleep, Sam saw the sun's first light peeking through the open aft port. He put on a pair of shorts and made his way through the cockpit and forward to the galley to make some coffee. Kathy was still tucked, undisturbed on *her* cushion. Sam just shook his head and fished around in the refrigerator for something to eat. When he pulled his head back out, he saw Kathy's bright orange webbed feet standing on the top step of the companionway stairs, her mottled brown and white tail resting comfortably on the surround to the hatch.

Sam waved at her, but she sat like a fixed sentry, watching him as he lit the propane stove, dug out a pan, and opened the cupboards to find seasonings. It wasn't until he cracked open an egg that she reacted noisily, stretching out her wings and puffing up her chest, all the while moving backward into the cockpit. She flapped off quacking indignantly, making her roost the top of the portside piling.

"That'll teach ya to invade somebody else's space, Kathy," Sam muttered as he sipped his coffee, standing on the companionway stairs, half in and half out of the boat. "What's the matter, old girl? Recognize one of your kin?"

"Who are you fussing at, Sam?"

Sam reeled around to see Jenny standing on the dock, her arms hugging herself in an attempt to warm up.

"You're up early," Sam said. "Want a cup of coffee?" He stepped into the cockpit, realizing how cold the early morning was on his bare chest, as he motioned for her to come aboard.

"Tea, if you have it, Sam. I just came down to check on the boat. I wanted to get the key from you." She grabbed the jib line and hopped over the safety line, obviously comfortable getting onto a boat. "Who were you talking to when I walked up?"

"Kathy." Sam pointed to the duck pecking at the top of the post.

Jenny laughed. "Girl trouble, Sam?"

"The only trouble I have with girls right now is that I don't have any." Sam jumped down to the aft cabin and grabbed his sweatshirt from the night before.

"Oh, Sam, are you all right? Is that blood?" Now that Jenny was close enough, she saw Sam's forehead and the dried drips of blood on his sweatshirt.

She reached her hand out to his head, and he bobbed away like a practiced boxer. "Oh, dear, does it hurt?"

"Only when it's touched…. It's nothing, Jen. I just knocked it pretty hard; that's all. You like honey in your tea, right? What is that, a British thing or something?" As he tried to steer the conversation away from his injury, he jumped down to the aft cabin once again to dig out a clean shirt before bouncing back up into the cockpit to demonstrate to Jenny that he felt fine.

"Yes, honey would be great, if you have it." Jenny stepped into the cockpit, still rubbing her arms for warmth.

Once again, Sam dove below and rummaged in the drawers before finding a red zippered sweatshirt with a hood on it, which he tossed up to Jenny. She gratefully accepted it and followed Sam to the galley. She settled into the cozy dinette settee to get warm while he made her a cup of tea.

The propane stove's warmth heated the cabin to a comfortable temperature. Sam had to pitch his earlier burnt attempt at eggs, so he proceeded to crack several more while toasting some English muffins under the broiler. He placed a bowl and small grater in front of Jenny.

"Here; make yourself useful," he said as he handed Jenny a block of cheddar. While she grated the cheese, he deftly chopped an onion and sautéed it in a little bit of oil. He found three red potatoes, which he chopped up into small cubes, and threw them in the pan with the onion, turned off the broiler, and sat down across from Jenny for a few minutes while they cooked.

"Are you thinking about sailing today, Jen?" Sam took a long sip from his cup.

"I thought I might see what will happen when I go aboard. *Stormy Monday* was really Lee's pride and joy, but we had some good times aboard. I don't know if I can be on her without him."

"Jenny, when it's time, you will. Do you want me to come with you?"

"No, Sam. This is one of those things I have to do. I am thinking about selling the boat. I want to see how I feel about that when I step aboard."

"Jenny, it's probably too soon to start thinking about selling. I mean, what if you miss the boat in a few months when you feel…better? Then what?"

Jenny looked into her mug of tea. "Sam, from a financial standpoint, I don't think I can manage to keep the boat and the condo, and I am not like you. I don't think I would be happy living aboard the boat."

Seeing that the potatoes were cooking nicely, Sam stirred the eggs and added them to the pan, plus a few spices, then the cheese. He covered the concoction with a lid, pulled the muffins out from the oven, and readied two plates.

"This is what I call my lazy-man boat omelet. Had I known I was going to have company for breakfast, I would have gotten some other things ready or something. This okay for you?" Sam handed her a loaded plate.

Jenny laughed. "And just who all did you think was going to eat this much? Thank you! This looks wonderful. Um, am I supposed to eat it with my fingers?"

"Oh, sorry. Forks and napkins are behind you." He pointed to the backrest of her seat, which opened up, revealing a jumble of utensils, paper goods, and rarely used cooking items like a garlic roaster, in addition to small power tools.

"Sam, you really should take a weekend and organize this boat. Lee always said everything had its place on a boat. Power tools and forks definitely do not go together."

"I know, I know; I need to do that one weekend." He didn't want to tell her his boat was more organized before the night Lee was killed. "You need anything else?" He pointed to her plate.

"No, this is…yum! I didn't know you could cook like this. Is there more hot water for tea?"

"Sure; help yourself." Sam watched Jenny as she poured more hot water into her cup and dumped a heap of honey in. "Like a little tea with your honey?" he ribbed her.

"A little," she smiled, and returned to the table. "So you don't think I should put the boat on the market, do you Sam?"

"It's up to you, Jen. I don't know what your situation is; I only know that it's a big decision that maybe you better wait on for a few months. Maybe see if you can enjoy it this summer, you know. It might help you get your mind off of…things. Has Chuck's wife called you? She said she might be able to help get some of your work shown to a larger audience at her gallery."

"No, but I don't think that's such a good idea now. I am just kinda fumbling around. I've been to her gallery, and frankly, it's filled with some high-end stuff. I don't know if my work is good enough for that place."

"I think you should let Lisa be the judge of that," Sam offered between bites. "She knows what her clients like. Besides, the way she talks, she could sell ice to Eskimos during the middle of a snowstorm!"

Jenny blew a little of her tea out of her mouth as she stifled a laugh. "You think Eskimos would like beach scenes?"

Sam smiled, then reached for the pan of potatoes. He offered the last bit to Jenny, but she declined.

"I can't finish what I have! It's great, though. I feel much better. I haven't eaten much since…." Her voice trailed off, and she stared vacantly out the hatch at the underside of the bimini. "Thanks, Sam. Umm, would you mind if I borrowed your sweatshirt for the day?" She rose from the dinette, clearing her plate and cup off the table and placing them into the deep sink. She started to wash them, but Sam chased her off the task.

"No problem, Jen. Don't worry about the dishes. I'll get it later. Here; let me get you the key to your boat. I checked on it and everything looks good. You shouldn't have any problems if you decide to go out today." He fished around in a plastic basket he kept on the shelf just over the port-side settee filled with coins and keys. He pulled out the single key to *Stormy Monday*. "I'll walk with you."

They walked down the dock a few slips to *Stormy Monday*, which tugged gently at her dock lines. A few people were already on the water, and still more were arriving at the dock for a day of projects or boating. Sam felt a tinge of envy. Living on a boat made it hard to go sailing frequently. Everything had to be stowed before he could pull away from the dock, and Sam wasn't sure he had a proper place for everything. *Someday*, he kept promising himself.

Stormy Monday was ready to sail, and after a bit of encouragement, Jenny stepped aboard alone. Sitting in the cockpit, Jenny slowly touched the steering wheel, gripping it tightly as if it might jettison away from her any minute. After a while, she moved around and opened the hatch boards, carefully placing them in a cloth sleeve mounted to the aft starboard bulkhead. Lee had made it so the boards wouldn't fly free below if the boat hit a wave wrong.

While Sam waited on the dock, Jenny went below to check the engine's oil and water. Once again in the cockpit, she started the engine and looked over the aft lines to see water pumping out. Everything checked out the way it should. She moved to the forward v-berth and got the cockpit cushions out, calling to Sam to help her.

"Sam, I think I might take her out. Would you mind helping to get her ready?"

"Not at all." He ran back to his boat's water hookup and unfastened the hose. He dragged it to *Stormy Monday*, and once it was hooked up there, he climbed aboard, pulling the hose with him to fill up a water tank.

Next, he helped Jenny place the cushions about the cockpit, and he swept off a few cobwebs from the mainsail cover before taking it off and stashing it below on the aft quarter berth. He then started to remove the spring lines.

"Jen, I have some bottles of water. I'll get them for you." He was off the boat before she could speak, dashing back to his own. When he returned, Jenny was again frozen at the wheel.

"Want me to get the lines?" he asked as he lowered a soft-sided cooler into the cockpit while still standing on the dock.

"No. I've changed my mind. I…I don't want to go."

"Whatever you say." Sam carefully retied one of the spring lines he'd taken off as he waited for Jenny to speak. Seeing that she was not ready to sail, he stepped aboard and sat down gingerly in the cockpit beside her. "Jenny, it's just not the right time to go out. That's all." He put his hand on hers, and she smiled, slightly comforted.

She looked past him, then motioned for him to get off the boat. "Sam, thank you for checking on the boat, and for breakfast. I think I would like to have some time alone. Do you mind?"

"No. I understand. Just let me know if I can help you." Sam marveled at how calm she was. Grace under pressure, he noted to himself, as he stepped over the safety lines and walked up the dock to his boat.

With another cup of coffee poured, Sam started cleaning up the breakfast mess. He noticed his coffee swaying a little, then poked his head up in time to see Jenny pulling straight out of her slip, her boat's turning creating a small wake in the marina.

"She's going to be just fine," Sam said as he sipped his coffee. "Brave girl." Then he returned to cleaning up the galley.

Sam fished the matrix out of his soiled jeans and tucked it into the tidy package hiding in the engine compartment.

CHAPTER THIRTEEN

Sam headed to the station to file an accident report on the loaner car. As he was finishing up the paperwork, he saw Chief Singleton's car pull into the parking lot, so he waited.

Chief was all fired up about something, judging by his pace.

"Morning, Chief," Sam called as Singleton blew past him in a huff. "Any leads?" Sam followed him down the hall to his office.

"Hey, Sam," replied Singleton as he flicked on the lights. "No, we don't have anything yet. What'd you do to the car?"

"I found my way into a tree; that's all. Sorry about that. I've filled out the necessary paperwork. Chief, I am ready to get on this case."

Singleton scratched his head for a minute. "Sam, I don't think you need to be on it. You and Lee were too close, and I think you haven't had enough time to get an impartial view of things. You still have several days off coming to you."

"Chief, I have to do something. I can't just sit around and wait."

"Well, then, why don't you focus your energy on something else? I have a big mess on my hands with the fire at the Golden Sun Hotel complex. The owner says it was deliberately set, but our guys are backed up so they can't track anything down. If you feel up to getting back to work, can you jump on that one?"

"Sure, Chief, but I want to help on Lee's case, too."

"Fine, but focus on the Golden Sun case first. We got enough guys on Lee's. Can't really spare any more, even if it's you." He dismissed Sam with a wave of his hand and grabbed the phone to indicate their unscheduled meeting was adjourned.

Sam was mad to be put off that way. The more he thought about it, the more it got to him. He headed to the impound lot, signed his own car out, and screeched away. The car was clean. Not a trace of what had happened was left. But Sam still drove straight to Vann's, a used car lot on Highway 17, just north of the Wrightsville beach turn off. A salesman attacked as soon as Sam stepped out of his truck.

"Howdy! My name is Bob. How can I help you today?" Bob slicked down a stray gray hair over his bald spot and reached for Sam's hand.

Sam declined to shake and, instead, started talking about his vehicle. "I would like to trade this for something else. It's got about 50,000 miles on it, runs great, and is clean, inside and out," Sam forced himself to say.

"You have the title on it?"

"Yep. What have you got?"

Bob smiled broadly and replied, "Whatever you need." He put his arm around Sam's shoulders and steered him through a row of used cars of various makes and models. Sam gravitated toward a red Dodge Ram 1500, and Bob pounced on his interest.

"This here is a fine truck. What did you say your name is?"

"Sam McClellan."

"Very good, Sam; this is the truck for you. I knew you were a truck man the second you drove onto the lot," Bob beamed.

Sam looked back at his own Blazer. Well, duh.

He looked at the interior of the Ram and then under the hood while Bob started it up and roared the engine for effect.

"May I drive?" Sam asked.

"Why, of course." Bob jumped out eagerly and ran around to the other side, his seatbelt fastened before Sam even had the driver's door closed.

Sam pulled out of the parking lot and headed north on 17, flooring it as only a cop in a chase would. He hit seventy miles per hour before the next stoplight and entrance to Topsail Beach. Bob held on for dear life as Sam jumped on the brakes, then did a U-turn in the middle of the road with the back end fishtailing at the speed.

"You have insurance?" Bob asked just above a whisper.

"Yep." Sam floored it again and drove back to the car lot, wheeling in at a high speed.

White-knuckled, Bob gingerly stepped out of the truck, clearly relieved to be back. Regaining his composure, he smoothed down the fly-away hair again and smiled. "You see? That truck was meant for you! If you have the title to yours, we'll go ahead and make a deal today!"

Sam looked over the truck one more time, and then he followed Bob into the trailer where bottle-blonde Glenda warmly greeted him like an old flame and offered him a cup of coffee as he sat at a small table filling out paperwork. After about twenty minutes, feeling like he had gotten a decent deal, Sam was off to a detailer across the street to get his "new" truck cleaned.

Half an hour later, as he was leaving the detailer, Sam saw Bob driving the Blazer into the entrance to the detailer, waving to Sam as he emerged from the truck. Sam was quick to step on the pedal so he wouldn't have to talk to Bob again.

CHAPTER FOURTEEN

Driving back down Highway 17, Sam thought about his conversation with Singleton. He exited toward Carolina Beach and headed toward the Golden Sun Hotel. Completed just a few months earlier, the new high-rise was an addition to an older motel with fifty-four oceanfront rooms. The complex stood as a landmark on the beach with two pools, beachfront rooms with balconies, a decent restaurant, and a gift shop. Since Sam had been out of the office for a few days, he knew nothing of the fire. And since he was not officially back on duty, he thought he would do an unannounced drive-by to see what he could uncover.

When he arrived on the scene, Sam saw that the boys had already been there and had cordoned off an area of the new section that contained fire damage. He circled around the parking lot, surveying the hotel and its proximity to the beach.

Sam parked near the two-story motel and casually walked into the lobby of the older low-rise. A pimple-faced teen leaning on the counter looking at a hotrod magazine jumped and stashed the magazine under the counter when he saw Sam approach the desk.

"You want a room?"

"No. Just looking around today. I have a family reunion coming up and wanted to book everybody here, but then I heard there was a fire, so I wanted to see how bad the damage is," Sam lied.

"The fire wasn't here. It was in the new part, but it wasn't too bad," the kid said, leaning on the counter again.

"Know what happened?"

"I heard someone started it on purpose to get back at the builder, or something like that."

Sam leaned on the counter, closing in on the clerk's personal space. "What good would that do? The builder just gets to build it again, more money in his pocket, and all that's covered by insurance anyway."

The clerk stood up straight. "You got a point there. I dunno; maybe the guy was stupid or something."

"Guy?" Sam let the word hang there.

"Well, I'm guessing it was a guy. Most of the construction workers were guys, and it just happened, so I don't really know what it was. Maybe you should talk with the police. Anyway, are you still interested in booking some rooms?"

"I would be interested, if I knew this place wasn't a target for repeat fires, or something," Sam replied. "Was there anyone around when it happened?"

"Yeah, Tracey was on the desk that night. Tracey Ellis." The clerk checked the schedule behind him on the wall. "She'll be on the desk of the other lobby this afternoon. You might catch her in the restaurant. They have a staff meeting there." Then he leaned over and confidentially said, "I didn't have to go to the meeting because I had to be on this desk."

"Maybe I will hang around and talk with her after she's done. In the restaurant?" Sam pointed out the door in the general direction of the restaurant.

"Yeah, just go out those doors, across the parking lot, and into the new building. The restaurant is on your left." The boy looked relieved to see Sam going.

"Thanks." Sam started to head for the doors, then stopped. "Oh, just one more thing. Did anyone get hurt in the fire?"

"No," said the clerk. "There was some damage to the offices, but nothing serious. The only weird thing about it was that was the same night some crazy nutcase drove down on the beach and tore up the pier a block down. Did you see that?"

"No, I didn't. Which night was that?" Sam turned and faced the teen.

"Two or three nights ago. It was actually early morning, and Tracey said she heard a car racing through the parking lot and then onto the beach right over there. See where the fence is down?" He pointed out of the window at the ocean side of the motel. "Tracey said she went to see what happened, and by the time she came back to the desk, she smelled the smoke coming from down the hall.

She got the firemen over here right away, so there wasn't much damage, like I said."

"What kind of a car was it?" Sam asked.

"Man, it was sweet: 427 four-speed, Camaro, silver with black stripes on the hood. I get hot just thinking about it."

"Sorry I missed that." He'd missed a lot during the past few days. Sam flashed back to the sound of the souped-up car he had heard leaving the Circle K the night Lee was killed as he walked out the door and headed across the parking lot to the high-rise. It was still early, so there wasn't much of a lunchtime crowd yet for the restaurant. Undetected, Sam slid into a booth toward the back of the restaurant, close enough to hear the table of hotel staff as they gathered for their meeting. The manager was going over the week's schedule. Once that was over, the group of employees disbanded to go to their duties. Sam picked up a menu from the table as a few employees streamed past him. One of them stopped to see whether he wanted to order anything, so he asked for coffee.

When a sprightly waitress returned with a mug, Sam asked her the same sort of questions as he'd asked the young clerk next door.

"Oh, wow, yeah, I heard about the car. I mean, like, everyone has heard of it, right? A bunch of us went to the pier that it hit, or, like, what was left of it." The waitress talked as bouncy as she walked, Sam noticed. "We were, like, that driver must have had too much of something, you know?"

"Did he get hurt?" Sam asked casually, as he glanced back over the menu.

"Oh, didn't you hear? The police didn't find the driver. The car door was open, the keys were gone, and the driver was gone, too. They already cleared the car out 'cause it was, like, a hazard or something." She waited patiently as Sam looked over the menu, then offered, "You looking for breakfast or lunch?"

"Just coffee, thanks."

With that, the waitress pulled out her pad of checks, scribbled what Sam thought looked like the word coffee and a smiley face, and placed it on the table. "Have a great day!" And she bounced off again toward the kitchen.

Sam left two dollars on the table, drank a few more sips of the black brew, and meandered back through the halls until he reached the lobby. An attractive woman about six feet tall stood behind the counter, tapping away at the hotel's computer keyboard as she balanced a phone on her shoulder.

"No, I am sorry; all of our oceanfront rooms are booked that weekend. We do have rooms on the other side of the building, though. Would you like one of those? Okay, let me see. Yes, I have two adjoining rooms for you, both non-smoking. Yes, that would be fine. May I have your credit card number to reserve the rooms? Yes…3451…yes…0221. Got it. Thank you. If you make it here before check-in time, you are welcome to use the restaurant. Okay, then; we will see you in two weeks."

Sam waited until she hung up the phone before approaching the desk.

"Hi. May I help you?" she called out to Sam.

"I hope so. Are you Tracey?"

"Yes. Who are you?"

"My name is Sam McClellan, and I am looking into the incident that happened here a few nights ago."

"You have to talk to the hotel manager. I'm the assistant manager, and I already told the cops everything I know. Are you an insurance agent or something?" She looked Sam over and offered a flirtatious smile.

"No, I am not with insurance. I'm a detective with the Carolina Beach Police, and I was just assigned to the case after a few days' leave. I suspect that the manager already told the other officers what he knew. I wanted to hear your version since you were on duty that night."

Sam pulled out a business card and handed it to the woman. She took the card and reviewed its contents, then stuffed it into the pocket of her khaki skirt. Sam noticed that her shirt was the same color as her blue eyes, and the contrast from her tanned skin made her none too difficult to look at.

"I can only talk for a few minutes. I have a lot of work to do." She turned her full attention to Sam.

"Let's start with the car. The clerk next door said you heard a car in the parking lot outside before it crashed through the fence. How could you have heard it in here? It seems well-insulated."

"I wasn't actually inside the lobby," Tracey offered. "I was taking a break and stepped out to smoke a cigarette when I heard a car screaming across the parking lot. The car came from the south side of the building, over there." Tracey walked to the end of the desk and pointed around the corner of a hall and out to the ocean. Yellow tape was running across the doorjamb to two of the rooms.

"Screaming?" Sam repeated.

"Yes, well, more like a rumbling. The police asked me to imitate what I heard…RUTTata, RUTTata, RUTTata—oh, this is silly. Anyway, my manager saw it and said it was a Camaro like one he'd had when he was younger. He said that it was a collector's dream…at least it was before it nosedived into the water.

"Then I saw it plow through the fence on the north side of the building, and the car jumped over what little dune there is there and ran into the base of what's left of the pier. The city never replaced it after Hurricane Fran got it, but they didn't pull out the pilings, either. By the time I climbed over the fence that the car knocked down, the car was halfway in the water. Like I told your buddies on the force, I ran back to the lobby, and as soon as I opened the door, I smelled smoke coming from the hallway. Alarms were going off everywhere, and people were running out of the place! It was a zoo! But the firemen got here in a hurry and put out the fire. We only had a little damage."

"Any ideas of what started it?"

"More like 'who'—the fireman who was in there first brought out a smoking file drawer and the computer's hard drive before another fellow turned the hose on the room. They didn't say, but I think somebody got in there and set the place on fire intentionally."

"Do you know what happened to it?"

Tracey just smiled. "You sure don't know too much about your case, Detective."

"Well, I just wanted to get your ideas. You were on the desk that night, so I thought maybe you saw something no one else did. Did you happen to see what the fireman did with the file drawer?"

"No. He just took it out of here in a heavy blanket of some kind—I guess to put the fire out without destroying whatever it was that set it off."

"What do you think was in there? I mean, what should have been in there—hotel records?" Sam leaned on the desk and smelled Tracey's perfume, a sweet scent of lilacs like his grandmother used to wear.

Just then, the phone rang. Tracey politely excused herself and answered it, turning back to the reservations computer.

Sam slowly moved away from the desk and down the hall to the first of the two closed doors. The doorframe was charred at its base. The lingering smell of smoke mingled with the stench of burnt carpeting as Sam opened the door and squatted under the yellow police tape. His eyes teared up for a second as he entered the room that had been an office. Charred remnants of an older model computer monitor sat on a warped plastic desk, and a four-drawer file cabinet minus one drawer leaned on its melted frame. Sam pulled hard at one of the drawers, but he couldn't get it open. He tried the second one down, and it budged, revealing its contents of charred bits of paper and folders. The next one was missing, and the lower one was so badly burned that it wouldn't open, either. Sam could see through the opening left from the missing drawer above it that whatever it held didn't survive the flames.

Sam poked around the room a few minutes longer, looking at the window casing, which was now covered with plywood. Halfway up the sliding window, the metal frame was bent. Forced entry. Whoever did this knew what he was doing. Sam started to pick his way back across the melted room when he saw Tracey standing in the doorway.

"I thought you were supposed to check into Command Central, or whatever you call it, to look at stuff," she said as she wiped her hands of non-apparent dirt on her skirt. "Find anything?" she casually asked.

"Nope. But I like to see a crime scene before diving into the evidence. You're right, we do have a 'command central' place, and I've already been there this morning. Still," he whispered, "I'd appreciate it if you didn't tell anyone I was here. I'm working undercover, so it's just easier this way."

"Whatever. You do it anyway you want, Detective. I'm just the hired help. Anything else I can help you with today?" She stepped back and motioned for him to come out of the office.

"No. I think I got all I needed here. Thanks for letting me look around. I want to be sure I don't miss anything as I start investigating." Sam offered his hand, and Tracey shook it calmly, but she didn't seem eager to let go.

Sam headed back through the lobby to the parking lot, then walked around the building to see where the car had busted down the fence and plowed into the water. There wasn't much to see, at this point.

Next stop, the fire station.

CHAPTER FIFTEEN

The firehouse's white stucco siding gleamed in the midday sun. Sam didn't make it over here very often despite its same-block proximity to the police station, but he knew everyone on the roster. Paul Martin, the fire chief, often held cookouts for the firemen and policemen at the end of the summer, as if to say, "We survived another year." The Golden Sun fire was the first apparent arson the town had seen in years, and the resulting commotion at the station was unusual.

"Hey, Jill, what's cooking today?" Sam called out to the dispatcher as he walked into the open bay.

Jill's office was just to the side of the station's two engines. To the right of her office were worn couches Sam guessed to be from the early 1970s, but they were comfortably positioned around a coffee table and high definition television.

Jill pulled off her earpiece and called back to Sam. "Hi, yourself. The guys are out back shooting hoops. What's up?"

"Just wanted to visit a minute with Eddie. Is he around?" Sam approached the small dispatch room, stopping to lean against the doorjamb.

"He's in the kitchen getting some lunch on. Help yourself—and bring me a plate when you come back through." Jill winked as she put her headset back on.

Only then did Sam realize she was listening to something good and groovy by Earth, Wind, and Fire. Sam picked up on the tune and headed through a screened door to a small but tidy kitchen filled with a commercial-grade stove and a refrigerator. Eddie was pulling the last of the sodas out of the refrigerator.

"What's for lunch?"

"Hey, man, your timing is great. The guys just took the burgers off the grill, and I'm getting the fixings out. Grab a plate." Eddie pointed to a dark-paneled cupboard, his thick arms and barrel chest filling his light blue T-shirt to capacity. Of all the guys at the firehouse, Eddie Sherman was the one Sam called most when there was a pickup game of basketball after hours. Eddie had been an all-star player in college, but a fall on the court, resulting in a bum knee, had forced him to choose another activity. Before he graduated, he started volunteering at the fire station, and he joined the crew when he finished his training program. Eddie was the station's technical guru, computer whiz, and all-around good guy. He had helped Sam out of a jam or two before, and Sam was betting he'd do it again.

"Thanks, Eddie, but I really came for some information. I wonder what you know about the contents of the file drawer or the hard drive that came out of the Golden Sun."

Eddie twisted the ends of his blond handlebar mustache for a moment. "Well, there wasn't much left of the stuff in the drawer. The hard drive, though, might still be salvageable. I haven't had a chance to turn it over to your guys yet because we haven't determined who gets it."

"It's evidence."

"You're assuming the fire was arson. So far, we're treading lightly on that. The manager and assistant manager are both smokers, and while neither of them claimed to have been in there, there was evidence of cigarettes. We're just checking out everything we can before we turn things over."

"That's not like you, Eddie. Come on; can't you give me a hint?" Sam was irritated. Why was Eddie holding out on him?

"Man, it's not my doing. Chief says we need to keep a lid on things now. I will promise you one thing, though—when I can release what I find out, you'll be the first to know." Eddie smiled sincerely, then hoisted a hefty cooler on his shoulder. "Sure you won't join us for lunch?"

"Yeah, I'm sure. Thanks anyway." Sam watched as Eddie strode to the back of the fire station. Sam could hear a basketball being dribbled, then a clang of a rim being hit. "Thanks anyway," he muttered as he walked out to his truck. *What's he up to?* Sam wondered as he headed back to his marina.

CHAPTER SIXTEEN

"Hey, there," Molly Monroe called to Sam when he was still 200 feet away on the dock. "I like your duck." She casually pointed to the persistent Mallard that was contently pruning herself on Sam's bimini despite Sam's heavy-footed approach.

"It's not my duck, and how did you find me?" Sam wasn't sure who to be more annoyed with—the fowl or the girl. He stepped aboard and tried to shoo the duck away from her roost.

"Well, it sure thinks your boat is home." Molly slipped off her red Keds and climbed aboard without waiting for an invitation. She watched as Sam tried in vain to shoo the duck away, then opened hatches to let some air in. "You know, there's an easier way to do that," she called as he moved forward to pop open the forward hatch.

"You an expert on ducks?"

"I grew up on a farm near Mount Airy—you know, Mayberry—and we had ducks all over the place. My brother and I used to throw rocks at them to get them to move, but Mom stopped that. Said it was mean. So we had to come up with a different plan."

"Yeah? What'd you do?"

"Stare at them. They thought we were choosing which one we wanted for dinner." With that, Molly stepped up on the raised coaming surrounding the cockpit and looked eye-to-eye at the duck. After a little mild quacking and some hissing, the bird moved off the bimini to the aft rail.

"Well, I'll be…." Sam was impressed.

"You got a beerrrr?" Molly asked, emphasizing the "r".

"Little early, don't you think?" Sam reached for a cold one and tossed it up to her as she made herself comfortable in the cockpit.

"Nice cushion design. Is there a patent pending?" She pointed to the cuts in the fabric.

"Something like that." Sam joined her in a drink, but he made his own water instead of beer. "How did you find out where I lived?"

"Friends in low places. Most everyone knows where cops live in a town this size. Your address isn't too hard to discover, if you know who to ask."

"And you, of course, do."

"Yep. I know lots of things. My brother was always in a bit of trouble, so I had to bail him out from time to time. Knowing the right person to help was a big deal when I needed it."

"Where is he now?"

"Davy Jones' locker, I guess. His body was never recovered, so I can only take the story for what it's worth." Molly took a long drink, clutching her green bottle tightly. "Still, I sometimes wonder. He was a good kid at heart; just not too bright about certain things."

"What was he into?"

"Drug-running for the big boys. I tried to get him to come work for me delivering boats, and he did it a couple of times, but I guess he thought he had to earn more."

"Big boys?"

"Dude, for a cop, you sure are dumb. That isn't your beat, is it?"

Sam felt his face grow hot. "My 'beat' is special investigations. I am a detective, not a beat cop. And beat cops don't deal with 'big boys,' anyway. What do you know?"

"Well, I got to thinking while I was drinking at the Barbary Coast. Maybe I got in your way that night because of karma."

"What?"

"I was supposed to be there. You were coming up from Southport, and I was too. Karma is what brings people together for a purpose. You said you thought you were in the way, and I started to think about what you might have been getting in the way of—what I might be able to help you with. And besides, maybe you could help me."

"Depends. What do you want help with?"

"I want to know more about my brother's death. If he was in somebody's way, then maybe we could work toget—"

"No." Sam cut her off. "I don't want a partner. I don't need a partner. The last one I had got his head blown off."

"Now see? You do care. I was beginning to think you didn't." Molly batted her eyes at Sam in an exaggerated fashion. "I asked around a little last night and got the word that your partner was killed not too long ago. Sorry, man; what a horrible way to go. Did he have family?"

Sam was silent for one full minute. "Why were you checking out my story, Molly?"

"Actually, I just wanted to know if there was something on you. I mean, if anyone knew anything about why somebody might be running you down on purpose. When I started talking, so did my friends." Molly fidgeted in her seat under the weight of Sam's stare.

"And what did you learn?"

"What you just told me, about your partner. Sorry about that."

"Anything else?"

"Well, that's why I came to find you today. I think you're getting into something deep, and I think my brother might have been sucked into the same trap. So I thought if you learned anything, you could, you know, share."

"If I find out anything, it's police information, not for public consumption, especially not for a vigilante sister."

"Even if it's your buddies on the force who are setting you up?" Molly's question hung in the air like Spanish moss on a live oak, its full gray length apparent, but not the many chiggers it contained.

"Talk," Sam said, leaning forward.

"There's this guy I know. He was a friend of my brother's, and he said there's something going on that your partner got messed up with. He didn't say how, but he had seen him around a few times down there."

"Down where?"

"Navassa. He wasn't supposed to be there, but he got in the way, so he was taken care of promptly. Anyway, my friend started putting two and two together, and he saw that the same folks involved with my brother's death were the bozos who got your partner. I suspect they're the same ones who have your number, now." Molly watched Sam's face cloud over.

"We're going sailing," Sam said quietly. He went forward to secure things and then called back up to the cockpit, "The key is on the hook in the aft cabin. Fire her up."

Without questioning him, Molly handed her empty bottle to Sam as he moved around the galley, then looked down the aft companionway where she saw a tarnished bronze hook with a key hanging on it. Sam watched as she took the wheel cover off, double-checked the position of the throttle and gear shifter, and then started the engine. He watched her check aft overboard to see what was coming out, take note of the wind's direction, and head for the lines on the port side. Sam could hear Molly working her way around the boat, removing lines in confidence.

Feeling the boat move, Sam glanced up from his task of storing all loose items below in the galley and watched Molly as she slowly backed out of the slip, casting the last line to the top of the starboard-side piling as the boat moved past it like a rodeo champ. He came topside in time to see her push the engine's gear shift forward slightly, nudging the throttle to get some forward momentum as *Angel* glided out of the marina's narrow fairway. She turned north toward the Myrtle Grove Sound, a thin channel of water between the mainland and Outer Banks lined with posh homes on one side and dredge spoil islands on the other.

Sam moved aft to take off the canvas cover from the mizzen. A random spider fell as he readied the sail and lines, then moved to the center of the cockpit coaming where he could reach the pull-cord on the StackPack containing the main. The engine's noise droned until they reached the shallow chop of Carolina Beach Inlet. Once in open water, Molly pointed the boat into the northeasterly wind. Starting aft, Sam raised the mizzen, then unfurled the Genoa. The wind pushing, urging, Sam raised the mainsail and returned to the cockpit. Molly pulled the air choke to stop the engine, refusing Sam's offer to take the helm.

"No, thanks; I'll take it on the reach; you work it back." Molly looked content at the helm to be on the water.

She looks different from the person who tried to pick my pocket, Sam thought. With her wavy hair, freckled skin that made her look more youthful than Sam guessed her to be, and her piercing green eyes, Molly was not unattractive. She'd never be mistaken for a beauty queen, but she was clever. She knew more than she was telling.

They sailed in silence for a while, Molly getting the feel for *Angel* as she steered slightly first to port, then to starboard, catching the wind in the sails. The Genoa's luffing soon subsided as Molly got it right, and the boat danced through slight waves, free from her marina slip's tethers, and doing what she was built for after a long absence from the waves. Light winds of ten knots made for a pleasant, easy sail. Sam was glad to be away from the slip, too.

CHAPTER SEVENTEEN

"Start from the beginning," Sam said over his shoulder, as he tightened the mizzen's halyard, and inspected the sails, which were long overdue for a cleaning. Brown spots left from mud daubers' nests created a polka-dot pattern on the sail, and Sam vowed silently to clean them all before taking the boat out again.

"Well, a lot of this is hearsay, but I think it's reliable," said Molly, keeping an eye on the two short pieces of fluttering yarn that hung from the bimini's metal frames, one on each side of the boat. The solid bimini blocked her view from the sails' luff tapes directly overhead, so these would do well to tell her when she veered too much off the wind.

"My friend Jimbo is a good guy. He and my brother did some things together when they were kids, and neither of them really ever grew up. But I think when my brother died, well, Jimbo got scared. Now, he wants to do right. So he started talking, hoping that word would get to somebody who could do something about it. I'm trying to do what I can to help him, see, and as it turns out, your partner was, too."

"What's this about?"

"Drugs. There are some big boys who run them up the coast. Drugs come in from Costa Rica, sometimes spending time in the islands, and sometimes coming into Southport. Word is that a fishery down there is the distribution point for the States."

"I can see that. Lots of trucking going on," Sam ventured.

"It's not just the trucks. There are a lot of 'tourists' who come through, and the guy who runs the place, Tripp Johnson, he fills their orders, so to speak, before they get to town. He lets the runners know what he needs. Then they go fetch the order. Jimbo was a runner with my brother."

"What about the Coast Guard? Don't they suspect something?" Sam thought for a minute about his own son. Was he facing the same stuff in his work?

"Sure; they stop a lot of boats, but they really are outnumbered to do any good. There are an awful lot of boats buzzing around. And it's not just the go-fast boats, or the shrimpers, though that's what most people think. Anybody can be a runner: kayakers, fishermen in small craft, even sailboats, though that's a different angle, better used for long-distance hauls."

"I'm all ears," Sam said as he leaned back.

"Well, it's not as difficult as it looks," Molly started. "I mean, anybody can be a mule, and the haul can vary, depending on the size of the boat. For instance, a twelve-foot Boston Whaler could bring in several hundred pounds, and that's the way it's always been. Probably won't change, either. The water is like the highway; anything goes. You know those huge cargo ships you see out there on the horizon? Some of the big dudes use those. Others, well, they'll hire guys like my brother to run it in. Even kayakers can do the job; it's just a question of dollars and risk, and like realtors are fond of saying, 'location, location, location'."

"Location?"

"Yep. Location can add to the variety. You know scuba divers sometimes have those extra tanks? Let me tell you, it's not extra air they are carrying. They dive down to a particular location, pick up what they need, bring it to the boat, and place it in a false bottom on the underside of the vessel without even breaking the water's surface. Pretty imaginative, right?"

"And then, of course, there's the shrimpers. Most people suspect them, and while lots of honest guys are out there, just as many are looking for a different kind of catch. They can stay offshore for long hauls, and then bring it in close enough for the little guys to get in on the action, so they act as middlemen and jack the prices. On the left coast and in the Gulf of Mexico, you got oil rigs, and they make for nice landmarks and drop-offs. Their pipes are good places to store stuff, too. Depending on their depths, divers can go get their loads, which are usually packaged in waterproof bags. Nice work for a diver."

"What about the Coast Guard?"

"Well, they are around, of course. But frankly, there's just too much of it going on for them to do anything about it. And there's so much water out there!" Molly made a sweeping gesture with her hand, pointing out the immensity of the task.

"I've talked to a few from time to time, and they sigh and shake their heads. They tell me that it's like the fishing story of the big one that got away: they might catch a little one, but the vast majority go unnoticed. It's a losing battle, and the chain of command knows it. Trying to catch the real punks is a drain on the Coasties. Their equipment is too slow and antiquated, and their manpower is insufficient. One Coastie told me he guessed that their catch-rate was one per one hundred. The press gets all excited, and our fearless governmental leaders start frothing at the mouth about one catch, but in reality, that's just the very tip of the iceberg. Besides, there's so much money to be made at the trade that there's always that temptation looming larger than life. That's what got my brother, and probably Lee."

"How did Lee get involved?"

"He just got in the way. He was helping some kids stay out of trouble by taking them sailing, so he had a reputation for being a good guy. One of the kids he was looking out for was the son of a reformed hooker in Navassa. He'd helped her get off the street, so when her own child started getting into trouble, she called Lee, and he stepped up to the plate to help this kid stay clean. He did a good job, too. That kid's now doing well in school, I hear.

"Anyway, when Tommy was killed, his girlfriend leaned pretty heavy on this woman for emotional support. She wasn't sure what to do, taking care of a little girl all alone in this mess. She's a cutie, my little niece is. I try to help Emily and—"

"Deloris?"

"How'd you know?"

"She sought me out at Lee's funeral. Your story was beginning to sound familiar," Sam said. "I told her to get out of town. She said something about Florida."

"Yeah, she has relatives down there. She and Tommy talked about opening a dive shop. Sounds pretty cool, you know?" Molly pulled the Genoa in a bit as she let the boat steer itself. "Hydraulic steering?"

"Yes. It's pretty good on the wind. The mizzen makes her sail to weather. Watch her fall off." As he spoke, the boat started to slow as she turned into the wind slightly, and the wind luffed the sail.

Molly righted the course and *Angel* picked up speed again. "I was thinking I might join them in Florida before this all happened. When did you talk to her?"

"Yesterday afternoon."

"Um-hum," said Molly softly. "Did she give you any leads as to what happened?"

"She suggested Lee knew. That's about all she had to offer." Sam thought about the notes and numbers he'd stashed away. "Does 211-8717 mean anything to you?"

Molly repeated them. "That's not a local prefix. No, I don't recognize it. Did you see that scrawled on a bathroom wall or something? 'Looking for a good time?'" Molly did her best Mae West impersonation.

"Something like that. Here; let me take the helm." Sam slid over toward the helmsman's seat. "You want some lunch? There's stuff below. Help yourself to whatever you can find."

Molly took the hint and headed below. She found a half-eaten bag of chips, some pretzels, and an apple. She also pulled two waters out of the refrigerator before coming topside and offering the lot to Sam.

"So what do you think Lee found out?" It was Molly's turn to fish for information.

"Whatever it was, it was hot. His desk at home got searched, and whoever was after it must have thought I got it because my boat got tossed on the same night Lee was killed." Sam pointed to the slashed cushion covers. "He was making a matrix of some kind. I just haven't had a chance to sift through it yet. That may have something to do with this mess."

"Where is it?"

"Tucked away," Sam said as he stuffed a handful of chips in his mouth. "What do you know about the fire at the Golden Sun Hotel?"

"What makes you think I know anything about that?" Molly sounded defensive.

"Because you seem to know a lot about what goes on in this town. Your friends, you know."

"I don't know all that much. I just focus on stuff that matters." She turned away and watched the horizon.

Seeing that he'd hit a nerve, Sam apologized. "Were you and your brother close?"

"Yep."

"Look, Molly; I think we got off on the wrong foot. We obviously have common information about certain things. Your brother and Lee were both into something they shouldn't have been into, and they both got waxed. Assuming it was a set-up, we might be looking for the same person."

"We?" Molly looked directly at Sam, her eyes flashing, but her mouth curling into a smile. "You mean 'we' should work together on this case? Like partners?"

"Don't get carried away, Molly. Let's just start with what we've got. If I find out anything more, I will let you know, and I want you to do the same. But you don't need to go find trouble for yourself. Understood?"

"Whatever."

"Let's start with why you were in Southport last night."

"I told you, I wasn't in Southport; I was delivering a boat for some guy on Bald Head Island from Wilmington. He got fresh with me on the ride home, so I decked him. He had a glass jaw, I guess, because when he hit the deck, he didn't get up again. I tossed an anchor overboard for him and then jumped overboard near Brunswick. I swam ashore and was looking for a ride when the guy with the deer lights came screaming by."

"And that's it?"

"Well, almost."

Sam got in her face. "Look; if we're going to work together, you have to tell me everything you know about this, or I can't help. What's worse, if you don't start being honest with me, you could get us both killed!"

"Well, don't get your boxers in a knot. I was getting around to telling you. I got to the marina on Bald Head earlier than the new boat's owner expected me, so before I met up with him, I did a little sightseeing. I walked over to the lighthouse. I wanted to see the view, so I climbed the stairs. Pretty spectacular, if you haven't been up there. You can see out to sea for quite a ways, something like twenty nautical miles.

"As I walked around the inside reading the signs about the structure and the history, I noticed a memorial plaque on the wall that commemorated the service of a woman cop who died on the grounds there. It reminded me of the story I had heard a few months earlier. There was little information about it in the article because, of course, it's *the island* and nobody *ever* dies over there. Anyway, that happened about the same time my brother got involved with the wrong crowd.

"I started thinking about that, and thinking there might be a connection to the guys who killed my brother. So this morning, I dug up the article in the newspaper's archives." Molly pulled from her shirt pocket a computer-printed copy of the article. She read the first paragraph to Sam:

> Melinda Southerby thought her new gig on Bald Head Island would be a peaceful change from her

stint as a police officer in Miami, Florida, but the job cost her dearly: she lost her life while off duty. After only two months on the force of the coastal North Carolina resort island, the Florida native was found shot to death at the base of Bald Head Island's lighthouse. She was dressed casually, and the Island police chief reported that she was not on duty at the time.

"So here's this supposedly experienced police officer who's joined the rent-a-cops over there. She's out for a moonlit ride in her golf cart, just enjoying the peace and quiet, right?" Molly put the paper down, pondering the circumstances. "The story would have us believe that she just got in the way of somebody who was doing something wrong there…certainly not a resident, though. She wasn't on duty, so she didn't have her gun or her radio to call for backup. That's what the story says."

Sam smiled. "But you've figured out the rest of the story, right, Sherlock?"

"Look; she drove to the lighthouse where the only lighting is the dim one on top and a few accent lights pointed back onto the lighthouse from its base for ambiance. She got in the way of something. Or someone. But what was she doing there? Was she supposed to meet somebody? A lover? Did she get a tip that there would be a reason to be there at exactly that time?

"And how come nobody heard the shot? There are houses all around there. Here's my guess: the gun was fired exactly as one of the ferries left the terminal and blew its horn! So whoever told her to come to the lighthouse and fired that fatal shot knew the boat schedule, or was watching the boat's lights, or had some inside information about when it would blow its horn before leaving the dock to make a much-ignored racket that covered the gunfire! And how come there wasn't a pack of dogs searching the island for a trace of dope, or a person, or something to help determine what all was involved?"

"Whoa, Monroe. You are getting a little carried away, here. Why is this story important to what happened to Tommy and Lee?"

"Because Jimbo was the lookout that night…and Tommy was in the creek behind the lighthouse, waiting for their 'friend' to meet the cop. If you stick with me, you see that she had connections in Miami, and she was planted on the island to ensure that the goods were going through the way they were supposed to. Jimbo said she was there to meet the locals and help make the connections with 'tourists' who passed through the island, then back to the mainland with their treasures."

"What went wrong?"

"She was stepping on toes. Her boss in Miami was reaching into the North Carolina territory. Johnson and friends didn't like it, so they sent a message to the Miami boss this way."

"Who was the trigger?"

"Jimbo says it was Tripp Johnson. He's scared now, and he thinks Tripp will be on to him as soon as he learns Jimbo didn't go down with my brother. He's been hiding out all this time, trying to get enough money to get away for good."

"So you are thinking Tripp took out your brother and Lee?" Sam said. "Why was Johnson after Tommy? He was doing a good job running the load, wasn't he?"

"Sure, but knowing Tripp wasted a cop—even if she was a plant—made Tommy nervous. He wanted out. Tripp wasn't about to let that happen…."

"So Lee found out about this from Deloris, and he wanted to get to Tripp…but Tripp got a heads-up somewhere along the line and pulled a fast one on Lee," Sam finished Molly's sentence.

Molly tapped the tip of her nose. The silence that followed the revelation was pierced only by the wind as it whistled through the rigging.

"Mind if I take the helm?" She moved in front of the wheel, and Sam slid off the seat.

"What does this have to do with Navassa?" Sam moved to sit on the port side.

"Well, it's all tied together, somehow. That's probably what your buddy was working on, too. Now whoever got him is after you." Molly pointed her finger at Sam.

"Yeah, I know."

"Now it's your turn to share. What were you doing on the road back from Southport last night?"

Sam trimmed the sails, stalling a bit. "I ate at Provision's, then drove home."

"Did you see anything? Talk to anybody? Play detective?"

"No, no, and no. I just went for a ride. Didn't tell anybody where I was going; I just went."

"And so you checked your car for a tracking bug, right? It was just coincidence that somebody tried to run you off the road, right?" Molly sat back and crossed her arms like a disapproving school marm.

"Just coincidence." Sam mentally kicked himself for not checking. The Altima he was driving was a loaner from the department. If there was a tracking device on it, Sam almost didn't want to know. "Come on. We're heading back in now." Sam pulled the wheel hard to port, and released the Genoa's furling line as they headed back to the dock.

• • •

While securing the boat, Sam's cell phone rang. "Hello. Yes, this is Sam McClellan." Sam clenched his teeth as he listened to the caller on the other end, repeating what was said for Molly's benefit. "You found a gizmo attached to the underside of my car? You don't say? Well, hang on to it. I'll be by for it later today. And don't call anyone else about this." His face gave away the sinking feeling he had.

"Another coincidence?" Molly ribbed.

"Another bug."

CHAPTER EIGHTEEN

"What's our next move?"

"*Your* next move is to go home and stay out of trouble."

"What? Dude, there's no way you're cutting me off like this. I need to help."

"You need to stay away from me and this mess, Mol. I can work faster if I don't have to worry about you."

"Worry about little ol' me? How sweet. Totally unnecessary, but sweet." Molly stood tall, her hands firmly on her hips. "I can take care of myself."

Sam didn't doubt that for a second. "Sure. But I don't have anything for you to do right now. Go home. Wait. I'll call you."

"I've heard that line before. And anyway, I don't have a phone, so you can't call me. Nope, I will have to check in on you a little later."

"No phone?" Sam was incredulous.

"No television, either. It rots the mind."

"How do you find your hot tips and leads, then?"

"Newspaper, and word-on-the-street news. And I go to the public library when I need to use the computer." Molly patted her shirt pocket, indicating the article print-out.

"Come on; I'll walk with you to the car."

"No car, either."

"How did you get here, then? I'm a long way from Fourth Street."

"A friend gave me a lift. You could offer to give me a ride home, if you're feeling charitable."

Once in Sam's truck, Molly gave him directions to Wilmington's Second Street.

"Just drop me off here. I need to get a few things in town, and this way, it's a one-way walk."

Sam did as he was told, leaving Molly in front of a small, antiquated, and rare city market. It was no bigger than many of the neighboring restaurants, but holding its own against encroaching development.

Sam headed to the station's impound to look for the Camaro.

"Sam, hey, I am sorry about Lee," George Alston called out as Sam entered the squatty warehouse. "He was a good man. I didn't get a chance to talk to you at his funeral, but I want you to know we all stand with you."

"Thanks, George," Sam said sincerely. George was true-blue, and in Sam's estimation, had seen it all over his long career with the force. Closing in on retirement, George was content to mind the evidence warehouse, tracking everything that came in, day after day after long, boring day.

"What can I help you with today, Sam?"

"I'm on the fire at Golden Sun. Wanted to take a look at the car that nose-dived into the ocean."

"Oh, that's already been taken to Wally's." George checked his log and nodded like a fake Chihuahua in the back of an Oldsmobile.

"When did it come in?"

"That same night. Ah, here it is," George pointed to his log. "Two in the morning. But it didn't stay long. Wally's guys came and got it."

"But the case is still open! Why are we disposing of evidence before the case is closed?"

"I don't know anything about that." George rarely wanted to know about any of it. He stayed content that way. "You better check with Chief. I'm sure he had all he needed on it."

"Thanks, George."

Sam drove to the tidy fenced-in lot of Wally's just a few miles away. Everything was close in Carolina Beach, though summer beach traffic sometimes made it feel as if everything were miles apart. Wally's sat on prime real estate; it'd been there forever and wasn't caving into developers who wanted his location for their own designs.

Wally Ebertson had passed the shop on to his daughter, Stella. In her late sixties, Stella ran a tight ship, with everything where it should be and everything accounted for. But Stella, Sam learned from her less-than-stellar employee, John Henry, was on vacation all week.

"She's gone to visit an uncle in Minnesota," John offered. "Something about cancer, she said." John was a fat, hairy man, one step removed from gorillahood, right down to his knuckles dragging on the sandy patch underneath his latest pickup: a shiny red corvette, probably towed for sport, knowing John.

"Where's the Camaro that came in a few nights ago?" Sam's eyes were scanning the neatly stacked rows of car remnants in search of the car. He wondered why Stella kept John around.

"She was ruined, for one thing. No way anybody ever gonna get that car back to running. Sand, grit, mud, water…." John marked off the offenses on his fat, grimy fingers.

"Where is it? I'd like to look at it."

"Stack twenty-five, Row B." John didn't bother to point it out, but he graciously waved his hand toward the general direction of the rear lot. Sam walked in that direction, counting off the stacks, then the ten-foot rows, as he passed them. There, one away from the top of the stack, was the crushed carcass of a car Sam could only guess was the Camaro.

Sam fumed as he jogged back to the gorilla-man. "Who gave the order to crush it? The case is still open; it's still evidence."

"Look, pal; if you don't like the procedure, talk to your boss. I just do as I'm told." John didn't bother to stand up this time.

"Who told you?"

"Chief."

Sam stormed back to his car without a word. Procedure. Evidence. He rolled it over in his mind like a Rubik's Cube as he drove to the police station. It didn't make sense.

CHAPTER NINETEEN

"What's going on, Chief?" Sam stormed into Chief Singleton's office at full speed, ignoring the growl Singleton made as he whirled around in his desk chair, the phone glued to one ear. "Put the damn phone down and give me some answers!" Sam grabbed the phone away from Chief and slammed it down on the receiver; then he glared at a startled Chief from across his own desk.

"What's gotten into you, Sam?" Chief shot back. He moved around to close his office door so the department wouldn't hear the ensuing shouting match; then he warily walked back to his chair and slowly sat. His desk phone rang again. This time, he answered it with a short, "I'll call you back," before hanging up.

"Me? I am just looking for some answers." Sam's hands balled into fists as he leaned on the desk. "I just learned that my old truck's bugged. Then, I see with my own two eyes a suspect's car that was lifted from the dunes at the Golden Sun has already been crushed beyond recognition over at Wally's. Whatever happened to proper procedures? I thought you assigned me to the fire case because you thought I could find some answers. But now I think you put me there to keep me out of the way or something. I am guessing my loaner car was bugged too, which means somebody was tracking me the night I ran into a tree. Help me out, here, Chief. What the hell is going on?" Sam crossed his arms over his chest as he stared at Singleton.

"First off," said Chief, taking a deep breath apparently to control his temper, "the car has been in the warehouse for close to a week. We dusted it inside and out, and it was clean. There's no room in there for ghosts, so we talked with Commissioner Martin, who signed the order. Next, we sent it to Wally's Wrecking to be crushed. *That's* standard operating procedure." Chief shifted forward in his chair and thumped a thick stack of papers on a corner of his desk. "Second, I have a caseload here like none I've seen before. Your piddly-assed attempt to find some answers at Golden Sun means nothing to me. I've got me a suspect, and I was on the phone trying to round up some more information to make it stick. Meanwhile, Andy tells me you are out sailing with some chickie. That's really being *on* the case, I'd say. And you are being watched because you are a suspect in Lee's murder. So shut your loud mouth and get your skinny ass out of my office. You are suspended, and I don't want to see you lurking around here until we get this solved!" Chief stood up with such force that his chair tipped over behind him as he pushed away from the desk. "I want your gun and your badge on the main desk on your way out the door."

"Suspended? You think I had something to do with Lee's murder? What are you, nuts?"

"Out! Now!"

"But I…. Shit!"

Sam nearly ripped the door off its hinges on his way out, and he shouted obscenities all the way to the street. Before he got in his truck, he dropped to his hands and knees to search the underside. Not seeing what he was expecting, Sam peeled out of the parking lot and headed toward the marina.

Before he reached his dock, Sam heard someone shout his name.

"Sam! Hey, Sam, can you wait up?"

Dillon Bates, the marina's smug young dockmaster, trotted toward him from the covered porch of the dock office. His pressed white polo shirt and khaki shorts were his personal uniform, even though the marina had no formal dress code for its four employees. His cropped blond hair was swooped and gooped up in the front, seeming to blow in a nonexistent breeze.

"What's up, Dillon?" Sam didn't slow his gait, forcing the young prepster into a run to catch up.

"Apparently, your lease." Dillon seemed pleased to be giving Sam the boot.

"What now?" Sam stopped to face Dillon. He was a full six inches taller than Dillon, and he noticed that the upturned swoop of hair helped to hide an encroaching bald spot.

"Your contract clearly states, 'No pets.' Sorry, man, but you got to get rid of the pet, or we have to get rid of you."

"I don't have a pet."

"Birds count, Sam."

"Bir...you mean the duck?" Sam couldn't hold back his laugh. "That's not a pet; that's a duck that likes to hang around on the pilings. I don't feed it, I don't cuddle it, and I don't pick up after it. Thus, it is *not* my pet."

"That's really not our concern. Besides, you are five days late in paying your slip fee, giving the marina owner another reason to turn it over to someone else who can pay. You have to go, Sam, and you have to take your *pet* with you."

"But it's not my pet! It's a duck. A wild duck. I can't take it with me because it's not mine!" No longer amused, Sam was agitated at this little runt of a guy telling him to leave.

"You signed the agreement. Right here, see? N-O P-E-T-S!" Dillon was having way too much fun with this as he held up the agreement with the clause highlighted in yellow for Sam's benefit.

Sam stomped toward his boat, and sure enough, there sat Kathy the duck, cozy on *her* seat in the cockpit. As he approached the boat, Sam tried to shoo her away, but she wouldn't budge. He grabbed a cushion and swung at her, missing as she flapped her wings and flew to the top of the aft rail. Sam didn't think; he just reached for the key and started the engine. The duck stayed put, and Sam started untying lines. Without a word to anyone, he motored out of his slip and headed out of the marina.

CHAPTER TWENTY

For the next two hours, Sam motored his way toward the Wrightsville Beach Causeway. The scenery varied from Myrtle Grove Sound to Masonboro Sound, from soaring hotel towers to glitzy McMansions to verdant wild wax myrtle trees and open sand dunes. At the causeway near the only bridge to Wrightsville Beach, Sam found a mooring field with a few open spots. It wouldn't be this way in a few hours, Sam knew, as the snowbird boaters made their boats fast for the evening. On either side of the causeway's protected waters were places to eat and shop, making it an ideal stopping place. Best of all, there was no fee to pick up a mooring ball there.

Sam had to hitch a ride with a passing dinghy to get to shore. Though the ride was short, by the time the battered motoring dinghy arrived, Sam was drenched.

Next, he thumbed it back to Carolina Beach to retrieve his truck parked at the marina. He thanked the driver for the ride and headed for his truck. Not knowing how to get back aboard since he didn't own a dinghy, Sam drove to the nearest Target store and bought a dry shirt and jeans. He'd have to figure out another place to dock, or buy a dinghy, an expense he really couldn't afford now that he was suspended from the force. A quick dinner at the Three Sisters' Café and a Bass Ale had Sam feeling a bit like Scarlett O'Hara: he decided he would deal with finding a new slip tomorrow.

It didn't take long to reach the Navassa exit from Highway 17. Not knowing where to look exactly, Sam decided to cruise the main street, which was all of four blocks long. He didn't know where to start, but he felt sure he had to trace Lee's steps to fill in the missing pieces that would help him figure out what had happened. Navassa was part of the puzzle. He just didn't know which part.

Navassa is little more than a crossroads, with all the amenities that stopping travelers need—fast food, gas, and a few sundries for the road—plus, an expanding belt of homes for Wilmington's commuters. The area was considered by some to be blight on the coast's otherwise glowing reputation until developers saw a golden opportunity. Despite the community's best efforts to present a clean, well-ordered community of look-alike houses, drugs were still abundant and easily had. Prostitution was a new one to Sam, but if Deloris were right, it was a booming business. Sam was vaguely aware of the kinds of kids Lee took out sailing from time to time. He silently praised Lee for his efforts. Sam felt selfish for not looking beyond his own little world, for not reaching out to someone else in need. He vowed to improve his track record.

Canvassing the streets, Sam headed into a dubious area of town. Even though it was early in the evening, Sam knew that *workers* didn't pay attention to clocks. They paid attention to dollars. After driving a few streets, he noticed a house that was better cared for than others on the block of dilapidated 1970s ranch-style houses. The grass was cut, the shutters neatly painted turquoise, and lights shining brightly on the young landscaping.

Sam circled the block and parked as far away from the house as he could manage and still see the place. For two hours, he watched visitors arrive and depart, clocking their stays at an average of thirty minutes each. In the fading light, Sam tried to imagine how far into this scene an observer like Lee could have gotten without getting noticed. He was jarred from his thoughts by the sight of a woman driving past him in a little olive green convertible Jetta.

"Molly?" Sam sat upright in his truck. "What's she doing?"

When Molly stepped out of the convertible, she was a sight to behold. She was wearing a tight sparkly purple dress that stopped at her thighs, and obviously uncomfortable high heels. Her dark hair flowed gently about her in the evening breeze, and she had on lipstick. Bright red lipstick.

Sam was out of his truck in seconds and composing a storyline in his head as he walked quickly to the house. He loudly coughed, trying to catch Molly's attention, and reached her as she waited on the front steps of the house. Grabbing her by the elbow, he growled lowly, "What's going on, Molly?"

Sam briskly escorted Molly away from the house, tightening his grip on her arm as they strolled down the street. He walked so close to her that if anyone were looking on, he should see a couple out for an evening walk. But Sam's ruse was unsuccessful.

Two guys jumped out of a battered black minivan and approached Sam and Molly with alarming speed. Pulling Molly tightly to his side, Sam whispered, "Not a word," and then looked straight ahead.

"Nice night for a walk," the one who looked like a defensive lineman sang out, without lessening his pace. He turned and in an instant was walking closely beside Sam.

"Come with us," the other one said as he maneuvered around to Molly's side, thereby steering Sam and Molly toward the van. "You from the Southport force? I know I seen your face somewhere; just can't place you."

Sam was confused. "I don't know what you're talking about. We're just lost."

"No, man, I seen you. You ain't visiting. You're a cop."

Walking slower as they reached the van doors, Sam grabbed Molly's arm so tightly that she yelped.

"Well, I am a cop, but I'm not here on official business. My girlfriend and I were on our way to a party, and we got the address confused. I realized our mistake just before she rang the doorbell."

"It's okay, man. But we don't do it that way here. If you want in, all you have to do is say so. Come into the van and we'll talk about it. Your…uh, *girlfriend* can come too." The defensive lineman planted himself behind Sam and Molly while the other slid the van's door open.

"Look; I don't know what you bozos are talking about!" Molly shouted. "My college roommate invited us to come to her party, and I read the directions wrong! This is where we were to meet, I thought…and now we are going to be late! Now if you don't mind, I have to find a bathroom real quick, or I am going to ruin my new dress. Excuse me, Mister. Honey, are you coming?" Molly called over her shoulder as she scooted past a surprised linebacker.

Sam shrugged his shoulders and trotted after Molly, who was walking as fast as she could manage in her ill-fitting outfit. A second after they both hopped into her car parked a few houses away, Molly hit the gas and the car took off with a jolt before Sam had his door completely shut.

The minivan's engine sputtered and coughed, then finally came to life, and its frame filled the rearview mirror of Molly's car as she headed for the highway. A string of green traffic lights increased the distance between the two cars, but the last traffic light before the highway ramp was yellow. Molly floored it. The linebacker tried to do the same, but a river of cars flowed with the opposing green light, sufficiently separating Molly from the minivan as she merged onto the highway, heading north toward the historic port town of Wilmington.

"What were you thinking?" Sam shouted when they reached the highway.

"Apparently the same thing you were!" Molly shot back at him. "May their alternator fall apart just as they reach the bridge, and their tires fall off too—which may happen, curse or no curse!"

Deftly swerving between cars at a speed that would frighten most drivers, Molly exited the highway at the entrance to the permanently-docked *USS North Carolina* battleship. At the end of the road, past the last parking lot for the battleship-turned-museum, lay the river and a full view of Wilmington's downtown waterfront on the opposing bank. Partially hidden under low-growing shrubs a few yards away was an old beat-up dinghy with chipped paint on its hull and a sack of clothes under a tarp. Kicking off her shoes, Molly ducked behind the bushes. She soon reemerged wearing jeans and a long gray cable knit turtleneck sweater. Molly quickly tucked her hair up under a blue Durham Bulls ball cap, shoved her other outfit in the dry sack, and pushed the boat out from under the bushes into the murky water.

"Coming?" she called to Sam as she jumped into the tender and took the oars in her hands.

Sam nearly missed the boat by leaping for it. He took an uneasy seat in the bow, incredulously watching Molly at the oars.

"What about your car?"

"Not mine." Molly was so nonchalant that Sam was afraid to ask whose it was.

CHAPTER TWENTY-ONE

"Where are we going, Mol?"

"Well, I figure your boat is marked, but so far, nobody knows about mine.... At least, I don't think they do." Her stroke was strong and steady, her course straight. "My boat is around the wharf, just past the chemical plant. I figure we should go there to sort things out and think out our plan of action."

"There you go again, we-ing all over the place. I told you I don't need a partner. And just what were you planning on doing—walking into that place and taking the next customer who flashed the cash? You could get hurt bad trying that kind of act."

"Oh, you're just jealous because I could get in without paying to get some information. All I planned on doing was talking it up with the girls. Reneeta had arranged everything for me, but we had to make it look like I was just visiting, dressed proper for a visit with the girls, see, but not the visitors. Then you burst onto the scene and nearly get us hauled away to who knows where by two gorillas who think they know you! Man, if those are your friends, you might want to pick some new ones."

"They weren't friends; they were cops. And that house was their house. Those girls were their moneymakers. They thought I was cutting in on the action!"

"Lee was in deep over his head, and he didn't even know it," said Molly, voicing Sam's thoughts.

"Um-hum. He had no idea what he was walking into, I bet."

Molly maneuvered her rowboat toward a forty-two-foot wooden Chris Craft motorboat. Its shimmering golden sides reflected the water in the setting sun's light, and its red coach roof sparkled to match the bronze ports. Tying the painter line of the dinghy to the boarding ladder, Molly gingerly stepped from the center of the tender to the ladder and climbed nimbly aboard. Looking over the stern rail to check momentarily on Sam's progress, Molly soon disappeared below and turned on the cabin lights.

Quickly, Sam made his way aboard the well-maintained yacht. He guessed it to be a late 1960s or an early 1970s model, with its wooden hull and original fittings. Assuming it was Molly's boat, Sam saw that she took good care of it. On the beamy aft deck were two captain's chairs with deep navy blue cushions piped in red cording. A varnished teak table made from a cockpit grate stood squarely between the two chairs. The teak cockpit coaming and handrails that surrounded the vessel gleamed, too, the result of hours of sanding and varnishing, Sam knew. The same proper navy blue and red fabric continued in the salon and galley three steps down where Delft blue tiles lined the interior of the galley's bulkheads and walls. Just ahead of the galley and yet another three steps down, Sam could see the entrance to the v-berth where Molly rustled through some drawers before coming back to the galley.

"Didn't take you for a stink-potter, Molly. Is this your boat?"

"Yeah, it's mine. I just finished her spring cleaning. Looks pretty good for an old girl, don't you think?" Molly pulled on some wool socks, and then got busy in the galley. "I don't know about you, but I'm starving!" Out of the upright refrigerator, she pulled two large king mackerel steaks, fresh asparagus, and crookneck yellow squash. She pointed to the settee and tossed Sam an onion. "Grab a knife from the top drawer and the cutting board from the counter and get to work. I want three thick slices for the fish and some chopped for the squash."

Sam did as he was told. He watched Molly as she passed through the cabin and went out on the back deck where she lit a small propane grill mounted on the aft rail. Returning to the galley, she marinated the mackerel in a mix of olive oil, mustard, soy sauce, ginger, and honey. Once she was satisfied with the progress of her side dishes, she took the large slabs of onion from Sam and placed them on the grill first topped with the fish. She closed the lid and returned to the galley where she continued chopping vegetables and wrapping them in a foil pouch before putting them on the grill, too. She started a pot of rice on the galley stove, and when it was simmering, she handed Sam a dark Guinness Stout. Deftly opening her own beer, she tossed the dolphin-shaped bottle opener to Sam and sat across from him in the salon. Once Molly had found a pad of paper and pen from a small cabinet above the settee, she jotted down the names of the area's surrounding towns of Southport, Navassa, Bald Head Island, the dates of Tommy's death and Lee's murder, and anything else that came to mind.

"You think those cops were running a prostitution ring in Navassa, right?" Molly took a long swig of her beer. "Do you think Lee got waxed because of them—or because of the drugs out of Southport?"

"I'm putting this thing together as you are, Molly. If the fine fellows we met in Navassa were in on the drugs too, and Lee found out while he was trying to help Reneeta or some of her friends, then he probably made the connection. Can we get your buddy Jimbo over here? There's got to be more to it. I just can't see it."

"Sure; I know where he is. We'll find him after we eat."

Sam looked over Molly's notes. He thought of his own notes and Lee's tucked away on *Angel*.

"Plates are in the shelf there, and silverware is in this locker," instructed Molly. "You serve up the rice and I'll get the rest." Molly got the mackerel and vegetables from the grill and loaded their plates. "If you need more, help yourself," she said as she placed it all in the galley's stove to keep it warm, then dove into her food. Not waiting for

Sam to comment, Molly offered the background behind her fish recipe. "This recipe came from a cook in one of the restaurants over on the beach. By putting the onions down first, their flavor gets grilled into the fish, and they make it a lot easier to get the fish off the grill when it's cooked."

"Great!" Sam said, genuinely appreciative. He hadn't realized how hungry he was until he got a taste of the food. It didn't take long, and he was out of his seat getting more, offering some to Molly. When they were done, he washed the dishes while Molly finished her beer.

"I almost hate to ask, but whose car was that we drove this evening?"

"Then don't ask. You probably wouldn't like the answer."

CHAPTER TWENTY-TWO

The row from Molly's boat at Bennett's Marina to Wilmington's main docks at the edge of Riverfront Park was an easy one with Sam at the oars. Molly bundled up against the approaching night's chill, and Sam warmed himself with each pull of the long wooden oars, a dull gray compared to the varnished yacht they rowed away from. Sam smiled when the gold-painted name on the stern registered: *Hullabaloo*.

Tying up at the covered wharf, Molly wove a skinny chain cinched off by a bike lock through the ends of both oars, the painter's ring, and then under the supports of the piling that the dock rested upon. They walked to the Barbary Coast Bar, where Molly was sure they'd find Jimbo. She received and returned a hearty hello from some of the guys seated on high stools at the bar. Then she led Sam to the far end of the well-polished mahogany bar where the lights were not so bright and ordered two beers.

"What's new, Reed?" she called to the bartender as he poured their beers.

"Same old, same old," the grizzly-looking man said, eyeing Sam carefully. "I don't think you've introduced me to your buddy here," Reed said as he wiped his hands on a towel slung over his shoulder. The towel came to rest atop Reed's cascading silvery hair.

"This is my cousin Justin. He's visiting from Oklahoma. I'm just showing him around town for a few days before he heads off to his new post."

Sam saw Reed relax a bit upon hearing Molly's explanation, making him wonder about the apparent protective nature of their relationship.

"Navy, eh? I wondered about your short hair." Reed pointed to Sam's head. "What's your next duty station?"

"I'm off to Norfolk for a while," said Sam, falling into the bluff as fast as he could think. I was hoping my *cousin* could show me around a little so I could, you know, pay my respects to her brother. We were close as kids."

Molly glared at him.

"Yeah, that was too bad about Tommy. We all miss him around here." Reed nodded toward Molly, then moved on to help another customer with drink orders.

"Okay, *cuz*, what now? Do you see Jimbo here?" Sam turned slightly to Molly, his voice lowered.

"Oh, he'll be along. He's a creature of habit. Well, many habits, I guess you could say. This is his place, and he surfaces when he needs something."

"How do you know he needs something?"

"The Jetta. He liberated it for me." Molly smiled as she sipped her beer, arms leaning comfortably on the bar's edge. "As a favor. I told him I'd round up some cash if he got me a car."

"So you went to the whorehouse to get it?" Sam was amazed at the lengths to which he guessed this woman would go.

"Well, not exactly. But I have friends who owe favors, and so we all help each other out. I was going there to get information and to collect money intended for Deloris. It was a contribution from the girls there who were all sorry to hear what had happened, and they've each been putting away a little for her from every trick since Tommy's death. But since you broke up our little tea party before it got started, I still had to come through with cash for Deloris and some more for Jimbo since he got me a car for our little adventure. I keep a stash aboard *Hullabaloo*, so I'll just give Jimbo some and give the rest to Deloris so she can take Emily to Florida."

"Sorry; I didn't know," said an embarrassed Sam. "But you really are asking for trouble. Maybe *you* need a better circle of friends."

"We take what we get and make the best out of it." Molly patted Sam's arm in a motherly manner. "Besides, you're going to get what you need out of tonight, don't you worry." She leaned back with a smile.

Sam looked away hurriedly, hoping to hide the blush of heat he felt rise to his cheeks. *She's coming on to me, isn't she?*

"So where is Jimbo?" He scanned the room, taking in the mix of yuppies and freaks. A few young couples in trendy dress-code black outfits bejeweled with silver clung to each other on a small, makeshift dance floor, while older salts held court among their comrades in the dark red-clad booths rimming the room. Periodically, a blast of cool night air announced the arrival of tourists looking for the "real" Wilmington. Sam watched as they turned abruptly back to the door when they summed up the patrons inside. Sam imagined that they all looked scary to newcomers. And in the midst of the growing crowd, Reed and two waitresses appeased them all with the wail of Lynyrd Skynyrd's "Sweet Home Alabama."

"There's Jimbo." Molly waved as a tall round-bearded man wearing a floppy hat ambled toward them from a bank of dimly lit booths.

"Hey, Jimbo! I want you to meet my cousin," Molly said as they followed Jimbo back to his booth. She slid in on one side, and Sam sat down next to her. Jimbo took his place opposite them.

Jimbo looked from Sam to Molly and back again. Turning to Sam, he said, "Hello, 'cousin of Molly'; name's Jimbo." He thrust out his hand for a shake.

"Justin," Sam said as they shook hands. "Molly tells me you knew my cousin, Tommy."

"Cousin?" Jimbo laughed. "Molly, who are you trying to kid?" Jimbo waved over a waitress and ordered a round of beers. "This guy's a cop."

"How'd you know?" Molly spilled the beans.

"I can smell 'em a mile away. Are you in trouble again, Molly?" Jimbo grinned.

"Not me, Jimbo. He's the one in trouble." She slowly pointed a finger at Sam. "I'm just trying to help him out of it before he gets what Tommy got."

"Oh, I see. How'd you get messed up with this, pal?" Jimbo helped the skinny waitress with her loaded tray by passing out the mugs and helping himself to the pitcher.

"Name's Sam McClellan. My partner was actually the one who got messed up with it. He was trying to help some folks to get out of the way, and he got killed because he knew too much."

"And now they're coming after you," Jimbo finished Sam's thoughts.

"Yep. Somebody thinks I know too much, too; but all I got are pieces to the puzzle. I'm hoping you can help me with one of them."

"Shoot."

"Well, we know what's going on, and we think we know what happened to Tommy. Tonight, we learned about something happening in Navassa that may or may not be connected…."

"It is," Jimbo offered.

"Okay, so there's that. My partner hid a sheet of numbers, perhaps a code, before he was killed. I wonder if you know what it means." Sam wrote the series of numbers on a napkin, 2118717. He turned it around for Jimbo to see.

Jimbo snorted. "That's the whole world to these folks, man. The route."

Sam looked puzzled.

"The triangle, man. The roads' numbers form a triangle!" Jimbo traced a triangle on the table, starting from a condensation circle his mug left on the wood. "The road into Southport, 211, is known as the local route for mules and carriers. The road between Southport and Wilmington, 87, is the regional route and pays lots more. And the highway, U.S. 17, is known as the route extending the reach far beyond the region, the highest paid route of all."

"That triangle is what somebody's protecting." It was more of a statement than a question that Sam posed, looking first at Molly, then at Jimbo. He drank from his mug and continued. "Tommy wanted to get out of it, but he couldn't get away fast enough. One of the 'girls' in Navassa called my partner in to help her get out, and he stumbled into the triangle; then he got eliminated. Now, whoever is in charge is coming after me. It fits." He hesitated before continuing. "Deloris told me you and another guy hid on the boat when Tommy was killed. She said you swam to shore, to Bald Head. How is it that you are still alive to tell me this?"

Jimbo looked around for a minute, then lowered his voice. "Because I'm dead."

Molly chuckled nervously for her friend.

"Dead?" Sam asked.

"Dead. I been hiding out ever since that night. They've come looking for me I've been told, but so far, I been keeping one step ahead. I am going to be leaving town pretty soon. Just need to get up enough money to last me a while. Molly, did you get what you said you would?"

Molly reached into her pocket and pulled out a small purple Crown Royale sack. She held it in her lap for a second before nodding. Without a word, she lifted both of her hands onto the table and placed them into Jimbo's outstretched hands, making a transfer. Then she leaned over the table and kissed him gently. "Use it well, Jimbo. And thanks for getting the car for me."

"No problem. You should see the beaut I've got lined up for my…vacation."

"Where are you going?" Sam asked.

"Can't say for sure. I plan to see where the wind's going to take me. I got all my stuff ready, and now that I got this," he nodded toward his hands, still folded on the table, "I guess I got no reason to stay." He took a long drink from his mug and started to get up. "You know who did it, don't you?"

"I have a hunch you do," Sam said.

"Yep. Johnson's your man," Jimbo whispered. "But if you have to get proof to take him down, you can start by getting in on the action yourself. You need to talk to Johnson's general manager. I just knew him as Mr. Walters. He's a retired shrimper in Southport who has a handle on schedules if you want to pretend to be runners. The only way to reach him, though, is to go to the source: Johnson's."

Jimbo stood tall, rearranged the now-exposed pillow stashed beneath his loud Hawaiian-print shirt, and tipped his hat to Molly. "Stay out of trouble, girl. And thanks." He patted a pocket he'd filled with the purple sack. Turning to Sam, he winked, "And you keep her out of trouble, will ya, pal?"

Sam nodded and raised his hand to salute Jimbo. "Will do. You stay out of trouble, too." Sam watched Jimbo amble away, tipping his hat to Reed as he exited the bar into the rush of cool night air.

"You would have done that for him at Navassa, wouldn't you?" Sam whispered to Molly when he caught her eye again. "Why?"

"Trust," she whispered.

"You are suggesting something?"

"Maybe. Maybe not. Friends like Jimbo are hard to find. He has gone way beyond the call of duty in trying to help me through this mess. He's helped Deloris and Emily. He's really a good guy, and I would hate to see anything happen to him. Right after the...accident, Jimbo headed straight for Deloris' place to be sure she was safe. The other crewman, Terry Cooper, hitched a ride on a sailboat heading north that very day they'd washed ashore, and nobody's heard from him since. Anyway, everything Jimbo had stashed away was taken from him when a bunch of goonies trashed his apartment a few days later. He knows who it was, but he can't do anything about it because he's afraid they'll kill him. He's probably right, so he's been hanging out in places they wouldn't think to look. Sometimes, he'd stay aboard my boat. When he told me what he knew, I figured he was a dead man. And since he's been good to me and what's left of our family, I wanted to help him out. Yeah, I would've done whatever it took to get him some cash. That's what friends are for. Just like you and your friend, Lee. You trusted him, and he was obviously trying to keep you out of this mess by not telling you about it. Now you are trying to avenge his death."

"Is that what I'm doing?"

"Isn't it? You're not on duty, and you're still digging. I'd say that qualifies as seeking revenge." Molly took a sip from her beer. "Now, if you'll excuse me, I have to go to the little girls' room." Molly scooted out from the booth and confidently walked through the bar toward the back of the room.

Sam looked at the bar's patrons. He'd driven by this place a few times, but he'd never taken the opportunity to come inside. It felt like a favorite old pair of sneakers: dirty, ragged, smelly, well worn, comfy…the kind of shoes that just can't be thrown away. The people at the bar looked much the same way. Molly probably fit in tight with them, except…except she was not like them. *She fits in this place because she knows the people, but she's not* one *of them*, Sam thought.

He blatantly stared at her as she returned. He noted her jeans fit her snugly, accentuating her small hips and legs, so thin that her thighs didn't touch when she walked. She had taken time to smooth down her wild hairs a bit and to put on fresh lipstick. This time, it was pale pink. Her cheeks were rosy from the drinks, and her eyes sparkled. He'd seen that look before, and he knew she would be easy pickings if he wanted to pursue things tonight. He quickly played "what-if" scenarios like fast-forwarded vignettes: if they went back to her boat, he could see how far things would go, or what if he played the gentleman and offered to sleep on the settee? Maybe he should forget the whole thing and call a cab to go fetch his truck and then drive back to…oh, right, no dinghy ride available out to *Angel*. Must do something about that.

Sam took another sip of beer before pushing his mug away. He stood when Molly arrived back at the table, nodding toward the door before she could get comfortably seated in the booth.

"Ready to go?"

"What's your hurry, Sam?" Molly looked dejected.

"I don't think this is a good place to discuss…plans. Come on; I'll take you back to your boat. I'll row," he offered.

"Suppose you're right," Molly brightened, "though we could make a night of it and go to another bar."

Sam heard the interest in her voice, but he shook his head. "Another time. We really should be careful, you know?" With a hand squarely on her back, he steered her toward the door and then down the street toward the docks.

Scanning passersby for any signs of recognition or trouble, Sam was running more scenarios through his head at a fast clip: what if somebody were tailing them… watching them? Maybe it was the power of suggestion, but for a split second, Sam thought he heard quickening footsteps behind him. *Nobody would try anything on this busy street of downtown Wilmington*, he thought. Still, he took Molly's arm, urging her to speed up.

Knowing they would be lost to the darkness of night as soon as they reached the black waters of Cape Fear, Sam's pace quickened. Then he remembered that the dinghy was chained to the dock, and taking time to unlock it might give a pursuer the upper hand. Sam pulled Molly into a small courtyard and quickly they were absorbed by the dark and the jazz music of the Waterfront Restaurant, just steps away from the riverfront docks.

"I thought you said…."

"Never mind what I said; just keep moving," Sam whispered.

The hostess greeted them with a perturbed I-don't-want-to-be-here look plastered to her ashen face, a stark contrast to her Gothic black outfit. "Two for dinner?" she assumed a voice as flat as her long, black hair. Her black fingernails clutched two menus like talons.

"Just drinks at the bar, thanks," Sam replied as he and Molly brushed past her and picked their way through tables toward the bar in the back.

Sam offered the only empty stool to Molly at the end of the bar while he surveyed the place. The front door was easy to see from where he stood, and just a few feet behind the end of the bar was the kitchen entrance. Leaning back on his heels, Sam could see that a door on the far wall of the kitchen was propped open by produce crates. *If* they had been followed, he and Molly could make their way out the back to gain some time.

If it were just his nerves chasing him around town, he'd laugh about it later.

"What's your pleasure?" The female barkeep waited for Sam to reply, her elbows on the bar.

Sam glanced in Molly's direction. Her irritation registered, and he promptly ordered two waters, much to the bartender's obvious annoyance.

"What's going on, Sam? You are acting like a teenager."

"Thanks for the compliment, Mol. I just thought we'd have one more for the river." Seeing her disbelief, he nodded toward the kitchen entrance. "And I thought we might have to take a detour to gain some time unlocking the dinghy."

At once, Molly understood. She slowly looked toward the front door at the exact moment the two linebackers from Navassa walked in. She reeled around, grabbed Sam's hand, and crouched down, pretending to search for a nonexistent contact lens. "How did they find us?" she whispered.

"Doesn't matter. They did," answered Sam. "Stay close. We're going to move through that open door in the kitchen and then cut up a block. Don't stop until I tell you to, understand?"

Molly nodded and pretended to find the errant contact lens for no one's benefit. Swiftly, she moved toward the kitchen, head down.

Sam followed. A quick backward glance through the windows of the kitchen's swinging doors confirmed that the two linebackers were on a search-and-destroy mission. He ducked and ran after Molly, ignoring the yells from the cook and prep-staff in the small kitchen.

"You know the parking deck at the Cotton Exchange?" Molly asked, once they were outside and dashing down the alley behind the restaurant. "Maybe we should hide out there. There's a flight of stairs up to the top deck, and we could keep an eye out for them up there."

"That won't do us any good if we get caught; no place to run," answered Sam. "We can cut behind the college, then back down to Front Street. That should give us a head start."

"Not if they know we are heading for a dinghy on the river!" Molly shot back.

"I don't think that's it," Sam explained calmly. "You lost them on the road. They may have found the 'liberated' car you ditched, but they would have no way of knowing we hopped into your boat from there. No, I bet they've been canvassing the restaurants and bars all evening and finally found us."

"But why would it be important enough for them to leave their 'post' in Navassa to hunt us down? For all they know, we were telling the truth."

"They took me for a cop, and they think I was moving in on their territory. If they called their boss, they learned it goes much deeper than just wanting a cut of their business." Sam thought about *Angel*. "Shit. Now my boat's definitely off limits."

"Your boat? What about mine? If they figured out who you are, don't you think they would know who I am and where my boat is?"

"Naw, there's no connection. You're not a cop. Keep moving." Sam wondered whether he spoke the truth as he nudged her in the back. "But just to be safe, let's get your boat moving as quick as we can and anchor out tonight."

Molly's abrupt stop caused Sam to slam into her back. "Houston, we may have a problem."

"What? Don't tell me the motor doesn't work."

"Well…" Molly whined, "it is on my list of things to fix. But don't worry; with a little bit of luck and a prayer or two, I might be able to get her started. And anyway, it's *motors*. We can get underway with one, but two would be better."

"You might want to start ranting some of those curses of yours to keep the guys off our trail." Sam pointed to a break in the college's buildings. "Down here."

The two slowed their pace to avoid attention as they approached the riverfront. Sam silently motioned Molly to wait while he looked for their pursuers. Taking a few steps out in the open, he saw people walking through the park, along the docks, and heading toward the Hilton. But he did not see the linebackers. Sam grabbed Molly's hand and pulled her close as if they were a "couple" strolling arm-in-arm toward the river's edge. When they made it to the promenade along the river, Sam peered over the top wooden railing atop the docks, then climbed over it and jumped down on a narrow dock below. He waited for Molly to follow.

Molly watched his antics, then walked a few feet to the left and opened a hinged section of the railing. She calmly climbed down the wooden gangway to the dock, gave Sam a smug look for her cleverness, and walked toward her dinghy.

Sam followed, frustrated that he hadn't noticed the hinged access to the docks below. As he walked, he kept his eyes trained on the railing to be sure they weren't discovered.

"We're in luck," Molly called as she unlocked the chain and untied the painter. "We've got an incoming tide, so it's going to be a fast ride."

Holding fast to the end of the rope still around the dock's piling, she stepped into the boat as it bobbed by the dock. When Sam got in, she released the line and fended off as a swift current tore them away from the docks and into the inky river.

Sam pulled the oars and guided the boat to keep it from bumping into anything as he rowed. At this speed, they would be back at her boat in no time.

CHAPTER TWENTY-THREE

Molly sat quietly as Sam rowed them back to B-dock at Bennett Brothers' Marina. She hadn't said a word since they boarded, and that made Sam a little nervous. For the short time he'd known her, she rarely stopped chattering. Looking at her from time to time, he could barely see her profile. There was little light now that they were well away from the docks' bright lights. He rowed toward the glow of lights at the marina, the same glow that began to illuminate Molly's face on their approach.

Not knowing what to make of the situation, Sam held his tongue as they came close enough to the stern of *Hullabaloo* to grab the boarding ladder. Sam held the dinghy steady for Molly as she stood in the center, deftly tying the painter line to one of the stanchions. Once aboard, Sam pulled the dinghy high onto the aft deck and secured it. He joined Molly, who was on her knees, precariously perched on the cockpit floor, leaning into the engine compartment. Stooped over the starboard engine, she was systematically checking the water, checking the oil, and checking the transmission fluid, then starting the glow plugs to heat the one engine that worked for sure before firing it up. She said a quick prayer out loud as the old engine sputtered a few times before turning over and stalling. Molly pumped fuel into the starboard engine by using a hand bulb as she started her praying again. On the third try, the engine roared to life. She followed the same steps, prayer included, for the port-side engine.

"May the eel grass and sand stay out of our filters," she chanted a made-up blessing.

"And may the anchor hold when we get where we're going," added Sam, as he moved forward to start untying the boat from the slip. "Where *are* we going?"

"To the Brunswick River," Molly called from the wheel house as he passed the window. "South of Wilmington. There's a lot of shoaling, so we will have to enter slowly." She hesitantly added, "I noticed one or two other boats coming to port as we were leaving the docks. Hopefully, we won't call attention to ourselves."

"Relax. It's too dark for anyone to see who's aboard. Stay to the far side of the river, if that will make you feel better."

"I will. We are going against the current so we will have an easier time of it on that side." Molly slipped the boat into gear and backed out of the slip effortlessly. She steered toward the far bank (but not too close) and made way for the Brunswick River.

Sam joined her in the pilothouse once they were underway, and he sat on the portside settee where he could watch the docks as they passed by. Using a pair of binoculars, he searched the waterfront for the linebackers. He didn't find them.

"Make yourself useful," Molly said, pointing to the binoculars. "Help me find the next channel marker. I am not used to running in the dark. I see the green marker over there, but I don't see the red."

Sam searched the dark until he saw a flash-flash of a small red light affixed to the top of a channel marker. He trained the flashlight on the square red sign until Molly acknowledged seeing it.

Molly slowed and turned onto the Brunswick River, picking her way by the ancient radar's sonar readings. "Been meaning to update this old thing, but at least I didn't get around to yanking it out yet." She watched the sounding register the water's falling depth until she saw a number she liked. "Here's a good spot. I'll hold her here until you get the anchor down."

Sam moved forward with one hand on the lifeline. He dropped the fifty-five-pound CQR anchor and galvanized chain to the appropriate seven-to-one scope, then waved his arms to indicate it was down, his silhouette made visible by the bow light.

He felt the boat shudder as Molly revved the engines in reverse until the anchor set, then shut them down. Sam watched her in the quiet of the pilothouse as she flipped open a green log book to note the date, time, and engine hours. She was all business with the boat, that was for sure. She disappeared below deck.

Sam looked up at the pitch-black sky, thankful to be on the water. "It's been too long," he muttered. "Must go cruising. Soon." He walked aft to the pilothouse and joined Molly below in the salon.

"We need to talk about our plan," she said matter-of-factly as she gathered mugs, sugar, and milk. A small kettle was on, and she had put teabags on the counter.

"I say we pay Mr. Walters a visit tomorrow. Ask for a job, and see what happens."

"Then what?" she asked as she poured hot water into his mug and handed him a teabag. "Suppose he gives us a job. What will that accomplish?"

"It could help confirm that Johnson is a drug source, and that's enough to get him off the street for a while until I can figure out how to nail him for murdering Lee and your brother."

Molly looked at her cup, then at Sam. "What can I do to help?"

"Just get us there tomorrow. You think this old boat of yours will make it?"

"Old is not bad, you know. I've been working hard on restoring this classic girl, and she's got a lot of life left in her." Molly smiled. "I'll get us there, no problem. Then what are you going to do? Just waltz in and ask for Mr. Walters?"

"Yep."

"And you are sure Johnson doesn't know what you look like?"

"Never met him before, so I don't think he does. Besides, he probably won't even be there. I'm going to see Mr. Walters, and you are going to stay aboard. It will look suspicious if we go in together. If I get hired to make a run, I'll be able to get some evidence. Then I call in the troops to flush him out…assuming I can find troops I can trust." Sam added some sugar to his tea, and he took a sip. "But what would be helpful is a tape recorder or something as proof that this is where it all begins. Do you have something I could use?"

"No. You'll just have it go it alone," answered Molly. Stifling a yawn, she took a sip of her tea and stretched out her legs under the settee table.

"Slack water will come about ten tomorrow morning," Molly said as she glanced at a small tide clock on the wall. It looked like the face of a regular clock with an additional ring of information defining tide movements of local waters. "If we leave any sooner than that, we'll be fighting the tide." She yawned again. "It's been a long day. I think I'll call it quits for now." Pausing, she looked thoughtfully at Sam. "You can have my bunk, if you want." After a few seconds of deafening silence, she added, "I'll sleep in the salon."

Sam smiled at her generosity, but he declined the offer. "I don't think I'm going to sleep much tonight anyway. I'll stay here and check on the anchor from time to time to be sure it's holding."

"Oh, it'll hold. CQR is short for secure, and that's fifty-five pounds of security up there on the bow. It's seen this boat through many blows," Molly explained as she got up from the settee and moved forward. "I'll be a minute in the head; then you can use it if you need it. See you tomorrow, Sam." With that, she slid out of sight.

"Thanks," Sam called after her. *Thanks a lot.* Then he mentally kicked himself for passing up an opportunity. He berated himself on his way up to the aft deck. *Sheesh, she practically invited you in, you idiot. What were you thinking? Maybe I'll give her a little time to get comfortable, then go ask for a blanket or something. No, too lame. It's getting cold up here. Would you mind if I...no, that's even worse. Let it go. We're going to have a long day tomorrow anyway. Got to get some sleep.*

But sleep was not to come so easily. The anchor didn't drag an inch, even with the change of currents, but the night surely dragged on. Sam lay there on the bunk in the salon, fitfully thinking about Molly. She was brave, strong, and smart. She wasn't bad to look at, either, once she got cleaned up a bit. But she had a dark side, one that ran counter to what he was used to in the women he dated. Maybe that was part of the attraction, something different. She drank too much, she ran with a rough crowd, and she had balls bigger than most men he knew. She clearly had compassion for her friends. Plus, she could handle a boat *and* an engine!

"Makes me tired to think of the possibilities," he thought. In the morning's small hours, Sam slept.

CHAPTER TWENTY-FOUR

Jarred awake by the sound of *Hullabaloo*'s engines rumbling to life beneath him, Sam quickly looked around, squinting in the morning sun.

"I thought you said we weren't leaving until ten!" he yelled at Molly, who smiled at him from the pilothouse.

"Dude, you overslept." Molly grinned as Sam plopped down on the settee nearby. "It's ten-thirty. If we leave now, we can make it to Southport in short order with this tide. See how it's racing past the marker over there?" She pointed out the nearest marker, its fixed pilings standing fast against a racing current. "There's a bakery down there I want to visit while you pay your respects to Mr. Walters. I am ready for some good bread."

"No way are you going sightseeing, Mol. You have to stay aboard with the engines running, just in case we need to move out fast. What happens if they identify me as a cop?"

"I'm going for a fast boat ride without you, I suppose," Molly teased. "All right, I will stay put. But we still need to get going. Here; I made you a cup of coffee."

She handed a steaming travel cup to the ruffled Sam. "You can have a few sips while the engines get warmed up. Then I need you up there on the anchor. I'll get my charts. Want an orange? I don't have much on board."

"No, this is good for now." Sam smiled gratefully as he sipped the hot coffee.

His eyes were still heavy from a rough night spent in the deck chair where he'd fallen asleep contemplating the midnight sky and Lee's path to death. He moved groggily forward to the pulpit and waited for Molly's signal for him to start raising the anchor.

Soon, *Hullabaloo* was underway, moving slowly into the south-bound channel of the Cape Fear River. They passed many north-bound snowbirds traveling back from their wintering-over places: Caribbean islands, warm waters, beaches, grandchildren. Each boat had the same brown-bearded stain at the waterline, a tell-tale sign of Intracoastal Waterway travelers. Some slowed down to limit their wakes as they passed *Hullabaloo*; some didn't. Most kept to their side of the channel with the occasional exception of a fast power-boater rushing to beat a bridge closing up ahead.

Sam noted that the majority of motor-boaters waved, while a good number of sail-boaters sneered. He mused that the rift between stink potters and rag boaters would never be mended, each thinking *their kind* was somehow better. Logically, Sam knew that all boaters shared an enjoyment of being on the water regardless of their crafts. But being a longtime sailor himself, he found he made the same generalizations that everyone else did, even if they weren't true. *Narrow-mindedness comes in many forms*, he thought, smiling.

Molly was comfortable at the wheel, often steering with her feet while sipping her coffee. She maintained a steady speed, frequently checking the radar and the buoys behind her to be sure she was well within the channel's unseen boundaries. When she found she drifted too far to starboard, she corrected her course and marked the drift and current point on a large chart beside her, which was held in place by two glass brick-like objects.

Watching her carefully, Sam asked for an explanation. "What are those things? And what are you doing?"

"These?" Molly nodded to the glass bricks. "They're ballast from some ancient ship. Several years ago, I was fishing with friends in a creek near the Fort Fisher Ferry landing. I cast my line too close to the shore and it got tangled up in the roots of an old tree. When I was untangling it, I found these. When ships used to ply these waters, they used ballast to fill their holds for better sailing, just like the lead in sailboat keels today. When they reached port and got a full cargo hold for the next destination, the ship's crew would throw the ballast overboard. Some colonial cities used the stuff for paving streets or building foundations, or for building wharves. These glass bricks found their way into the tree's roots, and as the tree grew up and out of the bank near water over the last century or so, the bricks were exposed. There were others, but I left some there for somebody else to discover. Pretty cool, huh?" She smiled as she held up one for Sam's inspection. "I've used them for a few years now, and they work well to hold charts in place. I sometimes think electronic gadgets like a GPS would be a great help, but I like the look and feel of the paper charts. These charts are old, so I continually update them when I find different depths or current pulls, like the one we just passed through." She gestured to scribble on the chart. "I also mark anchorages, like the one we stayed at last night. It's a lot easier to know where you're going to stay at the end of a long day's cruise."

"You've cruised a lot?"

"Not as much as I always thought I would. Taking out a boat like this costs money, and her upkeep ain't cheap, either."

"Reminds me of a few women I've dated along the way," Sam chuckled.

"Yeah, we women like our paint and powder, but this one's worth it." Molly patted the helm lovingly.

"Have you owned this boat long?"

"She was my dad's," Molly said after a moment.

"I thought you said you grew up on a farm," Sam quizzed.

"We did. Well, for a while, anyway. My parents tried lots of houses, lots of lifestyles. This one, living on a boat, was a great idea to my father, but my mother wasn't fond of the idea. It took me years to restore her, and I probably will be working on her for a few years more. I always thought…. Never mind."

"What?"

"Nothing."

Watching Molly's smile fade, Sam let it go. He headed below in search of something to eat and came back to the pilothouse with a box of crackers.

"Seasick?" Molly asked.

"Hungry. You know, there's a pretty decent coffee shop and a pricey little grocery store on Bald Head, if you want to go over there before we go to Johnson's."

"No, thanks. There's a place just beyond Southport, though. It's a good marina, and I think there's a little village. We'll get something there," Molly said. "I didn't know we'd be taking a little trip; otherwise, I would have stocked up. My life's been a little out of kilter since I met you."

Sam watched Molly for signs of how he should interpret her remark. "Yeah, things have been a little crazy these past few days. Did I tell you I got suspended? I'm a suspect in Lee's death."

Shock registered on Molly's face. "No freaking way! Are you kidding me?"

"Nope."

"Who do you think tossed your boat?"

"I don't know. But paybacks are coming, whoever did it."

"Do you think the gorillas in Navassa took your truck apart by now?"

"Probably." A sly smile crept across Sam's face. "For the first time, I'm thankful for that damn duck. Without her, my boat would be trashed again."

"What do you mean?"

"The gorillas won't find the boat when they come looking because I got kicked out of the marina for having a pet on board," Sam laughed. "Imagine that; the duck was useful after all!" Sam stretched out his legs triumphantly at the thought. "Mind if I take the helm for a while?"

"No problem," Molly answered, moving away from the wheel and down to the galley to refill her coffee cup.

CHAPTER TWENTY-FIVE

The sun was nearly straight overhead by the time they docked at Southern Village. The small inland development offered transient docking for boaters and long-term docking for residents of the upscale homes that dotted the well-tended marina. A bank of small shops and eateries sought to entice waterway travelers, though the position of the development just north of the Oak Island bridge afforded some protection from buffeting winds.

Sam and Molly had little trouble finding a spot to dock *Hullabaloo* in the middle of the day. With the last line fast, they wandered the storefronts until they found the South Bay Coffeehouse. A cup of coffee and a pastry later, they motored back to the north a few hundred yards to the small creek and town docks of Southport.

Molly found a tight but adequate slip on the main boardwalk nearest Restaurant Row and backed in, stern to the docks. Sam quickly lassoed lines around the pilings and loosely fastened them to the boat's cleats.

Once Sam stepped off the boat in the direction of Johnson's, he was swallowed up by a ground swell of people heading to lunch. After the group passed a small, bright yellow fish house, the swell lessened its pace; next, the tourist pack passed a battered blue fish house and restaurant, and the group shrunk more; finally, the remaining pedestrians descended upon Provision's, leaving only Sam to walk the remaining short distance to Johnson's in the mid-day heat.

Entering a perfectly square room decorated with fishing nets and crab pot markers, Sam was slammed with the smell of fish and saltwater.

A man standing with his back to Sam behind a raised Formica counter hosed down a long metal slab of a table, his long, silver hair flowing like a river down his back. The remains of the freshly cut fish swirled toward an open grate to the river below. A lone tabby cat, mangy but friendly, wound her way in between and around Sam's legs, hoping for attention or a handout. Offering neither, Sam moved toward the counter and waited for the long-haired man in high boots and rubber elbow-length gloves to acknowledge him.

Unnoticed, Sam looked around. On his right was a bank of shelves with seafood accouterments like tins of bright yellow cans of Old Bay seasoning and fishing poles. To his left was a small office with its door partially closed. The riverfront side of the fish house was open to docks lined with beat-up shrimp boats…and one gleaming white mega-yacht whose motor was running. The stern nearly jutted in through the open loading bay of the fish house. Sam recognized the name on her stern immediately: *Sa-*

brina. That's the yacht from my old marina, he thought. He expected to hear yelling, but he was disappointed.

"What can I help you with today?" the rubber-clad man yelled over the rush of water without turning around.

"Actually, I was wondering what I could help you with." Sam held his breath as the water stream stopped, and the man turned around to face him. "I've been told to come see a Mr. Walters."

"Walters? Don't know nobody by that name. Sure you got the right place?" The man put down the hose, his weather-worn face showing his years in the sun. He picked up a long fillet knife from the metal table and flung it into a nearby sink. Slowly, he approached the counter. He looked as mangy as the cat.

Sam saw what was left of rotting teeth when the guy smiled, and a stench came from his person that Sam was only too happy to be away from at that moment.

"Sorry; I must be mistaken. I was told that Johnson's was the place, and Walters was the man." Sam leaned away from the counter.

"Let me call around for you, uh, what'd you say your name was, son?" Toothless picked up the handset of a phone on the counter.

"No problem; I guess I got the wrong place. Don't go to any trouble, man."

But Sam's weak excuse didn't slow Toothless' dialing or calling out to another man who sat with his back to the door of the dark office.

As he entered the room with his ear engulfed by a Bluetooth phone earpiece, Andy Keller smiled and walked quickly toward Sam. "*I told you* you were worrying over nothing. Seems the pigeon's come to roost. Yes, here. I will bring him to you, and you can do what you like."

Andy walked around the end of the counter and thrust out his hand to Sam as if wanting to shake.

"Sam, good to see you. I heard you got suspended. Does that mean you are in the market for a new job?"

Stunned, Sam stumbled over his words as he pieced them together. "Andy, why? Why did you do that to Lee?"

"Business, Sam. It's all about business. My friend here would like to show you around the place."

Sam backed up, but his path was blocked by Toothless, who swiftly bolted the steel door to the fish house's main entrance. He crossed his thick arms and smiled a grotesque grin, the stench filling Sam's nostrils as the man moved closer.

"Look, ah, if I've come at a bad time," said Sam, feeling Andy right behind him, "I can call first the next time I visit." Sam jabbed his elbow hard into Andy's breastbone and ducked out of the way when Toothless dove for him, tumbling Andy to the slippery floor. Sam slid over the wet counter and out the back door facing the river dock where *Sabrina* stood idling.

Weighing his options, Sam quickly surmised that the dock surrounding the fish house merged with the outside dining area of Provision's, separated only by a waist-high railing. The fat man on *Sabrina* saw him as he emerged from the coolness of his pilothouse, phone attached to his ear, and mouth poised to yell. Hearing a commotion from inside the fish house, with metal scraping metal on the door, Sam jumped over Provision's railing and dashed through the crowded tables toward the main door. He was hedging that they wouldn't run after him the same way, but he didn't slow down to look. Within seconds, he yanked off *Hullabaloo*'s lines from their posts and scrambled over the aft rail.

"This doesn't look good!" Molly cried as she fended off one of the pilings before racing to the pilothouse.

"Get us out of here!" Sam watched as the Mutt-and-Jeff team ran from Johnson's and stretched for *Hullabaloo*'s transom just a second too late. Sam jumped up the short steps to the pilothouse where Molly was watching the depth sounder and working her way out of the slip.

"No-wake zone!" she called out.

"Now's not the time to worry about boating etiquette, Mol. Get going."

"Not me, you idiot, him!" Molly was pointing to the mega-yacht that was flooring it around a short bend, smack in front of Molly.

"Shit; it's *Sabrina*!"

"More friends of yours?" Molly sounded annoyed as she maneuvered to the creek's far side. The depth sounder's alarm screeched, so she veered back toward the mega-yacht.

"What are the chances?" she muttered as she pushed *Hullabaloo*'s throttle forward as hard as she could and headed right for *Sabrina*'s middle portside.

"CQR, don't fail me now!" she screamed as she rammed the fiberglass yacht with the heavy anchor before Sam could utter a sound. Just as quickly, she revved her engines in reverse, pulled out of the sinking mega-yacht, and thrust the throttle forward as fast as she could.

"They sure don't make them like they used to," Molly laughed as she steered her boat past the mess and raced to the middle of the channel while the fat man aboard *Sabrina* yelled obscenities and struggled to keep his footing on his sinking yacht.

"That's the guy I clocked the night we met! But that's not the same boat I delivered!" Molly yelled over the engines. "Do you know him?"

"He keeps his boat at the marina where I used to be."

"If he's involved, do you think he was keeping an eye on Lee?" Molly questioned.

"Maybe," relaxed Sam. "But what was he doing on Bald Head when you delivered a new boat to him? Checking on his territory?"

Hullabaloo sped up in the waterway as Molly weighed her options.

"I don't know. But we got to get some distance between us and them before I can think that one through. We could hide in one of the back bays between here and Wilmington, or we could make time out in the ocean if we headed out toward Bald Head and passed around the shoals." She chose to stay inside and veered north.

"It was a dirty job," Sam whispered.

Molly turned slowly to look at him. "A cop?"

"Yeah. One of Carolina Beach's finest. He was there. In Johnson's, like he was waiting on me. Shit. I can't believe they killed Lee in the name of 'business'. That's what he said, just before I hit him."

"Dude, I am sorry. May a thousand—"

"Don't, Mol. Just don't."

"Sorry." Molly checked her ancient chart for anchorages and laughed.

"What's so funny?"

"Well, it's that old game of cat and mouse. But it seems we have a cat on our trail who's more of a rat." She waited to see Sam crack a slight smile. "Here. Once we get to this area near Masonboro Island, we'll have a lot of options to hide." She traced her finger on top of Snow's Cut. She pointed to a narrow, shallow patch of powder blue on the chart bordered by the larger Masonboro and dots of smaller islands. "There are hundreds of back bays along in here that are too shallow for most. I can get us in and out quickly, and we'll just wait and see who passes."

"They'll be searching."

"Let 'em. I know these waters better than most. And if we need to, we can run through Masonboro Inlet to open water. I can take care of myself." She lifted her hands from the wheel for a second and moved away toward the long bench seat in the pilothouse where Sam had been sitting.

Sam jumped instinctively to take the wheel, and he watched amazed as Molly uncovered two rifles and methodically checked each one over before loading it. "I have lots of stuff stashed aboard, just in case." She also pulled out two bottles of tepid water and tossed one to Sam.

As the afternoon's sun heated up the pilothouse, Sam checked religiously for any signs of a following ship. He relinquished the helm to Molly and took binoculars to the aft deck. He marveled at the speed with which they passed Sunny Point Military Base. He checked the ferry as it made its way across the river to Fort Fisher, and he kept a sharp eye for any boat that seemed to follow their wake. He went below to rummage for something to eat. Feeling the boat slowing, Sam leaped back topside to see Molly steer the boat under the high bridge at Snow's Cut and into Myrtle Grove Sound. Molly continued north toward a narrow passage amid a thick stand of trees just south of Masonboro Island. Thinking she was running aground, Sam sprang forward to take the wheel, only to see a small tranquil bay emerge like an oasis.

"Wow."

"Look sharp," Molly pointed to the depth sounder. "It's shallow in here, but I know there's a spot further in. We just have to pick our way slowly."

"What if we have to get out in a hurry?"

"No worries. There's a cut just around that bend that shoots us to another bay, and I can work through these smaller passages back to the sound until we reach the inlet."

Molly kept the engines slow and nudged first to port, then to starboard, until she found the unmarked and ever-changing channel. "Good thing we've hit it on the rising tide. Otherwise…." Her voice trailed off as she found the place she wanted to drop anchor. "This is it. Unless they got a small Whaler, they won't make it in here anytime soon. Be a dear and drop anchor, please."

Sam obeyed and headed toward the bow. Once the anchor was secure by Molly's hand signs, he returned to the pilothouse.

"You didn't see anybody, did you?" Molly was noting their position on the giant chart.

"No. I suspect the scene you created kept them locked in for a bit. But Andy's going to call somebody; you can bet on it. They'll be looking soon. And now that your boat's known, we should probably get going."

"Where?"

"To the station. I need to know who else is in on it."

"You are kidding, right? You've got no idea whose pulling the strings and you want to march right in and have a chat with who? Your Chief? I thought you said your vehicles were bugged. No, dude, if you go in, you are on your own. I'm staying put." Molly stretched her legs on the bunk for emphasis.

"Suit yourself," Sam glared. "I'm taking the dinghy back to Carolina Beach. I'll come back for you when it's all over."

Sam purposefully walked out of the pilothouse and lowered the dinghy and oars to the muddy thin water below.

Within six pulls of the oars, Sam hit a sandbar. "How'd she do that?" he whispered as he got out of the dinghy and pulled it across the narrow bar. Once seated in the dinghy again, he found his rhythm and started to make progress. It would be a long row to town, a long time to think through his options. Sam rowed behind one of many bends in the neon green marsh-lined waterway that was off limits to boaters, working his way south, wishing for something of substance to eat.

Wrrrrrrzzzzz. The buzz of a small boat's engine jerked Sam's attention away from his empty stomach. Listening hard, he heard the sound speed up, then slow down before the explosion came, ripping silence and splintering wood in an instant. Rowing frantically back toward *Hullabaloo*, Sam's adrenaline rose as quickly as the neon green of the marsh gave way to glowing yellows.

The air thick with ash and diesel, Sam watched in horror as a black tower of smoke rose from *Hullabaloo*'s stern. Pausing only for a second to listen for the small craft's racing engine, Sam rowed as quickly as he could to the smoking, sinking wreck. He hit the sandbar again, this time yanking the dinghy onto the rise of wet sand and swimming as fast as he could toward *Hullabaloo*.

Fire leapt from the stern, making it too hot to climb aboard. The boat was listing to port, her wooden hull groaning under her own weight as she slid little by little into the waters. Sam made a quick lap along the starboard side, calling frantically for Molly.

No reply.

As the lower rail of the starboard-side life rails hit the water, Sam half-swam aboard. Through the pilothouse window, he saw Molly slumped over on the floor with water up to her mouth. Sam quickly pulled his way toward the pilothouse door, and with mighty effort, he yanked the door open. Inside, a swirling mess of mud, water, and sand hastily claimed every nook and neat place that had been the pilothouse. Sam lunged for Molly and hoisted her over his shoulder. He grabbed the flimsy water-soiled chart in his other hand and made his way back through the pilothouse door just as more water raced past. Now scrambling, now wading, now swimming, Sam found a foothold on the rail again and pushed clear of the sinking boat, pulling hard, sidestroke after sidestroke, carrying Molly up on his hip, until he was waist deep at the sandbar's edge. Sam laid Molly down quickly, then checked for signs of life before starting mouth-to-mouth resuscitation.

"Breathe!" he screamed at her.

"Dude..." she faintly replied, pulling his face toward hers. "My boat. Is she...?"

The question went unanswered as Sam held Molly upright so she could see for herself. Without a word, they watched the last of the flames shoot up and then sputter as murky water claimed *Hullabaloo*. Sam held Molly tight, from the first tear to the following surge of anger.

As the pale purple sky streaked orange and reached overhead, Molly stood tall. She gently picked up her soaked chart, pushed the dinghy off the sandbar, and gingerly climbed in. "It's time to go."

Sam took his place at the oars. Without looking at Molly, he rowed through the marsh and maritime forest of Masonboro Island.

CHAPTER TWENTY-SIX

Dick's Bay is a wide place amid low-slung islands. Exceptionally shallow, it is a good breeding ground for small fish and mosquitoes. Tonight, a good easterly breeze made Dick's Bay tolerable as Sam pulled to the lee shore of a smaller island. A single warped wax Myrtle rose from the sliver of sand, and it was there that Sam and Molly stopped for the night. Sleep, if it could be called such, was fitful as Sam leaned against the dinghy, listening intently for sounds that shouldn't be: a motor, a paddle, a stroke. Molly lay curled up beside his outstretched legs. She muttered in her sleep, woke slightly, cried, and passed out once again.

Morning brought warmth. At first light, Sam gently nudged her.

"Mol, it's time."

Molly opened her eyes, tossed the grit from her hair, and stood to stretch.

"What's for breakfast?"

"Pancakes and bacon," Sam played along.

"Good. I'm starved," Molly chirped.

Molly was first to the rowboat now several feet from the water's edge. She grabbed the painter line and started to pull the boat toward the water, then took her seat at the oars, and pointed to the stern.

"Push off, will you? We've got a long way to go on this tide."

Sam stretched, glad for a reprieve from the oars. Then he pushed the boat off the bar and hopped in.

"Let's head across the sound. We can hitch a ride back into town and get something to eat." Sam reached into his pocket, feeling soggy bills and hoping they were something other than ones.

"No, they'll be expecting that if they think for an instant we're still alive. We are going to take the town by sea. We can catch the tide's rush to the inlet, then let the current carry us south to the beach. They won't expect that."

"That's a long way, Molly."

"What's the matter, dude? Not up for a little exercise? Besides, I can probably find a friend to lend us some money, and maybe a car to get us to your boat, assuming they didn't torch her, too," Molly said sourly. "Then we'd have someplace to stay until we think things through, maybe get a change of clothes."

"I know just the place," Sam smiled.

The water's retreat from marsh to sea was swift, and they made good time. Molly was intent on hugging the shoreline through the inlet to stay out of the way of the charter and pleasure boats that morning, and she handled the oars expertly.

"Let me know when you want to switch," Sam goaded, knowing there'd be no safe way to change seats in the turbulent and fast water.

Molly didn't reply.

Once through the inlet's gauntlet, Molly rowed furiously along the coast. She soon found the slight southerly current she wanted and slowed her pace.

"Where's this place you are thinking about?"

"Lee's."

"And you don't think they have eyes on that place?"

"Why would they? Lee's out of the way, and his widow doesn't know anything. If she did, or if they thought she did, she'd be gone already. Besides, I need to check up on her anyway. There's the boardwalk…just a little farther."

"The boardwalk would be a good place to dock. Can we make it to her house on the beach from there?"

"Sure; it's not far."

Sam watched as Molly turned the boat toward the outstretched pier. The dinghy slid under the pier, unseen by passersby overhead. A few feet away was a dilapidated staircase with water-weary timbers exposed where there used to be treads. Sam pushed them from piling to slimy piling until they could make the stairs.

"They look rickety, but at least the boat will stay out of sight until we can come back for it," Sam offered quietly.

From their vantage point, they could see people moving on the boardwalk above, running, strolling, shadows filtering down between the planks' cracks. They heard children's screams and anxious parents calling to eager youngsters who raced from Ferris wheel to concession stand to arcade.

"Don't you think somebody's going to notice us climbing up from the sea, dude?" Molly whispered.

"That's the point," laughed Sam. "Kids do it all the time. And lovers. I've seen them. I've ignored them." Sam eyed the steps before lunging on the nearest remains of the lowest tread. "Come on. Time to get something to eat." He reached for Molly's hand, and together they tottered on the wavering wood, half-leaping from step to nearly non-existent step.

The boardwalk brimmed with children and their tag-along parents. Shrieks of laughter were muted only by the noise from the arcade's electronic wizardry and the Ferris wheel's mechanized organ music. As Sam had suggested, three daring youngsters were scooting away from their parents toward the edge of the pier where Sam and Molly scrambled up, and nobody took notice.

Sam kept an eye out for guys on the police force, hoping there were more good guys than bad among his peers. To be safe, he pulled Molly close to a group of tourists and gently muscled his way into the thick moving group that headed south toward Jenny's place.

When the swell subsided near a pizza shop, Sam and Molly stopped. Smells of grease met their match in garlic, and to anyone standing near their table, it would appear that the salt-encrusted pair had never eaten pizza before. Gorging on a large garlic, olive, and sausage pizza washed down by an amber beer, Sam and Molly briefly focused on their plates rather than their backs.

Satiated, the two headed back to the sunlight, hopped down on the beach hugging the pier, and walked as casually as they could toward Jenny's, occasionally weaving their way through bright beach blankets and striped umbrellas to the water's edge to cool themselves until there was no more pier to hide under.

"Jenny's place is the fifth one in the row. See the white porch? That's it." Sam nodded in the direction of Jenny's place. "You go to the back door just to be sure there's no one else there. If there is, just pretend you've got the wrong place, and get out of there fast. I'll join you after I check out the front."

Two buildings before reaching Jenny's, Sam left Molly cooling her feet in the waves and ran to the road front to look for signs of an unmarked vehicle parked suspiciously close to Jenny's condo. Relieved not to see any, he dashed back to the building's edge and waved to Molly, signaling for her to move toward the condo. Hoping that a lookout might not recognize Molly, Sam stayed put in the building's shade until she could signal to him that it was safe to enter the house.

Molly strode across the sand purposefully with her head up high, shoes in hand. She counted the units from the right side until she reached number five, the only unit with a white screened porch on the back. Not seeing anyone lurking about, she wondered whether Sam was just paranoid.

"Here's a recently widowed woman, trying to get her life in order. Cops would leave her alone, wouldn't they?"

Slowing her pace, Molly saw a slight figure sitting cross-legged on the porch's floor, lost in a sea of magazine clippings.

"Hello…" Molly called out tentatively.

"Yes?" Jenny looked up from her pile, scissors in hand.

"Are you Jenny?"

"Yes," Jenny said cautiously.

"I'm a friend of Sam's. I was in the neighborhood.…"

Jenny summed up "Sam's friend" with a screen door still between them.

"Come in," she offered, still not moving from her place on the floor. "Are you a sailing friend of Sam's? His boat wasn't in the marina when I got back from taking mine out the other day."

"I guess," Molly said genuinely. "I know he had to move the boat because of a duck, but I have no idea where the boat is now." Molly pushed her hair back from her face, aware for the first time that day how crusty she must look.

"Where is Sam now?" Jenny quizzed.

"He's around. He asked me to stop by first to see if.…" Molly paused and looked about Jenny's place a bit.

"To see if…?" Jenny sniffed.

"To see if you were alone."

"Very much, as you can see." Jenny motioned with her scissors to the cool, dark interior of the condo. "But why didn't Sam come himself, if he's so worried about me?"

"Because he thought there might be a guard on you or something."

"A guard? Whatever for? I don't require guarding."

"Not for you. A lookout for Sam, maybe. I told him he was crazy, but—"

"What's happened? Is Sam in trouble?" Jenny was alarmed.

"Yes," Molly said calmly. She reached for Jenny's arm to guide her indoors. She stood up but did not move. "I'm trying to help, too," Molly explained. "But we don't think they know what I look like, or if I made it out alive."

"What are you talking about? What's happened?" Jenny wrenched her arm away from Molly. "Maybe you'd better leave." Jenny moved toward the screen door.

"Wait!" Sam called, overhearing Jenny's raised voice. He darted toward the porch before Jenny could reach the door. "Jenny, it's me. I'm all right."

"Sam!" Relieved to see him, Jenny opened the screen door to him. "What is going on? Who's after you, and *who* is this?" She pointed toward Molly, then flopped her arms around his neck in a choking hug.

"It's a long story, Jen. Molly is, well, she's in the middle of it, too," Sam whispered. "Molly's brother was killed, and we think it was for the same reasons Lee was."

Jenny spun around and apologized. "Oh, Molly, I'm so sorry! I thought you were…well, never mind what I thought; how stupid of me!" She reached for Molly and hugged her tightly, too. "It's just been so overwhelming, and when you said Sam was in trouble, well, I just didn't think I could take any more."

Molly nodded. "I understand. I didn't mean to alarm you. I felt awkward, but Sam says we can't take any chances now."

"Well, I want to hear all about it. But first, you two get cleaned up. I can see you've had a rough time. Come on. I'll show you where the bathroom is." Jenny grabbed Molly by the hand and led her to the bathroom down the hall. "I'll get you some clothes. Sam, you can wear Lee's. Go pick out what you want and use my bathroom to get cleaned up."

Sam gratefully nodded and headed toward Lee and Jenny's bedroom. Lee's clothes hung neatly in the walk-in closet, and though he felt weird about it, Sam chose a pair of khakis and a red pullover. "Preppy, but clean," Sam smiled, remembering Lee standing in front of the barbeque grill on the beach last fall, wearing this outfit. Lee always did know how to dress.

Refreshed after taking showers, Molly and Sam sat in the living room with Jenny and told her everything that had happened, and everything they thought they knew. Sam had hoped for Jenny to fill in some gaps, but she had nothing more to offer than fresh coffee.

"I don't suppose it's safe to use the phone here," Sam said thoughtfully after some time. "It might be bugged."

"You think they're expecting you to call me," Jenny stated rather than asked.

"Afraid so. I suspect the connections go deeper than just Andy and the boys at Johnson's. I hate to think that, but all signs point to it."

"What can I do to help?" Jenny sat forward, hands open on her lap.

"You both need to stay put." Sam was firm.

"You're kidding, right?" Molly sneered. "There's no way I am just going to sit around and wait until you decide something has to happen, dude."

Sam shook his head. "I don't want you to be seen. You are safer here." Sam stretched, had another sip of coffee, and fumbled for his still damp sandals. They looked a little odd with his outfit, but they were comfortable. "Besides, if we have to get out of here in a hurry, at least I will know where you are."

"Well, you can't just walk out the door," Jenny pointed at Sam. "Every officer knows what you look like. Come into my studio. I have an idea."

Sam and Molly followed dutifully to Jenny's studio. She got out her paints and got busy on Sam's face. She momentarily vanished into her bedroom, then reappeared with a wig of long platinum blonde hair. She cropped it short, adjusted the wig on Sam's head, and continued to shape it into a haircut suitable for a preppy college-age kid.

"I wore this one on Halloween and didn't have the heart to throw it away," she said as she worked.

Afraid to look in the mirror, Sam patiently sat through Molly's smirks and Jenny's giggles. "Glad I can be so amusing to you two."

"You just look…" Molly started.

"Handsome," Jenny interjected. "Ruggedly handsome was what I was going for. Take a look for yourself." She ushered Sam to the bathroom mirror. "Your whiskers are good, but this will hide you better if someone sees you from a distance."

Sam couldn't believe the transformation. Though he'd always looked youthful, Jenny's artful hands made the illusion more real. He looked like a frat boy!

Jenny pulled out a hardware-store For Sale sign from the closet and handed it to Sam. "Now, put this sign in the Mustang's window," Jenny said, smiling as she gave the sign to Sam. "It'll look like you're just a kid taking a cool car out for a test drive. Where are you going first?" She dug through a few keys in the clamshell on her dresser.

"A pay phone. It's a long shot, but I want to call a buddy at the fire station."

"Do you think that's a good idea?" Molly was skeptical.

"I have to trust someone, Mol," said Sam, shrugging. "I'll be back as soon as I can. If you don't hear from me by tomorrow morning, you and Jenny get out of town as quickly as you can, okay?"

"We will," Jenny piped up. "We'll head to my sister's place in Raleigh and expect you to meet us there. She lives at the bottom of Byrd Street off of Glenwood Avenue. Do you know where that is?"

"Vaguely," Sam said, "but I will find you when I can. Take care." He thought about hugging them, but he opted to wave instead as he headed toward the garage where the Mustang waited.

CHAPTER TWENTY-SEVEN

Sam backed Lee's Mustang out of the short driveway and headed to Kure Beach in search of a phone. He parked near congested bungalows a few blocks inland of the beach, and he walked the remaining distance in as slouchy a stroll as he could manage to disguise his height. The late afternoon sun cast his shadow long on the pavement before him, and he slouched further until his back ached. As casually as he could, Sam stood in line for his turn at a phone booth. When the kid wearing baggy shorts in front of him finished his call, Sam took his place at the exposed booth, dialed Eddie Sherman's number, and held his breath.

"Sherman here."

"Eddie, this is Sam. Did you find anything in the computer from the hotel file?"

"Where have you been? I heard you were suspended! I've been looking for you for two days now."

"I really can't go into it right now, Eddie, but if you have something on this, I could use your help."

"Well, yeah. I guess you could. I did find out something that seemed out of sync. There were calls from one particular hotel room to two local numbers that turned up repeatedly on the hotel's automated operator system exactly two months apart. Same room, same numbers. See, all the numbers are stored on the computer's hard drive for billing purposes, and they are kept on file on the server for a period of two months after guests leave in case someone tries to skip out of the hotel without paying. Then collection agencies are enlisted and they challenge the people on the receiving end of calls made to try to find the whereabouts of the person who skipped."

"A tracing mechanism?"

"That's right. It's something a lot of hotels still use, though most won't accept calls this way. They want guests to pay on their own dime, their own calling card."

Sam was puzzled. "So someone has a favorite pizza joint and wanted it delivered when here on business. Or a girlfriend. What's so unusual about that?"

"Well, they weren't calls to a pizza joint. And it wasn't just one call to order a pizza. It was a bunch of calls made on consecutive days—sometimes five calls a day—over the course of a weeklong visit. There weren't any other calls recorded from this room, either," explained Paul.

"Who were the calls to?"

"Do you know the Blue Moon Gallery?"

"Yes, so it must be a buyer or an artist calling?" Sam didn't wait to hear a response. "Where was the other place?"

"Johnson's Fish Company down in Southport," reported Paul. "Seems like an odd combination, art and fish."

"Sounds more like fishy art," muttered Sam.

"What did you say?"

"Nothing, Eddie. When were the calls made?"

"As I said, two months apart. The last batch of calls was made just last week."

"Last week? You mean like Monday?" Sam was shaking.

"No, the night before your partner got it," Eddie whispered. "I am sorry to bring that up."

"Thanks, Eddie." Sam realized he was standing tall at the phone booth and slouched again. "Did you figure out who the room was registered to on those occasions?"

"The room was paid for with cash, and I already checked out the name of the guy the desk clerk was given. It was a phony. Sorry; that's a dead-end."

"Thanks. You've helped me tremendously. Would you do me one more favor? Please don't mention this to anyone else."

"I started the report, but I haven't turned it in yet. I'll hold on to it for a few days, if that'll help."

"Yeah, it'll help. Thanks. I owe you a beer."

"No sweat, man. And I like Budweiser just fine," Eddie replied.

CHAPTER TWENTY-EIGHT

Sam drove slowly back to Jenny's house, taking the most indirect path he could manage on the narrow island. Once the garage door came down, Sam ambled into the condo and was bombarded with questions from Jenny and Molly.

"What did you find out?"

"Who did you call?"

"Did anyone see you?"

Holding his hands up to stop their questions, Sam sat down and shook his head. A long silence hung thick like beach fog. Then he started his own questions.

"Jen, have you taken any of your paintings to the Blue Moon Gallery yet?"

"No, I haven't had a chance," Jenny looked sadly at her hands. "But what has that to do with all of this?"

"I suspect the gallery's connected to Johnson's somehow."

"How do you know that?" asked Molly.

"Phone calls, repeatedly from the hotel to both Blue Moon and to the fish company we visited in Southport," Sam pondered.

"Okay, so we know that Johnson's is bringing in the drugs, but what does a local gallery have to do with this?" Molly asked. "And the prostitution ring. You suggesting there's a tie?"

"I'm going to find out," Sam drummed his fingers on his leg.

"*We're* going to find out," Molly corrected him. "Your kind friends at Johnson's took my brother and my boat. I'm in this whether you like it or not."

"Molly's right, Sam," Jenny spoke softly. "Lee's gone, so I'm in. What's our next step?"

"Forget it! It's too dangerous," Sam shot back. "I lost my partner, and I am not about to lose you two. I think it would be a good idea if you went to your sister's house, Jen. Take Molly with you so I know you won't be in the way."

"Sure, dude." Molly folded her arms and sat back on the sofa forcefully. "I'll sit tight."

Jenny cleared her throat to ease the tension. "Would you like something to eat? I have some ham and stuff that friends brought over." She motioned to Molly to help her in the kitchen.

Molly acquiesced.

"Sam," Jenny called over her shoulder as she pulled the ham out of the refrigerator, "you can sleep on the couch, and Molly can sleep on the hide-a-bed in the studio. Perhaps tomorrow *you'll* know what to do."

CHAPTER TWENTY-NINE

Gulls screeched as Jenny tossed bits of bread—early-morning delights—upward on the beach. Sam watched her from the porch, coffee in hand.

She's been so strong, he mused, *even while she stays in the same house, sleeps in the same bed...and I have stayed in chaos so as not to think of Lee.* Sam glanced down at the burnt-orange Durham Bulls T-shirt he was wearing. Lee's shirt. "Must keep going," he whispered.

"Keep going where?" Molly stood only a breath behind him in an extra-large T-shirt, apparently from Lee's wardrobe also. Combing through her bed-rumbled hair with her fingers, Molly didn't seem upset by Sam's non-reply. She stepped back into the house and found a mug for herself before returning to the porch.

"Be careful, wherever you're going."

"I have no intentions of being anything but." Sam gently inched toward her, close enough to smell toothpaste on her breath, close enough to see the concern in her eyes. Close enough to kiss her.

"Good morning, you two!" Jenny opened the screen door before Sam had even noticed her returning to the house.

"Morning," Molly piped, suddenly aware that she was still the only one not fully clothed. She nipped momentarily into the studio in search of Jenny's loaner jeans and short-sleeved sweater.

Jenny went into the kitchen and busied herself with a breakfast of bacon and eggs. In another moment, Sam followed her to refill his cup and looked for bread to make toast.

After the three had eaten their fill, Sam reiterated his instructions and admonishments, and out he went.

CHAPTER THIRTY

Ignoring a few random stares and snickers from officers realizing who he was under the blonde wig, Sam barreled into Chief Singleton's office. Singleton was on the phone, his back to the door. His shoulders shuddered when Sam slammed it.

"I'll call you back, Hon. Someone just barged in." Singleton closed his cell phone and placed it on the desk before motioning Sam to sit, his poker face never flinching.

"And what's up with you, Goldilocks?" A faint smile curled on his tight lips.

"Oh, the usual." Sam slid into a chair away from the door. "Murder, mayhem, prostitution, drugs… for starters." Sam's voice dropped to a near whisper. "Once we get through that list, perhaps you'd like to tell me what you know about Lisa Owens."

"Chuck's wife. Stands about 5'4". What about her?"

"Much more to her than that, don't you think? Like her business, for starters. She travels a good bit, she says, in search of art for the gallery. You think she shops for something else along the way?"

"Wouldn't know." Chief looked at the files on his desk. "I don't know art much."

Sam pushed on. "Like I said, we'll get back to her. In the meantime, I've got this idea rolling around in my head, and it keeps bumping into notions I'm not sure what to do with. You know—murder, mayhem, prostitution, drugs." Sam prattled on, marveling at Chief's unflinching face. "Let's start with murder. Lee's death. It's really boggling me that we don't have someone in hand at this point. Worse than that, actually. It's pissing me off. And the further down I dig for answers, the more mayhem I find."

"For instance?"

"For instance..." Sam leaned back, his fingers forming a triangle for effect. "There are some nice girls down Navassa way. Their bosses are gorilla-sized cops who protect their interests by chasing me all over town. Know anything about that?"

Chief was silent.

"Or we could talk about some friends of one of our very own here who sell more than fish. A lot more. Should I mention that I've found a link to the rent-a-cop killing on Bald Head? Or should we just focus on a particular fire set to get us off the trail?"

"You've been a busy boy, Sam. You've got my attention."

"What I want is the truth, Chief." Sam relaxed his hands to his lap.

"We know about Navassa. It's about to go down, and the gorillas, as you call your brethren, are about to go down, too. It's not our jurisdiction, so all we can do is wait that one out. As for what's happening in Southport, I can't help your buddies on the force to choose their friends any more than I can pick out for you your clothes—or choice of hair color. I can call whomever you like in here, and we can ask him what's going on right now."

Sam measured his words like they were candy being doled out to a child. "I didn't mention that his friends were in Southport, Chief."

Silence.

"Oh, of course, that's out of our jurisdiction, too." Sam leaned forward and repeatedly traced a triangle on Chief's desk.

"It is."

"But Lisa's not, is she?"

"As in Chuck's wife?"

"The very same." Sam leaned back against the wall, then forward toward Chief. He noted the color of Chief's ordinarily ruddy face was getting deeper. He waited for Chief to speak.

"Come on, Sam. Let's take a walk." Chief slowly got up from his chair.

"No, Chief. I think I feel safest right here in the police station, amid the best force in North Carolina." Sam held his hand out in the "stop" position until Chief eased down again. Then Sam sat back, tipping his chair toward the wall, and stretching out his legs.

"Lisa is…well, she can be very persuasive," Chief started. "I didn't intend for it to all go this far."

Sam rocked on his chair, setting a rhythm for Chief's speech. He wasn't sure he wanted to hear a confession, but it looked like that's what he was going to get.

"I stopped in her gallery, looking for a gift one afternoon about a year ago. Didn't even realize who owned it until later." Chief's words were measured, labored. "She was so friendly, so knowledgeable about what was there that I felt good about spending some money, you know? I made up excuses to visit her again a few weeks after that, and then another time. Before I knew it, we were having coffee together; then…it just happened."

"What happened?"

"She…I…we started sneaking around. First, we just met at her gallery. Then it got more serious. My wife and I are having some trouble, and Lisa, well, she just seemed to care so much about what was going on; I couldn't stop it."

"Though I am not a man of the cloth, I am sure your confession makes you feel better. But that's not what I want to know about. I want you to tell me how she's involved with the fire."

"At Golden Sun? Lisa?" Chief's face drained.

Sam watched. "You're just talking about an affair." It was a statement more than a question.

"Yes!" Chief was defensive. "What else did you think I was talking about? She's not involved in anything wrong…well, you know what I mean."

"I know you're in deep with her if you can't see what's going on. I'll be in touch." Sam stood to leave.

"Wait, Sam. You can't…. Don't go. I want to know what else you've learned."

Sam weighed his options. "Chief, I'm still digging. I thought Lisa was connected, but maybe I was wrong. You need to deal with this…relationship, though. Sounds like it's clouding your vision."

Sam opened the door to leave, looking hard at Chief. He seemed smaller than usual.

Chief put his hand up, motioning Sam to sit again. "Let's talk."

"I've had enough of the infidelity crap, Chief."

"It's not about that. It's about Lee."

"I'm listening." Sam fell back into his chair and resumed his rocking.

"I found out more about Lisa during our visits than I wanted to know, but you're right when you say I'm in so deep. She's got me."

"Skip the drama."

"She's a mule."

"What?"

"Lisa runs up and down the coast 'in search of art' while carrying whatever her brother needs her to carry. The gallery is more or less a front."

"Her brother. And who is this fine fellow?" Sam asked, guessing before Chief answered.

"Tripp Johnson, in Southport. He got her involved shortly after she opened the gallery."

"So you know all of this, and you didn't stop it. Nice."

"I've been working on it. I need to stop Johnson, but the police down there are looking the other way, and it's out of my jurisdiction. I've looked higher up the food chain, but I get stymied there, too. This is really big."

"Why doesn't Lisa just stop?"

"Family reasons. She's threatening me with blackmail if I take Johnson down, and I am guessing he'd kill me or hurt my family if anything happens to her. When Lee was killed, I put two and two together. I confronted her about her brother's dealings and begged her to stop, but she wouldn't have it. Then she…she dumped me. I've been waiting it out, hoping to crack it from a different angle."

"Just how far is her range?"

"All the way up the coast. She has helpers who come into the gallery bringing stuff from Johnson, but I haven't been successful at nailing anyone yet."

"So you're working on it without her knowing?"

"Half-heartedly, I suppose, until Lee got killed. I think it was a message for me. You mentioned one of our finest was involved. Who?"

Sam hedged. "I was making a guess; that's all."

"Well, when you get it figured out, let me know. I can work with you from here, just me. You stay out of Lisa's space. I'll deal with her."

"I'll think about it." Sam was out of his chair again. "Stay off my back. I'll call if I need backup."

"Sam…"

Sam waited, his hand on the door.

"The bug on your cars…I didn't…."

"But it was convenient not to stop it?" Sam watched Chief look away.

"I didn't know it was done. There's someone else who wants you out of the picture."

"Yeah, I know. I just don't get why you're backing down for the punk."

"It's not someone here. It goes higher. I'm just taking orders, Sam. If I don't, I get canned…or worse."

"What I don't understand is how you can look yourself in the face every single morning and come in here like everything's fine. I thought you were bigger than that."

Sam pulled open the door and nearly mowed down Chuck Owens, who was standing just outside the office.

Chuck's face was magenta, his eyes darting back and forth, but his feet were frozen to the ground.

"You heard?"

"I heard enough." Chuck's eyes held Sam's.

"I'll take care of it, man." Sam placed his hand on Chuck's shoulder. "You're too close. Stay calm. I'm going to need your help later."

Sam moved past Chuck and sped up on his way out of the station. Chuck was a good guy; Sam felt sure. He probably didn't know anything about his wife's doings. Sam wanted to be a fly on the wall in Chief's office right about now, but he thought better of being in proximity to those sparks.

Taking the back street to the beach toward Jenny's, Sam watched his rearview mirror. He was not followed, so maybe Chief and Chuck were going at it back at the station. Things were moving fast.

Jenny's Jeep was not in the driveway, and Sam was surprised to find the condo empty. "Didn't think they'd leave so quickly, but it's for the best," he muttered.

He found a napkin on the kitchen counter with a number scratched on it, and a note with a telephone number on it: "Sister's in Raleigh. Come when you can."

Feeling better thinking that Molly and Jenny were out of harm's way, Sam returned to the Mustang. If the Chief were telling the truth, then Sam only had to look out for Andy. He hoped.

CHAPTER THIRTY-ONE

Jenny drove in silence. The plan they discussed was simple, but it would at least keep them busy. Maybe help, too. Molly sat quietly in the passenger seat, categorizing every weapon she'd ever had aboard her beloved *Hullabaloo*. She wished she had at least one of them now.

Parking at the end of the block of retail stores, Jenny popped open the Jeep's back hatch and pulled out a few of her larger paintings.

Molly went in first. She was greeted by a harried Lisa, wisps of hair escaping the loose bun on the top of her golden head.

"Welcome to Blue Moon," said Lisa, immediately walking toward her. "I meant to lock that door. I'm about to leave for a little while. Could you please come back later?" Lisa was trying to be courteous, but her agitation showed through the façade.

"Oh, dear, I really need to find a gift for my friend," Molly improvised. "She recommended your shop, you know, and since she invited us down for the summer, I just *have* to get something for her before we show up on her doorstep. I promise I won't take long."

Molly moved quickly through the door and off to the side to "study" the paintings on the wall. "This is lovely! Please tell me about this one."

Lisa's eyes rolled, but she walked over to Molly just the same and began a discourse on the contemporary work in front of her. Mid-sentence, she stopped at the sound of the entrance bell again.

Jenny struggled to get into the door, her arms full of paintings. She gently placed the brown craft paper-wrapped treasures against the opposite wall from where Molly and Jenny were standing and called out to Lisa.

"Hello, Lisa. I hope I haven't come at a bad time." Jenny waved a rolling five-finger wave.

"Hey, Jenny." Lisa excused herself from Molly and walked over to Jenny. "I'm glad to see you out and about. I was planning to call you in a few weeks. Now is not really a good time."

Jenny ignored her wave off. "I won't take long. I wanted to leave these with you so you could look at them when you have a chance. I hope they're up to the standards of the other works you represent. Like this one. This is gorgeous."

Jenny strolled along the wall to a signed and numbered Claude Howell print of one of his famous paintings and waited for Lisa to follow. The coral coloring of the blocky fishermen's nets looked stunning against the gallery's pale green walls.

"I am such a big fan of his. I didn't know you had his work."

"A few," Lisa replied flatly as she looked around for Molly, now nowhere to be seen. "This really is *not* a good time, Jenny."

Jenny feigned hurt. "Oh. Well, of course, I should have called first. I can see you are really busy here." Jenny made a sweeping gesture with her hand.

"It's not that. I was just heading out for a little while. I have an appointment."

"Looks more like a delivery, if you ask me." Molly stepped back into view from the gallery's office. In one hand was a small red leather carry-on suitcase. In the other was the handle of a matching rolling suitcase.

CHAPTER THIRTY-TWO

Sam headed south on the beach road, then cut back to the main drag. Two stoplights ahead was a small retail strip whose largest occupant was the Blue Moon Gallery. Parked at the end of the block of pale yellow buildings was Jenny's Jeep.

"They didn't," Sam said out loud as he pulled a U-turn on the street and parked behind the Jeep. Cursing himself for not having a weapon, Sam got out of the car slowly, taking in the situation.

Two large plate-glass windows facing the street revealed nothing of the gallery inside, thanks to rattan shades that were down. Sam glanced at his watch: ten-thirty. Shades should be up by now. Sam jogged to the end of the block and cut behind the strip mall. Counting the doors as he passed them, he found a deep blue one with scrollwork letters spelling out Blue Moon Gallery, a stark contrast of fancy compared to the windowless cinderblock blah of the rest of the building.

The delivery door was locked. Sam ran back to the front of the building and proceeded full force into the gallery. When his eyes adjusted to the darkened space, he found Jenny holding fast to Lisa's arms, pinning them back by the elbows. He smiled when he saw that Molly was nose-to-nose with Lisa, drilling her with questions.

Sizing up the situation, Sam slowly turned to lock the door. He stuck his head in the gallery's office, looking for a phone. *Chuck isn't going to be happy about this*, Sam thought as he dialed the number. His call was cut short by Molly's scream.

Sam dashed back to the main gallery to see a slick-looking blond man holding Molly in a headlock pose, a gun to her temple.

"One step closer and she's a goner." The sick smile on Molly's tormentor's face made Sam wince. Sam watched as the man hugged Molly tighter.

"Pity, really. She's my type, I hear tell."

Sam quickly played out scenarios in his mind. He looked to Jenny, who searched his eyes for direction. Sam nodded, and Jenny released Lisa.

"That's enough, Tripp. Let's get going." Lisa rubbed her arms, sore from Jenny's grasp. She moved toward the suitcases scattered in the gallery. "I've had enough of this town anyway."

Sam hedged. "Let me get this straight: you'd rather spend time with your brother Tripp than sell lovely pieces of art here in Carolina Beach? This is your brother, Tripp, right? What about your children? And Chuck? You think he's stupid or something?"

"Now that you mention it, yes. Of course, I'll miss the boys, but they can take care of themselves these days.

But Chuck, well, he was just a means to an end. This end." She held up the smaller suitcase.

Sam didn't miss a beat. "And the chief…was he a means to an end, too?"

Lisa stopped and stared at Sam. "Leave Dan out of this."

"Let me help you with that…." Sam started to lift the larger suitcase, but Tripp trained his gun on Sam.

"Don't move!" Tripp was agitated.

"Just helping the little lady, Tripp."

Tripp's smile widened. "She's no lady. She's my sister. Half-sister, to be exact. I've always wanted to say that."

Sam went with it. "Half-sister. On your father's side?"

"Sure. Dear ol' Dad was a busy guy in his youth. Now enough of this chit chat. Into the office." Tripp gestured with his gun. "This one," he said, his grip tightening around Molly, "she stays with me."

"Tripp, you are *not* going to do that here. Somebody might hear you. Let's take them somewhere else to do this."

Sam stalled. "Look, man, at least let the ladies go."

"Sure. I'll let this one go…with me."

Molly grunted as Tripp's arm tightened around her neck again.

"You must have it in for her family." Sam didn't move.

"Family?"

"Her brother. You wasted him on his boat."

"I waste lots of brothers. It's a matter of usefulness. When they are no longer useful…." Tripp shrugged.

Sam watched the blood race back into Molly's face as she wrenched herself to the right of Tripp, her hands both clawing at his arm. Tripp ignored her fingernails digging deep into his tanned flesh.

"Um, I like the way that feels, honey," Tripp goaded Molly. "You and me…we're going to have us some fun real soon. Why don't you save it until we're alone? You still have a use as far as I'm concerned," he cooed. "Unlike this place here, see. It's no longer useful." Tripp was clearly enjoying himself, pointing around the gallery like Vanna White presenting a winning phrase. "Now if you would be so kind as to move it, we'll get this over with. I have other things to attend to today."

Sam moved back a step into the office doorway, watching Lisa as she walked casually around her desk and reached to unlock the back door. Sam turned as if to help her again with her bags, his action being enough to divert Tripp's attention away from Jenny.

Amidst Tripp's shout of orders for Sam to put the bags down, Jenny lifted a cantaloupe-sized amethyst geode from a cream-colored pedestal standing in front of the Claude Howell and hurled it at Tripp. Her toss fell short, but it brought a shout from Lisa that momentarily distracted him.

In an instant, Molly leaned all of her weight forward onto Tripp's arms and mule-kicked him in the groin with her heel. Tripp squatted forward, his hands covering his privates, trying to regain his balance. Molly didn't give him a chance. She kicked him in the left kidney, bringing him to the ground as he reached for his lower back.

Molly snatched the gun away and pressed it hard to Tripp's temple.

Slowly cocking back the safety, Molly put her finger on the trigger. "For my brother."

"Don't, Molly!" Sam yelled.

"He deserves it!" Molly shrieked.

"But you don't deserve the consequences," Sam calmed. "Put down the gun, Molly."

Molly blinked at Sam as if seeing him for the first time. "He killed my brother." She slowly put the gun to her side, and her eyes returned to the heap of man at her feet. Molly gave him a swift kick in the side, then realigned the safety on the gun and tucked it into the back of her jeans under her sweater.

Not wanting to be left out, Jenny raced to the huddled mass while raising a tall turquoise pottery vase.

"Not the Sedberry!" Lisa screamed, her hands to her mouth in horror.

She cares more for her art than for her brother, Sam thought. *Nice sister*. Sam ripped Lisa's hands from her face and brought them to her back as he watched Jenny pause over Tripp. She was dripping with sweat, ready to pummel Tripp.

"Jen…" Sam called gently to her.

Frozen, Jenny didn't answer.

"It's over." Sam's voice was now just above a whisper.

Still Jenny didn't move, the vase high over her head.

The back door flung open. Chuck Owens moved in, gun raised, with his partner Mike Smith right behind him. Chuck's eyes were wild, but his actions were calm as he grabbed Lisa by the wrist and cuffed her.

"You have the right to remain silent..." he started slowly.

Lisa didn't respond.

Mike cuffed the writhing Tripp and pulled him to his knees.

"Jenny, it's over," Sam repeated quietly.

Jenny remained poised to strike.

Sam gently brought her arms down, the smooth-sided pottery vase still in a vise grip. "He's not worth it."

Jenny collapsed in his arms, sobbing, still holding the heavy Ken Sedberry vase.

Molly slowly took the vase from Jenny's grasp and put it back on its pedestal. Then she headed for the suitcases.

Molly gasped when she unzipped the larger one and opened it wide for all to see: stacks of hundreds, twenties, and tens, each stack neatly wrapped and secured by a thin blue ribbon like it was a party favor.

CHAPTER THIRTY-THREE

For two full minutes, Chuck and Lisa had a hateful stare down. The room was quiet, punctuated only by Jenny's sobs.

"Car's out back," Mike casually said, navigating a handcuffed Tripp around the splayed suitcases toward the office.

Molly carefully zipped up the large suitcase, stood it upright, and pulled out its handle.

"Don't touch it anymore." Mike's voice got everyone's attention. "Fingerprints and all."

"A little too late for that, Mike," Sam called over Jenny's shoulder, her wet face buried into his chest. "I suspect you'll find plenty of prints, but I wouldn't worry about Molly's."

Sam resumed his drawn-out shhhing to Jenny, more to soothe himself than her. Jenny's tears matched his feelings, plus the let-down of adrenaline after the rush. The answers had come. *Well, at least some of the answers*, he thought. *The rest will come. It's just a matter of cleaning house.*

Sam watched Chuck roughly shove Lisa toward the office door, then pick up his radio to call the guys from evidence. When they finished here, Sam knew the gallery would never look the same.

When Sam felt Jenny's sobbing slow, he gingerly pushed her away from him so he could see her puffy red eyes. Sam knew crying was cathartic. A release like this was important to her healing; he just needed to be sure she was all right.

His arm around her shoulders, Sam steered Jenny toward the front door. Molly followed a few paces behind. "We'll follow you back to the station," he called out to Mike and Chuck, who were working their way out the back door of the office.

"Don't go too far, Sam. We'll need you to answer a few questions about this mess." Mike's voice was barely audible from outside the back door.

Sam hoped Jenny or Molly would feel up to driving the Jeep to Raleigh for a change of scenery, even though all the action here was over. He watched Jenny's face to surmise whether she could drive yet. He opened the front door slowly, looking back to see whether Molly was coming. Jenny's gasp brought his attention to the door, where he froze. Blocking the doorway was a leering Andy Keller, backed by two scuzzy men. Sam recognized one of them—Toothless, from his visit to Johnson's Fishery.

The one with the toothless grin ducked past Andy, pushed Jenny aside, and tackled Sam, all within three lightning-quick steps.

Sam struggled underneath Toothless' weight, searching for a place to put a foot or a finger. Toothless was fast, and he pulled several wrestling moves in rapid succession, making Sam feel like he was being tossed in a laundromat dryer. His face squashed on the polished wood floor, Sam felt wet warmth ooze from his mouth and nose. Red. In front of his face. From his own face. That made him mad.

Sam managed to cock his head around in time to see Andy's other sidekick, Scuzzy Number Two, grab Molly and Jenny up by the arms as if they were rag dolls.

And to see Andy—leering at him.

Toothless began beating Sam. First his kidneys. Then his head. And then the lights went out for Sam.

CHAPTER THIRTY-FOUR

When Sam came to, he wasn't sure he wanted to be conscious. Not a place on his body felt right. Through swollen eyes, he could barely see around the gallery. He could listen, though. Listen for the floor creaking under the weight of someone. Listen for Jenny crying. Listen for Molly offering up a blessing or a curse. Sam heard nothing but the distant rushing of traffic outside the gallery's closed front door.

He slowly rolled onto one side and assumed the fetal position. He'd been left for dead. Again.

Only this time, he knew who did it to him. He felt for keys in his pocket.

Sam slowly managed to scoot his knees under him, resting his throbbing head on the floor. Child's pose. He fleetingly saw a memory of Frank sleeping like this, content. Safe.

Sam reached for a table leg, no doubt an art piece given its silky feel and contrasting end caps on the tapered legs. He gingerly raised himself until he was nearly upright. His hunch made him appreciate how his mother must feel as she managed around the kitchen in the early morning hours before his retired father woke up. *She has osteoporosis*, he thought. *She's had it for years. But she's safe in Raleigh. Far enough away from here. Safe. It's where Jenny and Molly should have gone. Then they'd be safe, too.*

Sam shuffled slowly to the gallery's office, peeking around the wall, separating it from the gallery space. An overturned chair, the desk, plus the usual office accouterments. No suitcases. No police. And no Tripp. No massive quantities of blood splattered all over the pale green walls, so Sam assumed everyone walked out on his own two feet. Or hers.

Lisa and Chuck had looked mad at each other during their confrontation, but Sam was getting the idea that it was all a show for his benefit. If good ol' true blue Chuck was in on it, there wasn't a straight brother on the force. There would be no backup, no one to help. Sam was on his own.

Sam leaned heavily on the back door leading to the alley. He couldn't hear car engines, voices, or guns firing. Through the fish-eye peephole, he saw nothing but the backside of another building.

Slowly, Sam opened the door and looked out in both directions. Clear. Using the building's wall for support, he crept toward the alley's entrance. Still no cars he recognized. No guns firing at him. Surely, Toothless and Sidekick wouldn't be so stupid to try something now in the bright light, would they?

Continuing around the building, Sam saw Lee's Mustang still in one piece. Sam cautiously slid in, hurting with every bend and turn as he got into the bucket seat and seatbelt.

Think. Think. Jenny and Molly in one car. Chuck in another, possibly with Lisa. Mike, Andy, Tripp, and the Scuz Brothers. Jenny's Jeep was still in front of the Mustang. Not seeing Lisa's Ford Taurus in front of the gallery, Sam assumed it was one of the vehicles underway. It could comfortably hold four, but if Lisa wasn't worried about comfort, maybe five. That left four people.

If Mike and Chuck came in their white Carolina Beach Police SUV, he'd look for that. The SUVs were an upgrade from the old Crown Victorias the force used to use. The small police force somehow had managed to convince the powers that be that SUVs were necessary at a beach town. Something about having to drive out on the dunes, though that rarely happened. So, no more Andy Taylor squad cars or Crown Vics.

Sam smirked at the thought of riding around with Barney Fife as he reached for the ignition. His lips were the only thing that didn't hurt. Sam's vision was not clear, but his focus was.

CHAPTER THIRTY-FIVE

Sam had only one place to go: the public library. Not a regular there, he wondered why people bothered during the summer when the beach beckoned. He instantly knew the answer when he stepped inside: air conditioning so cold Sam instantly felt chilled.

The petite gray-haired librarian had her black sweater snuggly clasped around her. Adorned with bright neon beach umbrellas, the sweater reached well below her waist, which was cinched with a bright turquoise fabric belt that matched her dress. On her nose sat bifocals as if they were a permanent fixture, just as she must have been at that front desk for decades.

Looking up from her computer, the librarian gasped when she saw Sam. She reached for the phone.

Sam painfully lunged at her hand before she could press a button.

"Please. It's not what you think." Sam was breathless. "I swear I won't hurt you or anyone in here! I'm a cop."

Sam felt for his wallet. Gone. Toothless was thorough. But not quite thorough enough. Sam held himself as straight as he could.

"I need to get online."

The librarian, whose name badge read Libby, cocked her head sideways, then shrugged. "Are you sure you shouldn't be at the hospital?"

"I promise I will go there next. Right now, I just need a computer."

Sam looked around, but he recognized none of the faces. They wouldn't think to look in here. But then again, they probably had other places to go. Sam just needed to know where to look.

Libby the Librarian got up from her seat and walked slowly with Sam to the back of the library. Off to the left was a *Carolina Room* filled with bookcases of books, maps, charts, and other reference material about the state. To the right was a small glassed-in room with a row of ten computers sitting on long tables. They were situated back-to-back, cables jumbled and tumbling, and all attached to the same spot on the floor with matching blue cables.

Thank goodness for DSL, Sam thought as he surveyed the other three computer users: a teenage boy with a really bad case of acne smeared on his face like grape jelly, a high school-aged mother with her sleeping baby close by in a stroller, and a man Sam tagged to be in his sixties, wearing what were probably his favorite clothes from his days in a hippie commune.

When Hippie looked up to see who had entered his presence, Sam felt the man's eyes drinking him in from head to toe; then he coolly looked away as if Sam were just another patron, despite his ragged appearance.

Nobody except Libby the Librarian seemed to notice or care that Sam was battered.

Libby excused herself and soon returned with a wet rag for Sam's face and a cup of tepid water.

Sam settled in a chair and familiarized himself with the login sheet taped to the frame of the monitor. In a few seconds, he was googling the United States Coast Guard. Two frames later, he was at the Vessel Documentation page.

The screen asked for "Vessel Name." Sam typed in *Firefly*, one of the boat names from Lee's matrix. *A long list of boat owners coveting the name as their own would be dismayed to see how unoriginal they were,* Sam thought.

In an easily read grid, each boat by that name had the owner's registration information: name, address, port of record, and renewal information. Bingo.

Second search: *Moonglow*, the other boat listed on the matrix. Bingo, again.

One *Firefly* and one *Moonglow* in Carolina Beach. One belonging to Andrew J. Keller and the other to a Mister Michael E. Smith. And both boats without current documentation. Shame on them.

Sam hastily thanked Libby the Librarian and assured her he was on his way to a doc-in-a-box as he passed her desk on the way out.

CHAPTER THIRTY-SIX

The Coast Guard Station was not very far from the library. Nothing was far in Carolina Beach.

Sam's lower backside was feeling a little less tender as he drove the short distance, silently hoping Libby the Librarian would forgive him for passing on the doctor visit at this moment.

Pulling into the parking lot, Sam paused. *How deep does it go, this mess? Are the Coasties in on it, too?* Only one way to find out.

Sam slowly climbed the building's three steps, each one reminding his stiff, hurting legs how to work. Hesitating, he pulled open the glass door to the station.

Joshua Mattingly, a.k.a. Hoops, was leaning back in his chair throwing an orange Nerf basketball into a small plastic hoop on the room's far wall. He closely resembled Cuba Gooding, Jr., and had on more than one occasion used his movie-star looks to hit on the ladies.

Finishing up his two-pointer shot, Joshua swung around in his chair to face Sam.

"Sam-Man, you're a wreck. Somebody's boyfriend find you?"

"Something like that, Hoops." Sam didn't want to go into the story. "I came across something I thought you might like to know about. Could earn you some recognition with the ladies and all."

Joshua leaned forward. He was all about getting recognition and time with the ladies. He thought joining the Coast Guard would be his ticket for sweet mamas falling for a man-in-uniform and all that, but after six years, he was disappointed with the returns.

"Speak."

"I saw these two really hot boats and was wondering who owned them."

"You in the market for a new boat?" Hoops interrupted. He was known as the Deal Man around the beach, always buying and selling cars, boats, bikes.

"Well," lied Sam, "I didn't think I was. But these two boats were moored out near where I was one afternoon. Both of these boats…well, I guess I can tell you. There were hotties draping themselves all over both of these boats, man. I was hoping to get invited to the party, you know what I'm saying, but that didn't work. So I came up with a plan. I'd meet the owners and get invited to their next gig. You know how boaters are. There's always a party. I figured if the boats went out again, the babes would, too."

Hoops grinned. "You're gonna get you some, bro. May I come along to partake in the next part-ey?"

Got him.

"Sure. All we need to do is to find the owners. Both had Carolina Beach hailing ports. One was called *Moonglow*; the other was *Firefly*."

"*Moonglow? Firefly?* What's next, *Tinkerbell?*" Hoops tilted his computer screen so Sam could read it over his shoulder and motioned for Sam to come around the desk. "Let's see what we see."

Hoops did a quick search in his database, and within seconds, he had both files pulled up.

"I love days like today," Hoops said with extreme satisfaction and a toothy smile to match.

"Why do you say that?" Sam played along.

"The two boats you saw. Their documentation is not current. Over here in this column, I can see they are not registered with the state, either. So that, my friend, is a big fat non-compliance fee per boat."

"Really? I had no idea," said Sam.

"Yep. So do yourself a favor, Sam-Man, and stay current."

Hoops printed out a short report, including all the contact information on *Moonglow* and *Firefly*'s owners. As he looked at the names again, he screwed up his face.

"Andrew J. Keller and Michael E. Smith. Mike? Andy Keller? These guys are on your team, Sam-Man. What's up with that?"

"I guess I wasn't invited to their party. A pity, really. Sorry to hear they're not staying current as law-abiding boaters." Sam worked Hoops back on course. "Now what are you going to do about it?"

"Never had to mess with guys I know before." Hoops scratched his head. "But in most other cases, we send them a warning letter, then go arrest them, if we can find them."

"Oh. Well, maybe in this case, since they're friends, you could go talk to them in person and see what happens," Sam suggested. "I guess we won't be partying anytime soon. See you later, Hoops."

Sam walked as straight and steady toward the door as he could manage. A visit to an urgent care center might not be a bad idea after all.

"Just a minute, Sam-Man. You can come along for the ride. Maybe if you talk to them first, they'll send in their documentation forms before I have to act."

Hoops rose from his chair, called to an unseen person behind a door next to his basketball hoop affixed to the wall, and walked with Sam to the door.

Sam noted that Hoops had a radio on his belt. "No gun?"

"Don't think we'll be needing one for Mike and Andy; do you?" Hoops seemed sincere.

"I think I'll take my car, Hoops. I'll follow you." Sam lagged a step behind.

"Suit yourself…. That your ride? Sweet, Sam-Man. Whenever you're ready to sell that tasty-looking little blue 'Stang, you call me, hear?"

"Will do, Hoops. Will do."

Sam followed Hoops' aging pale blue Lincoln Continental with the Coast Guard decals all over it, a sure sign the government wasn't funding this esteemed arm of law enforcement. At least not this station in Carolina Beach.

Ever since the 9/11 tragedy, the Guard's duties had shifted. Debate raged locally about the providence of homeland security versus keeping Carolina Beach the quaint beach town it had always been, with Coasties just part of the scenery. Several of Hoops' mates were reassigned to other stations, other duties, other cutters…wherever they were needed to fight terrorism. Such reassignments left Hoops' station short-handed and short-funded.

For some unknown reason, Hoops had managed to stay attached to the local station for all these years. Sam guessed it was because of his dealing ability: he could get the station just about anything it needed or wanted. Plus, Hoops wasn't afraid to chase a bad guy to play the hero role.

Sam was happy to oblige, allowing Hoops to take the lead in the quest for two *document_dodgers*.

CHAPTER THIRTY-SEVEN

Carolina Shores is one of those neighborhoods you wouldn't think existed. Turn off the main drag through town and onto Martin Drive and a canopy of shimmering leaves engulfs your car. Dappled sunlight plays on stately white stucco homes with red tiled roofs shaded by more pin oaks than you might expect to see in a beach town. Neon hibiscuses surround courtyards with gurgling fountains. Lawns of green give way to docks on canals that lead to the open water. And civility reigns supreme in Carolina Shores. Or at least appears to.

Carolina Shores was one of many annexations for the town proper, and it showed. It was one of the first neighborhoods to have underground utilities, all of them, and neat sidewalks, something few off-street neighborhoods had.

Mike Smith said he made a ton of money in real estate, thus he could afford to live in this neighborhood. His story was he'd gotten in before the prices went through the roof, before Carolina Beach had been discovered. Sam thought Mike must have bought when he was in diapers since the beach was the beach. Everyone wanted to live there.

Sam had been here a few times for cookouts, but he had not seen a boat before. That, he would have remembered. Perhaps it was a new acquisition. Sam was going to find out.

Sam parked behind Hoops, who parked behind Mike's white patrol SUV. Sam slowly followed Hoops up the manicured walkway, then veered off to the right toward the canal side of the house. Hoops followed.

"What's up?"

"Just seeing if the boat is here…. Maybe Mike sold it." Sam stalled. "Go ring the bell. I'll be right there."

Hoops did as he was told and headed back to the walkway toward the front door.

Sam peered into every window along the canal side of the house. No occupants. Everything seemed to be in place, from the large screen television in the living room to the tidy kitchen complete with espresso machine on the counter. Espresso…now that should say something about the man's tastes.

On the canal sat a ten-by-ten square foot dock complete with benches on either side of it. Under one bench was a yellow and white bait bucket and a small clear plastic case of fishing weights and hooks. Leaning up against the house, Sam saw a ribbed bottom dinghy, rough and battered, but inflated. Ready. There was no large boat at the dock.

"Nobody home, Homey," Hoops called to Sam as he rounded the house. "Would you look at that view? Mikey's got it made, Sam-Man. I didn't think you guys made much more than us."

Sam glanced briefly at the fluorescent yellow-green marsh grass lining the far side of the canal. *Good fishing in here*, he imagined. *Too bad I won't have time to enjoy it.*

"We don't, Hoops. At least not all of us do." Sam walked toward the dinghy. "Hoops, if you were going to go sailing, wouldn't you take your dink?"

"Depends on how far I planned on going. If I were to go a cruising, I would take it. If I were just out and about for a day sail, probably not. How about you? Do you have a dink?"

"I'm in need of one, actually. You think this would fit in your car?"

"Whoa, Sam-Man. I am not into borrowing like that."

"Even if your 'friend' forgot to register his dink as well as his big boat?" Sam pointed to the inflated pontoons that were clear of any registration stickers. "I just need to borrow it to get back on board my own boat."

"Small boats don't need to be registered if there's no motor involved."

Sam pointed to the small outboard motor leaning up against the wall.

"You get the front," Hoops conceded. "How come you can't get to your boat? I thought you were in the town marina."

"Long story. The short answer is I was out sailing and night came. I anchored and hitched a ride back in with a friend. Since then, I've been so busy I haven't had a chance to get back aboard." Sam felt sure his live-aboard status wasn't known to Hoops.

"Well, as long as you're just borrowing Mikey's dink, I'm cool with that. Wonder where he is? I guess I'll drive by Andy's house. If he's not there, I'll start the paperwork."

Sam and Hoops wrestled the dinghy on top of Hoops' car and tied the inflatable fast. Sam went back for the motor, disregarding Hoops' raised eyebrows. Sam gave him directions, and the two started for the Causeway Bridge in Wrightsville Beach. Sam hadn't been back to his boat in three days. He hoped it was still there.

CHAPTER THIRTY-EIGHT

Cars with car-top boats are not an uncommon sight in beach towns. In fact, it's a regular occurrence during summer months. Kayakers, windsurfers, and big-boat boaters all do the same thing to get their small crafts from one place to another.

What was curious about Sam's little procession was that the car carrying the small boat belonged to the Coast Guard.

Usually, all the Coast Guard's boats were docked near their station. Their ribbed inflatable could fit two of the dinghies Sam was borrowing inside it, and their fast maneuverable cutters docked nearby, always at the ready.

Following in the Mustang, Sam watched Hoops' brake lights flare as they started to climb the high-rising bridge over Snow's Cut, an east-west passage on the Intracoastal Waterway just north of the town of Carolina Beach. Great. A wreck.

Sam got out of the Mustang and walked up a few feet to Hoops' car.

"Thanks for coming, Hoops. Hope it's okay for you to be away like this."

"Just doing my duty, Sam-Man; just doing my duty." Hoops lit a cigar and took a long drag.

Sam moved away from Hoops' open window to get a breath of fresh air. Looking toward the top of the bridge where a blue light was flashing, Sam noticed a sailboat mast creeping toward the bridge.

Three steps forward, Sam saw it.

Toothless' long silver hair. Toothless stood at the helm, impatiently calling out to a small craft in front of him as he headed west toward Masonboro Sound.

"Hoops! Get on your radio! I saw Mike's boat heading west."

Hoops cupped his hand to his ear to hear Sam better.

Sam repeated: "Mike's boat! It's heading west."

"Not much I can do about it now, sitting in this traffic." Hoops obviously enjoyed another pull on his cigar. "Besides, you said Mike wouldn't mind if you borrowed his dink." Hoops pointed to the car-top treasure.

Sam threw his hands in the air. "Hoops, I wasn't going to bring you into all of this. It's a mess, and I need your help."

Hoops leaned over the seat toward Sam. "What's up, Sam-Man?"

"Mike's a dirty cop. He and Andy both. They are involved with a drug ring, and they took hostages when I tried to bust up their little party. They may be on that boat right now! Please. Do something!"

"What, no part-ey girls, Sam-Man? That's not like you to lie to a brother. But just the same, if Mike's doing wrong, we're gonna set him right. Tell me more." Hoops nodded to the passenger side door.

Sam obeyed and climbed in. The stench of Hoops' cigar reminded him of Lee. Methodically, he recounted everything he knew.

Hoops listened. Then Hoops reacted by grabbing his radio.

"Coast Guard base Zero-Three-Three, do you copy?" Static.

"You're on, Hoops. What's up?"

Sam recognized Hoops' sidekick Allen Morris on the radio. Hoops dispensed with the formal talk.

"Switch to forty-two."

"Switching forty-two."

Hoops tuned the radio into channel forty-two, a clear frequency not typically monitored by casual boaters or towboat operators. The curious could pick up all kinds of conversations if dialing around a radio, but Hoops' cryptic monologue was one Sam could barely understand.

"Looking for a rum punch. I'm stuck at Snow's Cut facing west. Can you pick up and deliver?"

"Copy. Can do. Want a single or a double?" Allen was on.

"Make it a double. One more thing. Could you check on my cat Moonglow for me? I left her with nothing for breakfast, and I think she's going to be spitting mad when I get back."

"Copy. Will do. Out." Allen's voice was replaced by static.

"Cat? Rum punch?"

"Yeah, Sam-Man. You never know who might be scanning the radio." Hoops slowly explained as if Sam were one tool shy of a tool shed. "Rum punch means possible drug runner. Single means unarmed, not much of an offense. Double, be prepared for the worst. My cat/dog/parrot/whatever's the name of the boat so Al can do a quick trace to ownership and alert bridge tenders, and 'breakfast' is code for hostage. When I 'get back', that's Hoops-speak for bring back up. Al's fast. He'll get some guys and take the cutter out for a spin. We're using the element of surprise here, so Mikey's pal will be none the wiser."

Sam shook his head. "He's probably armed, Hoops. He's got hostages. He sees a cutter coming, and what's he gonna do? Shoot and dump?"

"He won't have time. Not to worry, Sam-Man. We'll nail him. Anybody else with him?"

Sam thought about Scuz Number Two. "No, nobody else in the cockpit."

"Think they're all on board? Must be a pretty cozy group if all the hostages, *and* Mike *and* Andy are down below."

Sam counted on his fingers: "Tripp Johnson, Mike, Chuck, Lisa, Andy, Jenny, and Molly, one goon below, and Toothless at the helm. Nobody was sitting in the cockpit except Toothless, so either they were all down below, or…."

Sam didn't wait for Hoops to answer. He dashed back to the Mustang and did a seven-point turn to get off the bridge, the only road off the island. Sam headed back into Carolina Beach.

CHAPTER THIRTY-NINE

Sam floored it back to the city docks in Carolina Beach, slowing down long enough to cruise the small parking lot. No sign of the Owens' Ford Taurus. Driving slower down the road running parallel to the main road, Sam searched between every house and condo complex. Still no sign of it.

Sam headed back to the gallery. Parking in the alley behind it, Sam walked around the buildings that backed up to the gallery. When he got to the front of them, he saw what he had dreaded.

"Shit."

A public dock with slips for transient boaters jutted out into a cove surrounded by open green space filled with picnickers and play structures. Beyond the cove's entrance was an entrance to the Intracoastal Waterway.

Tripp and Company had come from Southport by boat. That's why there wasn't another car at the gallery. And that's why Mike and Chuck were so eager to wait just outside the office's back door, trying to stay out of sight, but prepared to leave as soon as the boat had arrived. *Clever*, Sam thought. He cursed himself for not checking it sooner. Whoever was on the boat had several hours' head start.

Sam was hopeful as he drove down a street leading to Chuck and Lisa's house. He turned off the main drag into a three-street subdivision of odd-looking contemporaries with hard angles and fogged skylights set in their rooflines. Reaching their house, Sam noted that the Owens' car wasn't in the driveway. The front door was wide open, though.

Sam cautiously entered. No one was inside, but it was clear someone had been: the house looked like a hurricane had pummeled it. Pieces of shattered pottery and glass lay on the tile floor. Furniture was upturned, cushions strewn about. The contents from a floor-to-ceiling bookcase were scattered, and the Oriental rugs were contorted off to one side.

Sidestepping the mess, Sam searched bedrooms, kitchen, and bathrooms. Every room had the mark of the same decorator.

Through the partially opened sliding glass door to a tidy patio, Sam saw the back of someone slumped in a lounge chair. Sam held his breath, then tiptoed out the sliding door. The figure did not move.

Cautiously, Sam slid around the side of the chair to where he could touch the man, who sat with a dazed look on his unshaven face, his countenance as rumpled as his clothes.

"You want to talk about it, Dan?"

Chief Dan Singleton didn't say a word, but he did turn his head to look at Sam. With tears streaming down his red eyes, the Chief shook his head.

"Look; I'm sorry she wasn't what you thought she was," Sam soothed. "She's made a real mess of things with her brother, and I know Mike Smith and Andy Keller are in on it, too."

Chief cut him off. "Andy…. I thought she really loved me. She was seeing him, too. She was using me—using us, trying to see who she could get to first."

"Lisa was with Andy, too? Aww, Chief, I didn't know. What about Chuck?"

"That's how I found out about Andy. After you left my office, Chuck stormed in, cussed me out, and cussed Lisa too. Said she was a slut, and he was not gonna take it anymore. Then just as quick, he stormed out of my office. I saw him grab Mike, and they left. I came over here to calm him down, to try to talk some sense into Lisa, but I walked in here and just lost it."

"You trashed the place?"

"I didn't mean to. It was rage. I…I really loved her." Chief started sobbing, rocking himself back and forth like a mama rocks her infant.

Sam sat down in a green plastic chair. A stainless steel grill was poised for action near a comfortable looking table and four chairs. Just a step off the concrete patio was a small garden plot with bright yellow squash blossoms open in the late day sun. This was where a family had gathered. Sam felt sorry for Lisa and Chuck's boys. They were away at college, so as Lisa pointed out, they could manage on their own now. Still, a family wrecked is a child ruined.

"Chief, we need to get going. We need to find Chuck and Lisa and Tripp. Come on. I'll tell you what I know. Maybe you can think of a way to stop this madness." Sam tugged gently on Chief's shirt. "I need your help, Dan."

Chief wiped his eyes. Slowly, he stood up, straightened his shirt, and looked around.

"I can't go back in that house. Let's walk around the side."

Sam thought that was the best idea, too.

CHAPTER FORTY

"Do you have a phone on you?" Sam walked shoulder to shoulder with Chief as they came around the side of Chuck and Lisa's house.

Without a word, Chief handed Sam his cell phone.

"Hoops, it's Sam. What have you got?"

"Sam-Man, you were right. Al and the boys got Mikey's boat. They came alongside, and just like you said, one stupid fool drew a gun on them. He was whacked, Al said, all high on something. He didn't look so good after their little visit, Al said."

"Was he alone?"

"No. Another two ratty-lookin' guys were down below working on a joint. Not anyone Al had ever seen before, he said. Look; I dropped the dinghy and the motor off behind the Causeway Diner, near the dumpster. I told the manager you'd be by to get it as soon as you could. Everything cool where you are?"

"So far. I got the Chief with me, and we're on it."

"What more can I do for you, Sam-Man?"

"Not sure at this point. Keep your phone handy, though. I left mine on board my boat, so I'm using

Chief's. I'll call again in case something comes up that you think I need to know about."

"Did they get Lisa?" Chief's eyes glassed over once Sam ended the call.

"No. Only Mike's boat and the Scuz Brothers, who, I guess, work for Tripp Johnson. They were the decoy to buy the others some time, I bet."

Sam wasn't sure how much more he should say, but he plunged ahead anyway.

"Seeing how Mike's boat was used to put us off the scent, I'm pretty sure Mike was in it from the start. Do you think he and Lisa—"

"Don't go there, Sam."

"Look, Chief; we need to know all the players, here. Why would Mike get a cut of it if Lisa wasn't, you know, involved?"

"Who said he's involved? Maybe he's just a hostage, like Chuck. Maybe Lisa's being held now against her will." Chief sounded almost hopeful.

"Not likely. She was a mule. You said so yourself. No, I think she's in it up to her eyeballs. I'm just trying to figure out how deep Chuck and Mike were in on it. It could make a difference for all of them." Sam eased into the Mustang and waited for Chief to do the same.

"Let's go find out." Chief was almost chipper.

Sam didn't like the look in Chief's eyes, but he decided having someone on his team—even someone half-crazy—was better than no one at all.

"Where's your car, Chief?"

"Down the street. I parked there in case Lisa had company…. I didn't want her to see me coming, I guess."

Sam drove past Chief's car on the way out of the neighborhood, then stopped and backed up.

"What kind of supplies you got in there?"

"Standard issue." Chief paused and smiled. "And a little something extra."

"Bring whatever you got. We may need it."

Chief returned to the Mustang in seconds with the standard issue Glock and a towel-wrapped pump action patrol rifle, unwrapping the latter briefly to show Sam.

"Impressive. From your own personal collection?"

"Something like that. Do you know what we're up against?"

Sam popped the trunk. Chief carefully laid his Remington inside and closed the trunk.

"Mike and Chuck are carrying their standard issues," Sam recounted as he drove south down the beach road and past the aquarium entrance. He turned right into the Fort Fisher Ferry landing's parking lot, got a ticket, and parked in a line waiting to board the ferry. "One of the hostages was able to make off with Tripp Johnson's gun at the gallery, but I suspect he's taken it back. I don't know about Andy. He wasn't showing."

Three cars were in front of Sam and Chief as they waited for the just-docking ferry to unload cars.

Without turning, Sam asked the question that had plagued him all day. "Chief, you said in your office that you were following orders. Whose orders?"

"Commissioner Martin. He said *he* was just following orders, but one can't tell with Martin. I didn't have the spine to stand him down. He said if I questioned him again, I'd be out, just like that. I've worked for a lot of years toward a comfortable retirement with full pension, and I wasn't about to screw that up because someone has it in for you. What did you do to Martin, anyway?"

"Not anything I'm aware of. Did he tell you to do anything other than bug my car or crush the Camaro before the case was closed?"

"No. But either way, I should have stood up to him. Shoulda told him no. You're a good cop, Sam. I see now you didn't have anything to do with Lee's death."

"Doesn't matter now. What does matter is we have to get to Johnson's."

The khaki-clad ferry attendant signaled for Sam to move forward. Sam slowly rolled the Mustang onto the ferry; blocks were set under his wheels, and he was instructed to turn his engine off.

When Sam and Chief climbed the ladder to the upper deck, they walked to a railing away from the other passengers.

"Who are we looking for, exactly?" Chief leaned over the rail.

"Lee's wife, Jenny Elliott; Molly Monroe, a...my friend who accidentally got messed up in all of this; Lisa, Chuck, Mike, Andy, and Tripp Johnson."

"What makes you think they're in Southport?"

"Two reasons. First, Mike let the Scuz Brothers, who accompanied Andy to the gallery, take his forty-two-foot sailboat *Moonglow* out for a spin. The Coast Guard picked them up heading south down the ditch, and they were armed and ready. Second, the fishery is the only place I can think of where they'd be holding hostages without anybody stopping by to see what's going on."

"Holding or disposing?"

"Probably preparing to dispose." Sam bit his lip, imagining what Jenny and Molly were going through. "Molly and Jenny surprised Lisa at the gallery. She was getting ready to take flight with two suitcases of cash. I can't believe she kept that much around."

"Can't just walk into a bank with two suitcases, now can you?" Chief was back to his old cantankerous self.

"Suppose not. There were plenty of places she could have hid it in the gallery. In hollow display pedestals, art pieces, wherever. She was getting ready to leave, so she gathered it all up. Did you find anything at her house?"

"Nothing out of the ordinary." Chief looked at the wake created by the ferry as it left the dock. "Really, I don't know what I expected to find. I was just so…." He slammed his fist on the railing.

"Yeah. I would be too if I were duped and used. Sorry. Let's keep going." Sam put a hand lightly on Chief's shoulder. "Tell me what she told you."

"About what?"

"About anything. How did you learn she was a mule? And how did you find out who her brother was?"

"One afternoon, I walked into the gallery and there he was. She didn't want to introduce me, but he was ballsy enough to. I watched him hand her an envelope. He said it was for a painting he'd commissioned by one of her artists, but he didn't look like the cultured type. When I asked her about it later, she couldn't keep up with his lie, so she said it was for something else, a fancy table she was expecting to be delivered by an artisan who lived in the mountains. Then she started, you know, coming on to me, so I dropped it."

"So how did you learn she was delivering for Tripp? Seems like something she wouldn't be too eager to discuss with the chief of police."

"She wasn't. I found out on my own. One night, we were supposed to meet at our favorite hideaway in Wilmington. She didn't show up, so I went looking for her. I drove by her house, and her car wasn't there. Then I went by the gallery and saw her. I was just about to get out of my car to ask if she was all right, but I stayed put for some reason. Maybe it dawned on me that what was going on between us was wrong. I was thinking I would break it off, but then I saw Andy coming out of the gallery right close behind her with his hand touching her back. You may have noticed I get kinda jealous when I think about her and anybody else. I couldn't think straight when I saw her hug him affectionately, the way she does…did me. I could feel my palms getting sweaty. I ducked down in my car so they wouldn't notice me. Then I watched as Andy helped Lisa load several boxes from his car into hers. When he drove off, I followed Lisa. She headed to

Wilmington, then out on to Highway 40, heading west to Raleigh."

"Where did she go?" Sam waited patiently as Chief calmed down enough to continue.

"There's a rest stop in the middle of the highway where the traffic passes, heading east and west on either side of it. Do you know it?"

Sam nodded.

"She pulled off there. I followed her and parked a safe distance away. I had even got out and snuck around a bush to get a closer look when she waved at this sleazy-looking guy who parked right beside her. He helped her transfer the boxes from her car to his; then they both drove away. I took a chance and followed the guy. His black Cadillac had New York plates. I wrote down the number, then followed him to the interstate and all the way to the ramp heading north on Interstate 95. I followed him for a little ways, then made a U-turn and came back down here."

"What'd you do with the license plate number?"

"Called it in, of course."

"And you don't think he was just an art lover?"

"Not a chance. I checked the sleaze-bucket out with a friend of mine. He's a bail jumper with a sheet as long as your arm."

"Sorry to hear that."

"Yeah. Me too." Chief walked to the other side of the ferry's top deck, close enough to a gaggle of tourists to signal that the conversation was over.

CHAPTER FORTY-ONE

By the time the ferry pulled into the Southport ferry landing, Sam was listing charges against Tripp Johnson on his fingers—murder, attempted murder, assault and battery, trafficking, prostitution. He looked at Chief as they were getting back in the car, lined in a cue to drive off the ferry.

"Think we can expect any help from the boys in Southport?"

Chief shook his head. "I don't know. These townies are pretty tight. And the Johnson family roots go way back. I can call, but we might be setting ourselves up. Let's take a look around. See what we think." A smile fluttered across his lips. "Besides, we have all the backup we need in the trunk."

Sam nodded. He focused on the narrow curving road leading out of the landing's parking lot and onto Moore Street, the riverside road heading into Southport.

The Mustang is holding up well, given what I'm putting it through, Sam thought. He hoped Lee wouldn't mind him driving it so much, but he had no other choice at this point. His truck was probably a carcass, still stuck in Navassa from the night Molly showed up in that tight sparkly dress. Sam tried hard not to think of Molly *that* way right now. He just wanted her and Jenny safe again.

Once inside the village of Southport, Sam paid attention to zigzagging tourists who crossed Moore Street, checking out menus of restaurants without so much as a glance at oncoming cars. *Tourists can be so aggravating,* Sam thought, as he stopped more than once to let another couple dressed in high-style cruise wear and frills pass. *Overdressed for the occasion and the place,* he noted. Sam also thought about his own empty stomach. But they had to keep going.

Down at the waterfront, traffic moved slowly as sightseers and restaurant goers drifted from eatery to eatery, deciding on which one to bestow their patronage. When Sam and Chief reached the corner of Restaurant Row, where Provision's meets the hungry world, Sam saw it.

The tan Ford Taurus station wagon was parked in front of Johnson's, the windows down. It was empty.

Sam parked nearby. He and Chief scanned the parking lot. Then they headed to Provision's dockside dining. Since it was early, there were still a few empty tables. From this vantage point, Sam could see part of the docks off Johnson's Fishery. No boats were there tonight.

Chief walked to the other end of the dining area. Then he was off like a shot.

Sam saw him running toward a white multi-towered Cabo Sportsfisher. When Sam jumped down on the dock and read the name emblazoned on the stern, he caught his breath.

Firefly.

Andy's boat glistened in the afternoon sun. The cabin door was open slightly, giving Sam a view of what made Chief jump so fast. A bloody hand was gripping the bottom of the door.

Chief was aboard in a second, pushing open the cabin door to a groaning voice. It was Chuck Owens. Just Chuck. No Lisa. No Molly. No Jenny.

Chuck's jaw was out of alignment, and his face a bloody mess where the nose should be. Below the neckline wasn't much better.

Chief and Sam tightly wrapped as many bleeding points as they could, and they tried to make Chuck as comfortable as possible without moving him. He was losing blood fast.

"Call an ambulance!" Chief screeched at a short preppy man standing on the dock nearby. Reaching for his flip phone, the prepster caught a glimpse of Chuck through the open door on the boat and shrieked. He fumbled his fingers until he found the nine and the one on the keypad.

"There's a man on the boat. *Firefly*. Uh-huh. No, I'm on the dock looking onto the boat. The dock. Next to Provision's. Yes. Yes." Then to the Chief: "They want to know his condition."

"Desperate! Tell them to get over here now!" Chief was redder than a Coast Guard cutter.

Prepster, now surprisingly calm, continued his call, giving as close a description of the situation as he could figure out.

Within seconds, the ambulance's wailing siren could be heard approaching through the narrow streets.

Chief and Sam stood back to let the emergency medical team do its thing, overseeing everything like a couple of supervisors in a factory. As Chuck was lifted off the boat, the questions began.

Chief took out his identification. "We'll talk at the hospital."

The EMT he talked with nodded and ran to the driver's side of the ambulance.

Chief nodded to Sam. "You stay here in case they come back. I'm going to the hospital with Chuck."

Before they could wheel Chuck to the ambulance, Chief gently fished in Chuck's pant pockets until he found the keys to Chuck's Taurus.

Sam shrugged, watching Chief spin out of the parking lot in Chuck's car, chasing the ambulance toward the hospital.

Then Sam headed for the fishery. Walking all around the facility, Sam saw that all the doors, streetside and dockside, were locked. If they had been here, they didn't stay long.

Returning to the Mustang, Sam was relieved to see that Chief's cell phone lay on the seat. He dialed Hoops' number.

"Hoops, I got another name for you to run down."

"Sam-Man, you getting yourself in all kinds of trouble, aren't you?" Hoops sounded relieved that Sam hadn't found too much of the wrong kind of trouble just yet.

"I'm trying hard to steer clear, but we need to find these folks. I'm running out of time and daylight, so I need you to find out the owner of one more boat. I only know the boat's name."

"Speak."

"Seawitch. I don't know the hailing port, but I'll bet you a beer it's Southport."

Silence on the other end filled Sam's ear.

Hoops spoke. "We got three down there. Any idea what kind you're looking for?"

"What have you got?"

"A twelve-foot Boston Whaler."

"No, it would have to be something bigger."

"A Hallberg-Rassy 342."

"Hum. That's big enough to carry five people, but I'm thinking a sailboat wouldn't be the choice vessel for a getaway. How about a long-distance motor cruiser? Something fast?"

"Sweet." Hoops let out a catcall whistle. "How about a forty-one-foot Beneteau Flyer with two Volvo engines? That fast enough for you?"

"That'll do. Owner?"

"Tripp Johnson. Southport. Need an address?"

"No. I seriously doubt anybody's home. Thanks, Hoops. I owe you one."

"You owe me three. One for liberating Mike's dinghy, one for delivering it for you, and one for lying to me to get me to do it. This one, you can have for free." Hoops paused. "This the boat you think your friends are on?"

"Yeah. I just don't know how I'm going to track them from here."

"You've called the right person, Sam-Man. I'll get you a fix on that vessel. You going to hold on to this number for the night?"

"Yeah."

"Good. I'll send out the troops from Oak Island. You hang tight and stay out of their way."

Sam feigned hurt. "You honestly think I would get in the way of the United States Coast Guard doing its duty?"

"Yes. Stay clear, Sam-Man. I'll call you when we have them in custody."

"I promise I'll stay out of trouble. I'll enjoy the evening from Provision's deck."

"Sure you will," Hoops answered incredulously. "Catch you later, Sam-Man."

Though Sam had promised, patience was not a strong suit for him. He pondered for a moment. Then he popped open the Mustang's trunk to fetch its contents and jogged back to *Firefly*.

CHAPTER FORTY-TWO

Hot-wiring a boat is a lot quicker than hot-wiring a car. On a car, a thief has to remove the left side of the steering column. His screwdriver finds a round cup-like mechanism, and the car starts right up. A common auto-body shop tool called a *dent puller* is attached to the steering wheel, and the thief wiggles it back and forth until the ignition lock pops. Procedures may vary from car to car, but getting one started without a key is generally not a problem.

On a boat, the engine can be started by hand in the engine compartment. Wires are exposed, sure. But on a boat, it's more a matter of using a starter button or hand-cranking one or more belt wheels, depending on the model, than crossing wires. A starter button, like the one Sam found on *Firefly*, is particularly easy and helpful when changing the oil—or chasing bad guys.

Sam untied the dock lines. Within seconds, he was clear of the no-wake zone in front of Provision's and working his way toward Bald Head Island.

On any other evening, a night on the water—even in a fast boat—was a glorious mingling of fresh air and scents and sights. White Ibis settle down in their tree-top nests like ornaments on a Christmas tree planted on spoil islands created from dredged sands. An occasional dolphin leaps high enough to be seen, even in the brackish Cape Fear River. And the neon yellow-green marsh grass reaches up toward the Crayola orange, purple, and yellow sky, colors brilliant in the setting sun's wake.

This particular evening, Sam noticed none of it. He veered to the right of Bald Head Island toward the Atlantic's open waters. The island's octagonal brick lighthouse, a relic of days when whale oil was carried up spiraling stairs to keep the lamp lit, and the tall black and white column of a lighthouse on Oak Island, could be seen from the channel. An imaginary line strung between the two lighthouses signaled the river's end and the ocean's beginning.

Boating around Bald Head is treacherous, even for boatmen familiar with the shifting shoals visible in shallow waters that flail a long serpent's tail of sand from side to side, depending on which storm hit it last. During the daylight, fishermen pick their way through the channel, mindful that what appears on a chart may not be what's under their keels. At night, all bets are off.

Sam held his left hand up to the sky, his thumb parallel with the horizon. He noted where the sun was on his ringless ring finger. At this time of the year, each finger between the sun and the horizon represents fifteen minutes. Another hour of daylight, tops.

He flipped the navigational lights on. He scanned the radio for conversations. First to the Coast Guard station, next to the weather station, where a computerized voice referred to as *Mechanical Mike* sounded off tides, times, and weather forecasts of waters stretching from Norfolk to Georgia. Finally, the scan button reached a frequency most commonly used by recreational boaters. Nothing much to listen to, unless you want to hear news of the catch of the day.

Sam set the radio on scan and listened to snatches of various conversations as he sped along the Oak Island side of the channel. When he saw the initial red open ocean buoy, fear crept up his spine for the first time that day—not for his own safety, but for Molly and Jenny's. He wondered how far behind he was.

From *Firefly*'s starboard side came a deep rumbling and a flash of orangey red. The Coast Guard cutter flew past him and waved him off.

Had Hoops said something? Sam ignored their signals to back off and followed in the cutter's wake for a moment before speeding up. Sam heard their admonition over the radio, but he ignored that, too. They knew who he was; Hoops would have told them. Running alongside the cutter, Sam didn't bother with pretenses when he scooped up the radio's hand-held mic and waved it in the air.

"Switch to forty-two," he tried not to yell.

"Switching forty-two."

If anyone heard the demand, he wouldn't know it was a Coast Guard cutter. That's just what Sam wanted.

A voice shattered the static on channel forty-two. "We'll take it from here, copy?"

"I hear you. But I will not turn back. They are armed and dangerous, and they got hostages."

"Concur," answered the efficient voice. "This is not your ballgame anymore, cowboy. Turn back."

"I'll be your backup, but I am not laying off."

Sam veered back behind the cutter. *Firefly* was fast, but it didn't have the tracking devices the cutter had. Sam would let them take the lead to find *Seawitch*. Sam vowed to be there, too. Sam switched back to scan mode and dropped his pace a little, giving the cutter two hundred yards as it headed due southeast twenty degrees to open water.

Forty-five minutes left until dark engulfed the ocean. If they stayed close to shore, they could follow various towns' markers and lights. Sam turned on the helm-mounted GPS and watched the numbers increase as he ran in deeper water. There was no radar on board, so he'd have to rely on the cutter's direction. Sam figured that with these electronics on board, *Firefly* must have been Andy's toy for fishing near Frying Pan Shoals. Sam marked his fuel and hoped the gauge was accurate.

CHAPTER FORTY-THREE

An old song by Little River Band drifted into Sam's head. He marveled at how the lyricist romanticized the ocean at night. Sam was sure the moon didn't look like any lover he'd had, but the sentiment was nice. A cool ocean breeze, the open ocean, and not but a few stars overhead could make nearly anyone wax poetic, but Sam was focused on the stern lights in front of him. The rescue boat was moving fast. Sam wanted to ride shotgun, but he kept a respectable distance as they chewed up space between them and their target.

About an hour running full out, Sam noticed the rescue boat swerving to the east. He did the same. There, about five hundred yards ahead, are the low profile lights of a fast cruiser.

This time of year, most cruisers are heading north or they are heading to the deep South, toward Venezuela, to avoid hurricanes. For a boat that size to be offshore at this time of year could mean a lot of things, but not many of them good.

Dousing all of *Firefly*'s lights, Sam brought the boat to idle as he watched the Coast Guard approach the boat in question, its high wattage searchlight trained on the vessel in question. Cutting through *Firefly*'s radio's static, Sam heard the efficient voice he'd talked to before. He listened intently.

"Southeast-bound vessel, this is the United States Coast Guard. State your name."

No response on the radio, but it was clear the message was received. The boat sped up. The rescue boat followed and closed the distance between the two boats.

Running without lights, Sam veered slightly east of the chase vessel. A radar would pick him out of the dark sea like lint on a black shirt, but Sam guessed he'd be a gnat compared to the wasp about to sting whoever was running away from the Coast Guard. It's *never* a good idea to run from the Coast Guard. It makes the boys in blue nervous, and they bring out the big guns for reassurance. Sam only hoped their guns were bigger and their fingers faster on the triggers than the delinquent fingers they were chasing.

Efficient Voice again tried to raise a response. This time, a pale rattled voice answered.

"Help us, please!"

Then static.

Sam recognized the voice in an instant. Molly. She was still alive. "Us" rang in his ears. He couldn't sit by and wait it out.

Without turning his running lights back on, Sam turned *Firefly* back toward the vessels to the south and west of him. Slamming the throttle down, Sam thought through his "what if" scenarios once again. If he rammed the boat he guessed to be *Seawitch*, he could injure Molly and Jenny and probably injure or kill himself, trashing both boats in the process. The Coast Guard would be standing by, and it might be able to fish them all out of the water, but at night, even in a calm sea like this, that could put the Coast Guard at risk, given the possibility of flotsam or fire from two crashing vessels.

Sam passed the Coast Guard rescue boat and ran alongside the runaway boat. Its deep red hull looked like tar, the same as everything else at night, but Sam caught a glimpse of a reflective name on the side as the rescue boat's beam made a sweep: *Seawitch*. An unseen bullet flew past Sam's ear. He ducked, taking the steering wheel with him as he veered to the east away from *Seawitch*.

"Great. I've been spotted," thought Sam. The Coast Guard's light illuminated his boat instantaneously, just long enough for it to be seen. Sam felt around the cockpit with his foot for the two guns he'd brought along for such an occasion, but he only found the pump action patrol rifle. He scraped it up to his side as he crouched at the exposed helm.

If he could make it up to the boat's tower, he could probably pick off whomever he needed to. But he'd have to be at a near standstill to do that, and all three boats were moving fast.

Sam watched the rescue boat's lights as the boat moved ahead of him again. Sam steered *Firefly* aft of the rescue boat, dodging behind it, and he started his approach toward *Seawitch* from the other side.

Sam saw it before he heard it over the roar of *Firefly*'s engine. A flash of rapid pinpoint gunfire from *Seawitch*'s stern knocked out the rescue boat's searchlight.

Firing on a Coast Guard rescue boat? These guys are nuts! If these guys—former comrades and "friends," plus whatever whacko Tripp might be—are stupid enough to fire at the Coast Guard, they might be stupid enough to try anything.

Sam smiled at his own stupidity as he raced forward to cut in front of *Seawitch*. Getting rammed by a boat going full out is never an ideal situation. But it was the only way Sam was sure he could distract whoever was doing all the shooting.

He pushed the throttle all the way down and leaped overboard into the inky water. Surprised by the cold splash, Sam dreaded his stupidity instantly. If the crash didn't get Molly and Jenny, hypothermia would.

The terrific sound of crushing, colliding fiberglass and metal took Sam's breath away as he watched *Seawitch* plow through *Firefly*'s mid-section, both halves up-ended, pointing to the early night sky like glaciers. Shining in the rescue boat's auxiliary spotlight, *Firefly*'s aluminum tower seemed suspended in mid-air, now floating, now crashing on *Seawitch*'s stern, its tube legs striking someone aboard *Seawitch* on its return to earth. *Seawitch* continued moving forward at a terrific pace with both engines running at full speed, but Sam saw the rescue boat close the distance between it and *Seawitch* rapidly. *Seawitch* must be taking on water to slow it down like that.

Minutes. Sam knew he had minutes before the chill claiming his feet would climb his legs. He swam toward the two boats, watching the rescue boat cautiously approach *Seawitch* the last few yards.

Shots rang out from *Seawitch*, followed by cussing and a failed attempt to revive stalling engines.

The rescue boat's spotlight illuminated *Seawitch*, showing the fear of the three men clinging to the cockpit's sloping topsides.

Three men. Tripp, Mike, Andy.

Sam swam faster. He looked again. One woman. Which one? The Coast Guard's rescue boat slowed to a stop five yards from the wreckage. Cautiously, guns still poised, the guardsmen started rescue operations for the people they saw aboard with the assist of a smaller motorized inflatable, shuttling them back to the larger rescue boat.

Sam wanted to yell out, but he kept swimming. Pieces of fiberglass drifted by his arms and legs, and an occasional metal fitting or bracket floating by on a hunk of wood grazed his face as he trudged through the slight ocean chop.

When he came into the sphere of the rescue boat's spotlight, Sam stopped to catch his breath and to watch the rescue. Mike came without a fight. Andy, battered and bloodied on his forehead, nearly collapsed into a rescue team member's arms. Tripp was nowhere to be seen.

One of the Coasties noticed Sam and lowered a rope ladder off the rescue boat's stern. Sam gratefully acknowledged it with a tired wave and started to doggie-paddle toward it. Exhaustion tugged at his arms and legs, but Sam kept moving, reaching forward for the boat until he felt the back of his left leg burning.

"Too early in the season for man-o-wars," he whispered, reaching his hand to his leg. He felt warmth ooze from his leg and felt the searing pain. In a quick glance at *Seawitch*, Sam gawked at a smiling Lisa, rifle in hand, standing tall on the sinking boat's precariously tilted aft railing.

Lisa didn't falter or flinch when the boat lurched or when the Coast Guard yelled at her to put her gun down. Smile never fading, Lisa raised a Colt 45 to her temple.

For a moment, Sam marveled at how graceful death could be. Lisa's head pulled the rest of her into a slow-motion arcing dive toward the water.

Andy shrieked when he saw this final act of Lisa's caught in the bright searchlight. He flung himself toward the water, rocking the small inflatable. Two Coasties yanked him back and held him securely. Another Coastie climbed aboard the sinking vessel.

Exhausted, Sam gave his last ounce of strength to reach the larger rescue boat. A burly Coastie met him on the ladder and lifted Sam up the rest of the way. Safely aboard, Sam was smothered in blankets and bandages.

For an instant, the brilliant blast illuminated the night, wrenching the tiredness from Sam's bones as he flew to the railing. *Seawitch* was a fiery mess of exploding debris, shards of fiberglass, and splintering wood leaping skyward in a display that would rival most fireworks. It would be the last thing Sam remembered seeing as he collapsed on the rescue boat's deck.

CHAPTER FORTY-FOUR

Six o'clock. Sam stared at the clock, not quite recognizing what it was. Six-oh-one. A faint sound of voices drifted by. Sam focused on the solid door through which they came. Mauve curtains hung on a track just inside the door.

Six-oh-two. Sam's head hurt, his leg throbbed, and every part of his body ached as if he'd been run over by a car.

The voices grew louder, and one, attached to a tall man dressed in a white coat, came through the door. His well-trimmed red mustache reminded Sam of Rhett Butler.

"Welcome back!" Rhett said, looking over a chart. "We weren't so sure you'd be joining us today. How are we feeling?"

"Like *we* shouldn't be here. Where *is* here?" Sam looked at the clock again. Six-oh-four.

"Dosher Hospital. Dr. Henderson at your service," the gentle doctor said, offering a short bow and a generous smile. "You lost a lot of blood. We've got a nice cocktail for you to relieve some of the pain so you can rest this morning."

A nurse moved behind Dr. Henderson like his shadow. She pumped the contents of a syringe into a tube streaming from Sam's arm, then changed an IV bag attached to a tube running into the same blue plastic tip sticking out from the back of his wrist.

Six-oh-six.

"Rest," soothed Dr. Henderson. "You'll be out of here soon."

Just as efficiently as he'd come in, Dr. Henderson left the room.

The nurse finished her required fussing about, and a technician exchanged places with her to take Sam's temperature and blood pressure. They were efficient in their leaving, too.

Six-oh-nine.

"No need to mince words when actions suffice," thought Sam.

Taking in the wallpaper border dominated by shrimping boats, Sam clawed his way to a memory of what happened the night before. He pressed the nurse-call button on the bed railing, and an efficient but pleasant voice drifted through the speaker. Efficiency must be part of the job description.

"How can I help you?"

"Is Chuck Owens a patient here?"

"One minute. I'll check."

Silence.

"Yes. He's in ICU."

"I need to speak with him."

"Not today, sir. He's in critical condition."

"How is he?"

"I'm not permitted to say, other than telling you his status is critical."

"Thanks."

Sam watched the sun's filtered rays dance on the wall nearest the clock. Six-fifteen. His head felt heavy again, almost dizzy. Then Sam slipped into healing sleep once again.

Six-sixteen.

CHAPTER FORTY-FIVE

Dr. Henderson was his cheery, efficient self during his late morning visit to Sam's room.

"Hello, Mr. McClellan. How are we feeling now?"

"I suppose *we* are feeling better. Are you at liberty to talk about another patient if it's a police matter and I'm the police?" Sam was hopeful.

"Generally, no. But if you were to ask me about a dear, dear friend who, let's just say for sport, was brought in severely beaten, I'd probably be able to tell you his chances for survival are better today than they were last night without breaking any rules of patient confidentiality. But I don't suppose you would ask me such a question, would you?" Dr. Henderson offered a smile as quick as his step around the bed.

"I wouldn't dream of it," Sam smiled gratefully. "And what's my condition?"

"Generally, pretty good. We were able to stabilize you last night, and you're on the mend. You'll be fine in another few hours or so. Hypothermia, bullet wound, dehydration…all make for a winning combination, I'd say. Get comfortable; rest." There was that soothing tone again.

"Did my Coast Guard friends bring anyone else in last night whom you feel I shouldn't ask about?"

"Not that I'm aware of," Dr. Henderson said. "We're a small staff, and I was the Emergency Room doc on call last night. There were no surprises, other than you and your friend in ICU."

Sam felt he had to ask. "Is there a morgue here?"

Dr. Henderson looked up from his chart. "Mr. McClellan, this is Southport. *Of course* we have one. It's not a tourist attraction we publicize, but we do have one. After all, people *do die* here." His smile returned to his face.

"Were there any new tenants arriving last night?"

"I couldn't say. But when you are feeling up to it, you can go visit Dr. Jerry Huff yourself. He'll be able to tell you of new tenants."

Just as with Dr. Henderson's earlier visit, the shadow nurse entered the room, followed by a technician.

As Dr. Henderson reached for the door, he looked sternly back at Sam. "You're a lucky man, Mr. McClellan. Had the Coast Guard not been right there, you'd not have lasted much longer."

Then his smile was back, and he efficiently marched out of the room.

When the shadow nurse and technician left, Sam pushed the hydraulic-powered bed's control buttons until he was comfortably sitting upright. Turning on the ceiling-mounted television on the opposite wall, Sam surfed until he found a local news program. A static image of a Coast Guard rescue boat overlaid with the Coast Guard's emblem stared back at Sam as he increased the volume of the perky newscaster presenting the story as if it were a weather report.

"…the incident report said. Debris from the wreckage litters Yaupon Beach, and the Oak Island Beach Police have cordoned off all northern beach access roads. Visitors are advised to choose a different beach since they will be turned away until the investigation is complete. Now we turn to Harold with the Sports. Harold?"

• • •

Waiting for a doctor's okay to get released from the hospital is never easy. For Sam, it was excruciating that afternoon. With every creak down the hall or opening of a door, Sam cast a hopeful look at his own room's door.

Every hour, he checked the local news stations. Scattered reports added up to a big fat "We don't know what happened," leaving Sam more worried than ever about Jenny and Molly. When they say "full details in an hour," Sam hoped they'd have more. But hour after hour, it was the same thing, like waiting for a hurricane to make landfall. No one quite knows where it's going to land, so news anchors scare everybody along the coast with guesses.

Sam watched for another two hours. Then he reached for the phone.

Hoops picked up on the first ring. "Sam-Man! How are you? Where are you?"

Sam was glad to hear a friendly voice on the other end. "Dosher. The doctor says I have to stay a little longer, but I'm ready to go now. What's the word? I need to know everything. Did everyone get off the boat?"

"I don't have that report, but I can get it. What's your room number? I'll call you back."

Sam struggled to read the numbers on the phone's handset. His head throbbed whenever he turned it, and trying to read made him dizzy. "I'm in room one-twenty-four. You'll have to give me the short version when you find out. Thanks, Hoops. I owe—"

"Naw, Sam-Man. You don't owe me anything. Just get well, hear?"

"Will do, Hoops; will do."

Sam tried to get up to walk around, but catheters were stuck in places he couldn't reach, and tubes jutted out from more than one place on his body. Defeated, Sam fell back on the pillows and stared at the ceiling. By the time Shadow Nurse and a technician entered the room to proffer up more bags of medicine and fluids, Sam was asleep.

CHAPTER FORTY-SIX

Sam woke later that afternoon to sunlight flitting through the window's shades. Within minutes, Dr. Henderson marched in with his entourage.

"Good afternoon, Mr. McClellan. Let's take another look at that leg and get you on it again."

A second technician, a male this time, entered the room with a pair of crutches for Sam to try. He adjusted them to fit Sam when he saw how tall Sam was.

"I want you to start slowly, get the feel of these things first," Dr. Henderson explained. "No races, if you please. Your leg is going to take several weeks to heal, but you'll need to start therapy so you don't forget how to use it. Now, let's get you out of bed. Exercise is important for you."

Dr. Henderson's entourage got to work removing tubes and the catheter. After twenty minutes of fussing with bandages, they left the room with various admonitions about going slowly and resting often. The nurse said if he were a good patient, Sam would be released that evening.

And that was all the encouragement Sam needed. Cautiously, he swung his legs over the side of the bed and propped himself up using the crutches. He struggled to arrange the scant hospital gown, then took his first tentative step.

At first, Sam did exactly as he was told, hobbling slowly around the room. Soon, he had the hang of using crutches, so he headed for the intensive care unit. He felt up for company. Sam hoped Chuck did too.

Dosher Hospital is a narrow two-story affair. Like its larger cousins, it shares an antiseptic smell, but it is easily navigated because of large signs and limited departments vying for a patient's attention.

Sam found the intensive care unit. He tried his best to look casual as he hobbled the corridor of glassed rooms until he found Chuck, being attended to by a technician or a nurse; Sam couldn't tell which. He waited for the technician to leave, then slipped in beside Chuck's hospital bed. He eased himself into a small chair. Chuck had more wires attached to him than an old computer.

"Chuck, it's me. Sam McClellan. Just checking on you, man."

Cracking open a swollen, bruised eye, Chuck's battered mouth twisted into what Sam guessed was a pained smile.

"Sam. You look like you should be in the hospital."

"Yeah, I know." At least Chuck still had a sense of humor. "Chuck, I need you to tell me what happened after you and Mike left the gallery."

The slight smile left Chuck's face. "Oh, that. Sam, I'm really tired now. Can this wait?"

"No, it can't. I need to know exactly what went down. I'm guessing since you were beaten to a bloody pulp and left for dead, you weren't part of the original plan."

Chuck closed the one eye he could open. "I didn't know anything about Lisa's...involvements until you had your little visit with the chief. It was far more than I wanted to know." Chuck sighed heavily. "I was raging. Mike caught sight of me and grabbed me by the arm. I blurted that I was going to the gallery to put a stop to Lisa's messing around. I really thought that's what it was all about.

"When we got there, you and your girlfriends were already having a field day. I didn't want to believe any of what I overheard Chief tell you, but when I saw Lisa's suitcase full of dough, I knew he was telling the truth."

"Did you know Tripp was her half-brother?"

"Yeah, I knew. But I was clueless about his operation until I saw him on the gallery floor beaten by...what's your girlfriend's name? We weren't formally introduced on our little side trip to Southport."

"Molly. And she's really just a friend. Tripp killed her brother, and she wanted revenge. What happened when you left the gallery?"

Well, I put Lisa in cuffs, took her into the office, and was going to take her out the back door, like Mike suggested. Mike cuffed Tripp. Or at least I thought he had. They came into the office too. When I heard a commotion in the front gallery, I moved around the desk to see. Then Mike hit me on the head with the butt of his gun. The next thing I know, I'm down below on a fast-moving boat, *my* hands cuffed in front of me."

"Who was with you?"

"Molly and Jenny were down below with me. I had no idea who was topside at that point, except Andy and Lisa were making out right there where I could see."

"What happened then?"

"Molly pretended to fall on me when we stopped for fuel. She transferred a gun to me. I don't know where she got it. She took her time getting up, like she was giving me time to get ready. I propped myself up against the pedestal of a table behind her.

"Then Andy came down the companionway steps. Molly leaned way over to the right and I got off one shot, but missed. Andy tackled me. I think he would have killed me, but Lisa stopped him, believe it or not. I don't remember anything beyond that."

Sam replayed the scene in the gallery. Molly had grabbed Tripp's gun and tucked it in her jeans. Good for her! Why Tripp didn't remember he'd lost it was irrelevant.

"Huhum."

Sam looked around at a stern-faced nurse clearing her throat.

"Visiting hours are over," she said without stripping her stare from Sam.

"I was just leaving." Sam nodded to Chuck and put his hand on his shoulder. "I'm sorry you had to go through that, Chuck. Get better."

"Thanks, Sam. You didn't tell me what happened to you."

Sam didn't have the heart to tell Chuck about Lisa's marksmanship. "I'll tell you on our next visit. You take care."

As Sam exited, he saw two carbon copies of Chuck coming down the hall. His twin sons. Of course. They were home from college. Sam was glad they'd be able to help Chuck heal.

As Sam hobbled down the hall, he thought through everything he'd done since Lee's murder. He played the "what-if" game again, knowing that his scenarios were irrelevant at this point.

CHAPTER FORTY-SEVEN

Before Sam could reach his room, he saw Chief Dan Singleton coming around the corner.

"There you are," Chief called. "I've been waiting for you, and I was about to give up. Come on."

"Where are we going?"

"The morgue. I called, and they said we could come take a look to see if we know anybody there." Chief slowed his walk so Sam could keep up on his crutches.

"That was a stupid thing to do, you know." Chief pointed at his leg. "The report said you were shot by gunfire that came from a sinking boat. You want to tell me what happened?"

Sam recounted the story. He watched Chief's face redden at the mention of Lisa firing on him, then turning a gun on herself.

"She got what she deserved, I suppose. Let's go visit her." Chief quickened his pace as they approached an unmarked elevator leading to the basement morgue.

Like the rest of the hospital above it, the morgue was long and narrow. A rabbit-warren of ante-rooms and offices led to a cavernous dismal gray room surrounded by shiny metal cabinets. The smell of formaldehyde was so strong that Sam had to catch his breath before entering.

A battered desk sat in one corner and behind it was Dr. Jerry Huff, himself as gray as the room he occupied, pouring over a stack of papers. His bifocals slid the length of his pointy nose as he looked up to greet his visitors.

"Dr. Huff?" Chief bellowed as he entered the room, his voice's small echo returning to Sam's ears as he followed a few hobbles behind.

"Yes? Oh, you must be the fellow who called. The technician said the police might be stopping by."

"Yes. I'm Chief Dan Singleton of the Carolina Beach Police, and this is Detective Sam McClellan."

"I see you are a guest of our fine establishment." Dr. Huff pointed to Sam's hospital gown.

"I am. And the food is definitely four-star quality."

Dr. Huff rolled his dark eyes and rubbed his hand back through thinning hair. "Sure. Now, how can I be of assistance?"

"We would like to know about anybody who came to visit here last night." Chief wasn't wasting any time.

"Okey-dokey. Let's see if you recognize our current contestants."

Dr. Huff shuffled through some of the papers until he found a hardbound log book. Behind him was an ancient computer, obviously off.

"Ah, yes. We had three from last night. Two men, one woman. Sad. Very sad. But hey, it keeps me employed." A flicker of a smile blossomed.

"Two men, one woman," Chief repeated. "Do you know their names? What were the circumstances?"

"Names, no. Circumstances, yes. Perhaps you can identify some or all of them?" Dr. Huff walked toward the cabinets, his gait stilted by a limp. His small frame made reaching the top drawers a challenge, which he overcame by using a stepstool.

The first drawer he slid open was full of sheet. "Domestic. Wife shot him." Dr. Huff was curt.

When Dr. Huff pulled the sheet partially away, Chief shook his head. The partly removed sheet revealed a very large black male.

Dr. Huff recovered the body and slid the drawer back in place. He walked around a corner where two tables lay side by side.

"I'm still working on these." He pulled back the cover from a petite male, this one of Asian descent. "Bar fight. He lost."

Chief shook his head again and moved to the other table. Audibly sucking in his breath, he pulled back the cover.

Sam noted the relief that came over Chief's face. "Who is it?"

"Not anybody I recognize." Chief stepped away so Sam could see a Caucasian woman, small in features, but clearly not any of the three women they were looking for today.

"Domestic. She lost." Dr. Huff casually pointed out matching marks on her neck. "Happens all the time. This one was from Bald Head Island, if you want to know. The husband *said* he found her that way, but the police think otherwise. Don't see anything you like today?"

"Afraid not," said Chief. "But I want you to call me if you get any more."

"Looking for anything in particular?" Dr. Huff sounded a bit like a retail sales clerk.

"A woman and a man, for starters. Boating accident. Possibly two other women." Chief glanced at Sam as he listed the other two women's descriptions.

"Ooh," cheered Dr. Huff. "It sounds positively tantalizing."

Dr. Huff was a little too gleeful for Sam. He turned his crutches around and headed for the door.

Chief gave a thank you and followed Sam. He cleared his throat and talked quietly as they walked toward the elevator that would take them back to the land of the living.

"I'm going to be resigning, Sam. There will be a full-scale investigation. I know I'm going to be kicked for not acting when I suspected something, so I'm letting someone else step up to the plate. Before that happens, though, I want to see you back on the force."

Sam hobbled a little slower as he got onto the waiting elevator. "Chief, I'll stand by you, no matter what comes. You were stupid to get involved with Lisa in the first place, but fortunately for you, stupidity is not a crime."

Chief smiled. "Stupid. Yeah, you could call it that."

"I need to know what happened to Molly and Jenny, first and foremost. Next, I want to see Mike and Andy pay for what they did to Lee."

"I'm working on it now."

"After that, you can call it whatever you want, but an extended vacation would be nice."

"Ditto that."

"Where will you go when you resign, Chief? You think you and your wife can patch it up?"

"Don't know. Trish is pretty mad right now. I told her what happened. Felt like I had to since it's about to be under public scrutiny. She left yesterday for the mountains. When it's all over, maybe we can work things out."

"Well, good luck." Sam was sincere.

They exited the elevator and Chief escorted Sam back to his room. Sam pondered whether there were any other places in town where bodies would be taken, but Chief assured him the local morgue would be their best bet for locating those they sought, given how they died.

Sam heard the phone ring as he said goodbye to the Chief just outside his hospital room. It was Hoops.

"Sam-Man, how you feeling?"

"Better, once I hear what you've got."

"Fine. Dispense with the niceties. The report is that the rescue boat picked up survivors from a sinking vessel; cause of the explosion still under investigation. There was a collision, but you know that already, don't you?" Hoops didn't wait for a reply. "There were no bodies recovered from the wreckage."

"No bodies? But that's impossible! I saw Lisa Owens put a gun to her head and do a swan dive."

"Did you happen to notice her scuba tank?"

Sam whipped his head around at the sound of a familiar voice.

"Molly!" Sam leaped off the bed toward her, nearly falling as he hugged Molly.

Jenny was walking into his room two steps behind Molly, a grin plastered to her bruised face upon seeing Sam lip-lock Molly.

Molly looked dazed when he pulled away and grabbed the phone.

"Hoops, I'll call you back. I have visitors." Sam threw the phone down and bear-hugged Jenny. He held her hand and scooped Molly's in his other hand, leading them to two chairs sitting opposite the hospital bed. "Tell me what happened!"

Jenny started first. "We felt you needed a little help, so we tried to flush Lisa out at the gallery. Molly went in posing as a customer in need of a last-minute gift, and I went in with my paintings a few minutes later. We had her cornered by the time you arrived."

Molly picked up the story. "We figured we were okay when Chuck and Mike showed up, but Mike was in on it. He and Andy beat Chuck up pretty bad, then hauled us off to a speedboat that was waiting at the pier behind the gallery. They didn't know I still had Tripp's gun, and when I got a chance, I gave it to Chuck. He tried to get a shot off, but missed. Andy flew into a rage. I think he would have killed him, but Lisa stopped him."

"You went to Southport?"

"Yeah, after fueling up. Then Mike and Andy hauled Jenny and me off the boat and put us on a larger one, a Beneteau, I think."

"They beat Chuck to death, Sam," Jenny sobbed. "Right there in front of us."

Sam smiled and held her hand. "Chuck's here at the hospital. They did a job on him, but he's a tough guy. He'll be all right." Sam paused as he gently touched her bruised cheek. "What did they do to you?"

"Chuck's alive! Thank goodness they didn't kill him." Jenny's sobs slowed. Then she continued. "I hit my face on Tripp's scuba gear. I could hear the Coast Guard telling us to stop, and Tripp started pulling small tanks and stuff out from under one of the settees. Tripp and Lisa pulled on full-body wetsuits, and Tripp put all the money from the two suitcases into dry bags. He was telling Lisa to tether one to her leg as soon as they got topside. They were getting ready to jump overboard when the boat was broadsided. When I fell over, I landed face-first on his tank. He had to push me off to get out of there."

Molly chimed in. "I was pulling Jenny up the companionway steps when I saw Lisa fire a gun at the water. She held a gun up to her head. I waited for the shot, but it didn't come. Then she dove into the water, with the tank, tether, and treasure. Tripp was slithering off the other side of the boat like the snake he is."

"When we got to the aft railing, the Coast Guard was taking Mike and Andy back to the rescue boat," Jenny explained. "We were scared they didn't know we were there, but they came back for us. We both thought you were dead back at the gallery. It was only when we got to the rescue boat that we saw you there, passed out. They took us to an urgent care center on Oak Island, waited around for us to be seen, then took us back to my condo. All the way back to Carolina Beach—on the Coast Guard rescue boat! They told us you were here at Dosher."

"We had to walk to the gallery to get Jenny's car," Molly interjected. "Otherwise, we would have been here much sooner. That, and we didn't wake up until about noon today." Molly's smile was back. "May a thousand—"

Sam wouldn't let her finish. He pulled her to his side and kissed her hard.

Jenny giggled, then reached for a cup of water on the bedside table for Sam. "The nurse at the station down the hall said you were getting out of here this evening. We thought you might like a ride home."

Sam looked at Molly, then glanced at Jenny. "Molly doesn't have a home anymore." Then turning to Molly: "I'm sorry you got hurt in all of this."

Molly's back straightened. "I won't be homeless for long. Besides, I think I have a place to stay for a while." She smiled.

Sam's mind raced with what-ifs again.

Molly seemed to hear his gears shifting. "With Jenny. I'm staying with Jenny. And it looks like you will be too until we can get you back on board *Angel*."

Sam smiled. "I have a dinghy, now. Seems Mike was in a generous mood, so I borrowed his. I'm sorry about your boat, Molly."

"No sweat, dude. I'm going to raise her." Molly brightened. Then she leaned over and kissed Sam's cheek. "Thanks for the affection. I was beginning to think Tripp was the only one who'd pay attention to my good looks and natural abilities."

Sam's ribs hurt when he stopped laughing. Then he helped Jenny and Molly gather his things to go.

CHAPTER FORTY-EIGHT

Late morning sun flooded the living room, tickling Sam's face, urging him to open tired eyes. Squinting, he saw Jenny and Molly on the porch, coffee mugs in hand. He was thankful they had rescued him from the hospital, and hopeful there was an extra cup of coffee.

Hobbling crutchless to the kitchen, Sam found a mug and joined the girls on the porch where he took in a majestic view of sky, surf, and sand cluttered by neon umbrellas and coolers.

"Morning."

"Feeling better?" Molly piped up.

"A bit. My leg is still throbbing a little, but I'll manage."

"You sure you should be up without crutches?"

"They're a pain in the butt. I'll be fine."

"Good." Jenny dragged her gaze from the ocean's gentle swells. "Then you cook breakfast. Molly, did you know Sam can cook?"

"I do declare!" Molly feigned surprise. "Another wonder."

Sam smirked and hobbled back to the kitchen. Pulling eggs out of the fridge, he realized how hungry he was for some real food. Soon Jenny and Molly joined him in making and enjoying a huge breakfast.

As the last dish landed in the dishwasher, Jenny instructed Molly to help herself to something to wear, and she helped Sam find a clean shirt, along with giving him instructions to drop his dirty clothes in the bathroom hamper.

"Don't know how you're going to manage to get around on your boat. We'll need to move it to a marina so you don't have to row. Where is it?"

"The Causeway. The dinghy is supposed to be behind the restaurant near the dumpster. A Coast Guard friend left it there for me. And I'll be all right, once I get aboard."

"You are a stubborn cuss, aren't you?" Jenny scolded. "Perhaps Molly could be helpful on your boat?"

Sam changed the subject. "Okay if I wear this one?" He pulled out a deep Navy blue T-shirt with Rensselaer Polytechnic Institute emblazed on the front.

"Sure. Take it. It was Lee's favorite. His father went there, and they enjoyed going to a game every now and again when they visited in New York."

"Oh, Jen, I didn't know. I'll find a different shirt."

"It's all right. Really."

Sam pulled on the shirt and watched for Jenny's reaction. He got a smile out of her.

"I need to fetch my truck. It's still in Navassa."

"It may not be in one piece anymore, Sam," Molly interjected from the doorway.

"I know, but I still need to get it. I'd like to go check my boat first, though, if you don't mind. Then we can head to Southport to get Lee's Mustang and see about my truck."

"That's fine." Jenny reached for her car keys. "Better grab your crutches. You may want them on your boat later."

• • •

The dinghy was indeed where Hoops said it would be, leaning up against the dumpster behind the Causeway Restaurant. The trio struggled to get it to the bank of the river, but once it was on the slope, they managed it easily to the water's edge, holding fast to the painter line while a limping Sam climbed in and snapped the oars in waiting locks.

"You may need these," Molly cajoled him as she threw Sam's crutches into the dinghy. "Maybe keep them for fishing sometime."

"We'll wait for you in the restaurant, Sam," Jenny called as she walked back up the short bank to the diner.

"I won't be long," Sam answered, sitting in the dinghy, taking in the view of his boat between strokes.

A few strong pulls and Sam maneuvered the dinghy aft of *Angel*, bobbing patiently on her anchor. Sam reached for the stern-mounted ladder and tied the dinghy's painter line; then he hoisted himself up the three steps of the boarding ladder to the deck.

Half-sitting and half-limping over the railing, Sam looked at the bank where Molly still stood. He could see she was shading her eyes, looking not toward Sam but another boat nearby.

Three steps forward to the edge of the cockpit, Sam saw the wooden boards were removed from the forward-facing hatch. Before he could turn around and get off the boat, a hand shot up through the open aft hatch, catching Sam's ankle and tripping him. He fell face-forward into the cockpit, yelping when he hit the port-side locker with his left elbow.

From his prone position, Sam could hear Molly yelling something, but the coaming was so high from his vantage point that he couldn't see her. Rolling on his back in an attempt to shake lose the hand that held fast, Sam's nose brushed a hard metal barrel.

"Up. Slowly. There's someone I want you to meet." With eyes full of hate and a voice to match, Lisa casually waved at Molly on the shore from her place in the forward companionway. "Too bad your girlfriend didn't come aboard. I was hoping to have a little conversation with her over her choice of friends." Her gun was at Sam's nose, hidden from view of the bank.

"I could say the same of you," Sam said, slowly sitting up. His good leg was being held fast. He saw that the hand holding it was attached to Tripp, emerging from the aft cabin, quite pleased with himself.

Sam inched his way toward the cockpit slowly, feeling the constant pressure of Lisa's gun in his face. Tripp let go of his leg, allowing him to sit up on his knees on the teak cockpit grates.

Lisa slowly sat on the bench nearest to Sam, revealing who stood silently behind her. Standing on the companionway stairs to the main salon and smiling at Sam was the loud-mouthed yachtie from Sam's former marina.

"I don't think we've ever been formally introduced. I'm Marcus Johnson."

"As in Johnson's Fishery?"

"Dear Old Dad," called Tripp, nodding as he stepped behind Sam and pushed him forward toward the main salon.

"Or 'Daddy,' if you like," Lisa chimed in.

"The same." The Fat Man ignored his children and plowed ahead. "You have been a busy fellow. Tripp and Lisa have told me all about the gallery incident. And, of course, I know you have a penchant for wrecking boats and businesses." His warped smile revealed gold-capped teeth. "*Sabrina* was my favorite boat, you know. I was surprised she could be destroyed so easily by an old hulk of a boat like the one you were on." He sighed for emphasis. "Well, it's time to put an end to all that mess."

Sam noted the silencer on the end of Fat Man's gun as he used it to motion Sam to come below.

"Let's take him for a little ride, Dad. It's too crowded here." Tripp motioned at the waterway.

"Besides, I'm getting hot," Lisa chimed in. "Let's take a ride to someplace more…intimate in the air-conditioned boat."

"Now, Lisa, dear, this will only take a moment," soothed Fat Man, as if calming a toddler's tantrum. "Then we'll be on our way."

"Dad, this old tub will sink if you start shooting," agreed Tripp. "Let's at least get far enough out so we can take care of him off the deck without any mess to clean. I'm so sick of cleaning up guts. Let's take your boat."

Like a statue, Tripp waited for his father's orders. He seemed to Sam more like a teenager seeking parental approval than the leader of a drug ring.

Tripp only moved when Fat Man acquiesced with a nod and a short "Fine."

Tripp yanked Sam's shirt backward toward the aft deck. "You heard what he said. Let's go." Then turning to Fat Man: "We'll meet you there, Dad."

Sam climbed slowly back up to the aft deck, the one step seeming like Mount Everest in its height. He quickly scanned the bank for Molly, but he didn't see her. To his other side, he watched Lisa and Fat Man dismount *Angel* into a waiting motorized inflatable tender. He hadn't noticed the tender before from the angle he'd approached, but he saw it now as it raced toward a two-story yacht of blinding white.

Tripp pushed Sam down the aft ladder, nearly tumbling him into the bouncing dinghy. Then Tripp turned his back on Sam to hop down the ladder himself.

In a fleeting rush, Sam grabbed one of his crutches and slammed it into Tripp's side, knocking him half off the ladder. Tripp regained his grip and pulled a gun on Sam from his higher vantage point.

"Try that again and I'll take care of you right where you sit, just like I popped your partner." Tripp carefully made his way into the little boat. Without looking away from Sam again, he untied the painter line with one hand. "Now row." Tripp pointed to the gargantuan hull a few hundred feet forward of *Angel*.

Sam marveled at the gleaming gold lettering on the high transom: *Jezebel*. Named for Lisa, no doubt.

"Your father likes big toys, I see—to compensate for how little a man he really is beneath all that blubber, huh?" Sam took his time rowing, goading Tripp. "I guess he told you what you were doing was okay, didn't he? He must tell you lots of things. Like how to run the business."

"Shut up."

"He's the boss man, isn't he? He's calling the shots, and you're just his little gopher. I see how this works. Must have been fun growing up with him as your guide."

"Just row, Mouth."

Sam didn't let up. "Must piss you off that he loves Lisa more, doesn't it? I mean, she's getting all the glory, isn't she? You're just down here doing the dirty work. You know, if you had been smart, you would have alternated hotels where you met to take his orders. Then you wouldn't have had to torch the place." Sam was reaching. "But Dear Old Dad figured if anyone was going down, it wasn't going to be him. That's what he was stopping by to tell you, wasn't it, the day I came to visit you at the fishery?"

"Just shut up! You don't know what you're talking about!"

"Oh, I think I do. You and Lisa slid over the side of *Seawitch* like a couple of cowards because you couldn't handle the mess you'd made. What did you do—swim to this boat? Or perhaps to his house? Let me guess. He's got a place on Bald Head Island, and you ran home to Daddy. You're like a bully on a playground, and you gotta do it to show your old man you're big enough for his affection." Sam dropped the oar handles and waited. It didn't take but a second.

"I said SHUT THE F—"

As he spoke, Tripp stood up to swing at Sam, but Sam was faster, whipping a crutch across Tripp's face. Tripp's gun flew into the water as he slumped over the inflatable side of the dinghy, his head landing in the brown silted river.

Pondering only for a second, Sam grabbed the painter line and tied Tripp's hands behind his back and to the plank seat in the dinghy. Then he pulled Tripp's head out of the water, smiling at the blood trickling down Tripp's chin. "That's for Lee, you slime bag."

Sam picked up the oars and pulled the last two strokes to *Jezebel*. With the tip of an oar, he pushed Fat Man's dinghy aside from the boat's long ladder and used a bungee cord to secure the dinghy to *Jezebel's* massive boarding ladder.

Peeking over the transom, Sam relaxed at what he saw. Fat Man was sprawled on the enormous deck, head cocked to one side and his tongue hanging from his bloody mouth. Lisa, down on her knees, was begging Molly not to shoot her with her own gun.

Sam labored over to Lisa. He yanked a plastic tie strap from the underside of an overstuffed yellow-striped cockpit cushion and fastened Lisa's hands behind her to the pedestal of a large teak table.

Then Sam tenderly squatted in front of her. "I think I'll let Chief Singleton take care of you from here. It's not his *jurisdiction*, but I bet he and the local boys can work something out."

Pulling himself up by the table, Sam entered the pilot house and called the Coast Guard to report the incident.

When Sam finished giving the particulars, he hobbled back to Molly, still frozen over Lisa. Sam noticed for the first time she was drenched.

"You want to tell me what happened?"

"I recognized his boat. This boat," Molly said without emotion. "It's the one I delivered to the fat one on Bald Head the night you and I met."

"So you decided to go swimming again."

"Yep. I made it over the transom just as I heard their dinghy motor revving up from the other side of your boat, so I hid in the pilot house. When the guy got close enough, I decked him."

"Glass jaw?"

"Thankfully. Little Miss Lisa here was so surprised that she nearly threw her gun at me," Molly added. "And here we are."

"And here we are." Sam inched closer, Molly's strength and resolve apparent. Sirens wailed on the water and in the Causeway Restaurant's parking lot. Sam saw Jenny waving from the shore.

CHAPTER FORTY-NINE

"Sam-Man!"

"Hey, Hoops." Sam stretched out on his cockpit cushion, measuring tape in one hand, phone in the other. "What's up?"

"Just wanted to check on you. I got the full report here, so you can come by next time you're in town."

"Thanks, Hoops. I'll get it when I can. I'm car-less right now. Mine was trashed in Navassa."

"What are you going to do?"

"I thought I might go sailing. I've taken a leave of duty since the investigation is over. Now that August is here, I thought maybe I'd finally head up to Norfolk. My son's stationed there, and it's been a while since we had a chance to visit."

"Too bad he's not stationed here with me. Then you could come see him anytime you wanted." Hoops was sincere.

"Yeah. Actually, I think I'm ready for a break from the beach. Things have been a little nutty."

"I hear ya, Sam-Man. Listen; we're having our end-of-summer barbeque tonight. Can you come?"

"Sounds good to me, Hoops. I need to say goodbye to a few friends, anyway. Can I call you later if I need a ride? I already sold my truck."

"Sure. You call, I'll be there to get you. Take care."

"You too. And Hoops? Thanks for your help in all of this. I owe you one."

"Fine. You can bring the steaks."

"Fair enough."

Sam got back to his measuring. This last cockpit cushion was giving him fits because its tattered cover was shredded beyond recognition. He had had to strip what was left of it and make a new pattern before he could make a new cover for it. This time, Sam chose a smart blue, green, and white striped fabric. Matching the strips at the corners was harder than he thought it would be. Anxious to finish his project, Sam wanted to return Jenny's sewing machine and her inverter charger this morning when she came to pick him up.

Jenny had eagerly agreed to run Sam around, collecting supplies for his cruise, and Sam was pleased to give her something to focus on this week. Now that the investigation into Carolina Beach's police force was over, Sam sensed Jenny's adrenaline waning. He watched her grow pensive, so he came up with a list of things he "needed her help" with, and it seemed to be working. Today was her last trip to the Causeway moorings to fetch him and run him around.

Looking up from his frustrations, Sam saw the Acapulco blue Mustang pull into the Causeway Restaurant's parking lot. He brightened when he recognized Molly in the passenger seat.

Rowing to the bank with the sewing machine safely between his feet, Sam played what-ifs in his head. His desire was clear, but the path to it was not.

"Thanks for the ride, Jen. Hi, Molly. Long time no see."

"I've been busy." Molly looked down at her red Keds. "Been working on *Hullabaloo*."

"How's it coming?"

"She's up, but she's a mess. Hoops pulled some strings for me and reported her as a hazard to navigation. My buddies own a boat small enough to get into the shallow waters, but big enough to have some megacompressors. We filled her with giant balloons to get her up, then pumped her dry and towed her back to Boat Works in Wilmington. It's going to take some doing, but I'll get her going again. My friends are taking pity on me and doing the work at a greatly reduced rate. I'll have to deliver a few boats to pay for her, but since a lot of snowbirds get tired of cruising once they finish the islands, I'll have work bringing their boats home again."

Sam took it in for a second. "So you don't have time to take a sail?"

"Not really. I've got three boats lined up over the next six weeks. I caught a break today because I…. Well, I wanted to come and give you a special blessing before you started your trip."

Sam put the sewing machine into the trunk and got into the backseat as Molly blessed his boat first and then him.

"May the sun always be shining, a fair wind at your back, and the waves kind as you sail to…where are you going?"

"Norfolk. To see my son."

"Right. As you sail to Norfolk and beyond for new adventures untold."

"Thanks. That sounds vaguely familiar."

"It's a variation of an old Irish blessing," Jenny chimed in. "Lee used to paraphrase it before we set sail every weekend." She smiled as she drove. "Where are we heading?"

"West Marine. I need to get oil and a filter. Then to the grocery store, if you don't mind. Thanks for running me around today."

"I'm happy to do it. When do you think you'll leave?"

"I was going to leave tomorrow, but Hoops called. He's having his famous 'Summer's Over' party tonight, so starting tomorrow may be a little rough. You two should come to the barbeque, too."

"Of course we'll come," Jenny answered for Molly, who sat, unusually quiet, in the front seat.

"Just let us know when. Molly's staying with me until her boat is habitable again. Frankly, I'm happy to have the company. A party would be fun."

Sam's phone rang. It was Dan Singleton.

"Sam, I thought you might like to know. Tripp Johnson finally broke. They hadn't planned to dive from the boat so soon. Tripp said *Seawitch* was rigged to blow up when they were farther away from the coast. They were going to let Mike and Andy roast, if you can believe that! Molly and Jenny would have been unfortunate additions to the barbeque, but that didn't seem to bother Tripp too much. What did make him mad was how you spoiled their little party. We got 'em right up to Commissioner Martin. He's none too happy about our discovery, but that's his problem, now. Thanks for your help in breaking the case."

"Glad to do my part. Did you get my letter?"

"Yeah, I passed it along to the new guy. He wasn't happy about losing you, but I think having Chuck back made it a little easier."

"How is Chuck handling things?"

"He seems resolved. He got a promotion, you know. About the time I was leaving, he started piecing the case together for the D.A. He's still pretty mad at me because of, well, you know, my fling with Lisa. I hope he'll get over it, though. I really didn't mean to hurt him."

"I hear ya. Affairs are never meant to hurt anyone. But in the long run, we just end up hurting ourselves." Sam took in his own words, letting each one sink deeper than a weighted fishing hook. "Give him my best next time you see him. You heading back to the mountains?"

"Yeah. I just came down to close on the house here. We got a little place, a cottage, my wife calls it, so we'll be fixing it up to storybook standards for a while, I suppose. It's a little cooler in Blowing Rock. If you feel the need to get away from the water some time, come visit."

"Thanks. I will."

Sam relayed what little news Dan Singleton had to offer, hoping Jenny and Molly wouldn't mind revisiting their ordeal.

Molly smiled. "May a million fire ants infest Tripp's cell as he sleeps naked on the ground."

Jenny and Sam cheered.

CHAPTER FIFTY

After Sam stowed his provisions and tied down the dinghy on the forward deck, he fired up *Angel*'s engine. Unhooking his line from the mooring ball, he checked the current. At this speed, he'd make it back to Carolina Beach in time to catch a transient slip at his old marina.

The afternoon's trip gave Sam time to think, time to plan. It was the first time in four years he had opened a chart book to plot his course to Norfolk. Seeing the contours of shoreline and depths charted on paper revived his hope of cruising.

Disappointed that Molly had so flatly turned down his invitation to go sailing, Sam paused when he realized it had been about as vague a proposition as he'd made in recent history. Molly was different. Something stirred inside when he thought about her and about what possibilities might be ahead for both of them. Sam actually thought about attempting a relationship—a good, solid one—with Molly…if she were interested, that is. So far, he couldn't quite tell.

While tying *Angel* alongside a long unsheltered transient dock at the edge of the marina, Sam was pleased to see the docks were fairly empty. No sign of the squirt of a dockmaster anywhere, making sliding into the marina unnoticed (and unaccounted for) all that much sweeter.

Sam showered in the dockside bathhouse, reveling in the hot water that flowed over his tanned body. The past few months had been a time for answering far too many questions during the investigation. Yet he'd had enough time to take *Angel* out, including taking the boat on one "shakedown" run to Bald Head Island where he had walked to the top of the lighthouse for the fantastic view. Sam had rented a golf cart and toured the island—all of it. When it was over, he pondered what difference that simple ride might have made with his ex-wife. Maybe something, or maybe nothing at all. Either way, when he returned to a cold beer on his boat, he felt relieved to be free of that relationship so he could focus on something new…perhaps with Molly, he pondered.

When he was shaved and dressed, Sam walked the few blocks to Jenny's condo in the sticky heat of August with a cooler in hand. In a few more weeks, all signs of visiting tourists would disappear. In a few more weeks, the humidity would disappear, too.

• • •

"I got some steaks for us, Hoops. And I'm bringing friends." Sam spoke into his phone from the quiet of Jenny's porch. A few roasted beach-goers lingered on the sand in the late afternoon sun.

"Great! You need a ride?"

"No, I'm set. You ready for company?"

"You bet, Sam-Man. Come anytime. I got a few guys here already, so we'll have a nice crowd. I'll fire up the grill and get the fixings."

Sam, Jenny, and Molly took the Mustang to Hoops' house two miles away in Kure Beach, a continuation of the spit of sand on which Carolina Beach sits. A dozen or so people milled around the sound-side patio, beers in hand. Sam noted a mix of Coasties and others there, and he wished he'd bought more food.

There was plenty, as it seemed to be a potluck affair. Sam chatted with almost everyone, then breezed toward a quiet Molly, sitting in a corner like a dejected high schooler at a dance.

"Everything all right?" Sam offered her a Yuengling.

"Fine." Molly didn't smile, but she took the beer. "Thanks."

Sam plunged ahead. "What's the plan?"

"Plan?"

"Where do we go from here?"

"We?" Molly brightened. "I thought you didn't want a partner."

"I didn't think I did. But now I'm not so sure." Sam gave Molly his best smile, hoping she'd get what he was trying to say.

"Well, when you figure it out, you let me know." Molly got up and smoothed her skirt, one she borrowed from Jenny since all of her things were mud-encased or mildewed from *Hullabaloo*'s sinking. Now toe to toe with Sam, she whispered, "Partner."

Sam stepped back, no longer sure of what he'd unleashed. "I just thought maybe we might go sailing or something. I'm heading up to Norfolk to see my son, and I thought when I come back—"

"I probably won't be here," Molly interrupted, realizing her blunder. "I'm heading to Florida to see Deloris and Emily. *Hullabaloo* is going to take some time to fix up, so I'll probably spend the winter with them."

"Oh. I see." Now it was Sam's turn to feel dejected. He wished he could decide what he wanted with Molly. The attraction was real, but he didn't want to commit to anything long-term. Still, to be summarily rejected stung. Sam tried to cover his disappointment.

"Well, if you change your mind and want to convert from the dark side of powerboating, you let me know. We'll go sailing."

Molly glared at him. "Don't bet on it. Powerboats rule. *Hullabaloo* got you out of more than one jam, as I recall, so don't slander powerboats."

"Mol, I didn't mean anything by it." Why was she so upset?

"Never mind. Thanks for the beer. Have a great visit with your son. And I really did mean every word of the blessing today. I hope you travel safely." Her smile returned.

"Thanks. And I hope you get the boat back to where you had her before. She's a great boat. Really."

Sam watched for a flicker of the earlier attraction he'd recognized in Molly's eyes. He wasn't sure how to read her tonight. He watched her raise her hand in a tight salute before disappearing around the side of the house.

Sam pondered briefly about going after her. Before he could move, Jenny tapped him on the shoulder.

"Lovers' quarrel?"

"We weren't lovers, Jenny. I'm not sure what we were, or are, but I can assure you we weren't lovers."

"Too bad." Jenny voiced Sam's thoughts, then grabbed up his hand and dropped a key into it. It was the key to the Mustang.

"I want you to have it." Jenny was beaming. "I'll keep it safe until you return from your cruise. The key will stay in the conch shell near the garage."

"I don't know what to say, Jenny. That car is worth a good bit of money. You should keep it. Or sell it for cash."

"I've made up my mind, Sam. I want you to have it. Lee would have wanted you to have it, too. Now, I won't take no for an answer, and that's final. I've already signed the title over to you."

Sam hugged her. "Thank you, Jenny. I'll treasure this gift. Not just the car, though it's sweet, but the gift of knowing you think highly enough of me to give me something so precious. Thank you."

"You are welcome. Thank you for finding out what happened to Lee. Now go get Molly." Jenny pulled away from Sam's embrace. "I'll get a ride home."

Sam nodded. He quickly made the rounds to his host and friends, then headed for the Mustang. He looked up and down the street, but he saw no sign of Molly.

Driving to Jenny's, Sam thought of the many nights he'd spent hanging out there with Lee. Tonight, there were no lights on. Sam pulled into the darkened driveway. He hid the key in a conch shell by the garage door, then walked to the marina. He had hoped to see Molly once more. But then again, he wasn't sure what he'd say to her if he did.

CHAPTER FIFTY-ONE

Her silhouette startled him. As Sam walked toward *Angel*, he could just barely see her shape sitting on the aft rail in the dim light of the marina's transient dock. Two steps closer, and he was sure it was her.

"What are the chances?" he muttered.

Sam flapped his arms and hissed, but Kathy the Mallard didn't budge from her perch.

"Well, at least I won't get kicked out for having a pet this time. Kathy, you can stay the night. Again. But in the morning, I'm leaving. You'll have to leave, too."

Kathy raised her head in apparent acknowledgment, then hopped down on the aft deck atop a nest of coiled line for the night.

. . .

The next day, in the calm of early morning under a pale blue sky, Sam secured everything below and above for his cruise. He was happy to be getting underway, despite his fine-feathered traveling companion's presence, yet something nagged at him. Still, he poured a travel mug full of black coffee before washing and storing the coffeepot.

It was a fair day for sailing. Wisps of skyward mare's tails signaled approaching wind—a good omen. The weather report on the radio confirmed it was a good day to get going, so Sam fired up the engine and moved topside to untie the three lines that tethered him to the marina—and to Carolina Beach.

Starting forward, Sam noted the wind coming off the dock. He untied the bow line first, planning to let the wind pivot *Angel* from the stern. Moving back toward *Angel*'s midsection, Sam leaned down to let go of the line when he heard Molly shout.

"Wait!"

Seeing a large box in her arms, Sam's heart soared. He retied the dock line and helped her aboard, setting the package in the cockpit.

"I'm glad I caught you!" Molly panted. "I wanted to talk before you left…. I want to apologize for last night."

"It's okay, Molly."

"No, it isn't. I was childish last night, and I'm sorry."

"You want to talk about it?"

"It's simple, really. I'm just jealous you are pursuing your dream. And I'm essentially grounded."

"You don't have to be, Molly. You could come with me. We'll do some sailing on the Chesapeake; then you can catch a bus back here to continue working on *Hullabaloo*. I'll be back after a while." Sam stepped closer and put his hand on Molly's, searching her face for a glimmer of hope.

"I can't. I have too much to do on the boat, and I really need to get those deliveries done to pay for her repairs and restoration." Molly bit her lip. "Another time?"

"Another time, then." Sam kissed her quickly on her cheek.

Molly climbed off the boat. Looking aft, she saw Kathy. "Your first mate?"

"Apparently so. She'll fly off when she figures out I'm heading north, not south."

"Maybe. Oh, the box is a care package Jenny and I put together for you. Enjoy it, Sam. And keep in touch." Molly untied the line from the dock and tossed it to Sam, then mirrored his walk aft to get the last line.

"You too, Molly. You too." Sam waved one last time before putting the boat into forward gear, forward to Norfolk.

THE END

PREVIEW OF THE NEXT SAM MCCLELLAN TALE:

STUNG!

Sam McClellan smelled popcorn. He walked across the polished wooden floors of the clubhouse toward the smell into a bright kitchen with hideous blue cabinets. A spindly man with a scraggly ponytail and matching beard greeted him without turning away from the microwave.

"Hello. Can I help you?"

"I'm looking for the dockmaster."

"Looks like you found him," the man said over his shoulder. "Name's Ed Caglioni. You need a slip?"

"If you could pull me into one, that'd be great. My engine died so I anchored out in the creek. I'm guessing it's the fuel pump."

"Fuel pump, eh?" Ed pulled the finished popcorn out of the microwave and turned to face Sam. "What makes you think that?" He shoved a greasy hand into the bag of popcorn he was holding, then offered it to Sam.

Sam declined with a shake of his head, even though his stomach was growling loud enough to be heard.

"I checked everything else…the filter's littered. I haven't been out in a while…."

"And you didn't know you were supposed to check it all out before you left the dock," Ed interrupted crossly. "You know that's the most expensive part of the engine. What kind you got?"

Sam folded his arms. "I did check things before I left the dock, and everything was fine. And yes, I realize it's going to cost me. Can you help me or not?"

"Aww, don't get all upset. I just see so many people hop on boats without a clue about how to manage 'em. We don't need to pull you into a slip to fix it, though. That'll save you some money. Let's go look at the calendar and I'll see when I can get to it."

"Are you the only mechanic around?"

"I'm the only one you want working on your boat around here, I can tell you that." Ed strolled—no, strutted—across the sitting area of the clubhouse and into his office. "We got bathrooms with showers here, and washers and dryers, if you need 'em. Ordinarily, they're reserved for folks in the slips, but since I'm going to work on your boat, you can use 'em."

"Thanks. When do you think you can fit me in?"

When he replied, Ed sounded suspiciously like Deputy Barney Fife from an old television show. "Weeeellll, I got a bottom job ahead of you, so it may be Tuesday before I can install it. What kind of an engine is it?"

"Volvo. I'll get the manual for you. Tuesday of next week?"

"Yep. That's the soonest I can get to it. I charge fifty bucks an hour, and once I get the part, it's gonna take me about a day. That suit you, er, what did you say your name is?" Ed motioned with the popcorn bag for Sam to sit in a ratty chair unlike the fine ones out in the lounge area.

"Sam McClellan. And it has to be done." Sam sat down and stretched out his long legs.

"Where are you bound?"

"Norfolk."

"Edenton's a little out of the way," Ed offered as he filled out a work order form.

"I have an aunt here in town. I thought I'd come for a short visit."

"Oh? Who's your aunt?" Ed turned the paperwork around for Sam to sign, and he smiled a toothy grin under his popcorn-encrusted mustache like a shark about to take a bite of his prey.

"Lou McClellan. I haven't seen her since I was a kid, so I'll have to borrow your phone book to find out where she lives."

Ed's smile suddenly vanished and his voice grew cold as he sat upright. "No need. She's on Oak Street, just a few blocks up from the river on the other side of our main street in town, which is actually Broad Street. You saw the dock at the foot of Broad when you sailed in, so it's a short walk from there." Ed paused for a second and leaned in toward Sam conspiratorially so Sam could smell a mix of fuel and alcohol on his breath. "Are you coming now because of what she did?"

"What did she do?" Sam was puzzled.

"She murdered her neighbor. Nicest guy you wanta meet, and she turned her killer bees lose on him. Killed him just a few days ago. Says she didn't do it, but everyone in town knows she hated him."

"Why did she hate him?"

"Well, for years and years, your dear aunt and Harvey Bishop were real friendly toward each other. They were so friendly, in fact, he'd asked her to marry him, town folk say. Well, she said she'd think about it. While she was thinking about it, his daughter shows up—a daughter he never knew he had—and Lou got all mad at him. She told everyone in town he was a pervert, and she was sick of being his neighbor. She was hoping to turn the town against him, but his family's been here a long, long time, and he wasn't about to go anywhere. He tried to calm her down, but she never did let up. So it don't surprise me one bit that she offed him."

"You seem to know a lot about the case," Sam said, standing up to leave.

"Yep, everybody knows all about it. Edenton is a small community. We're like a family, see. Sign here, and I'll order your pump."

"So you turn on one of your own just like that?" Sam glared at Ed Caglioni as he walked out without signing the work order.

"I can't order your part until you sign!" Ed called after him. "Look; I'm sorry about your aunt, but don't let that get in the way of getting your engine fixed."

Sam slammed the clubhouse door so hard that its glass-pane rattled as if it would shatter. Untying his dinghy's painter line from the dock, he hopped in and cranked the motor. Sam exited the marina, creating as much of a wake as his small two-stroke outboard could manage; then he sped past his boat and down the creek toward the town docks of Edenton.

ABOUT THE AUTHOR

North Carolina author Laura S. Wharton writes sea adventure/suspense/mystery novels for adults and mysteries for children. Award-winning adult titles include *The Pirate's Bastard* (historical fiction), set in colonial North Carolina on the coast; it was nominated for a Sir Walter Raleigh Award for Fiction. The award-winning *Leaving Lukens* (historical fiction) is set in 1942 as World War II encroaches on a small North Carolina coastal village. Her newest mystery, *In Julia's Garden,* will be released in 2015.

She's also the author of four mysteries for children, including *Mystery at the Phoenix Festival*, the award-winning series, *Mystery at the Lake House #1: Monsters Below*, and *Mystery at the Lake House #2: The Mermaid's Tale*, and *The Wizard's Quest*. All of Laura's books involve adventure, fun, a little history, and sailboats. (Laura is a recovering sailor who could backslide at any moment!) Laura Wharton lives in Mt. Airy, North Carolina, with her husband and son, fellow author William Wharton.

Learn more about Laura and her books at
www.LauraWhartonBooks.com.

ACKNOWLEDGMENTS

I hope you have enjoyed reading this book as much as I enjoyed writing it. I thank the following people who contributed their expertise and support: the kind folks at Broad Creek Press, most excellent editor, Tyler Tichelaar, and Fusion Creative Works for their cover and interior design.

A shout-out is necessary for the service men and women who lose their lives in the line of duty battling villains like the ones in this book. Whether they be police officers, firefighters, or military personnel, they do what the rest of us can barely comprehend—and all because it's the right thing to do.

No story would be complete without saying a huge thank you to my parents, who have always shared with me their love of the English language. Growing up in a house full of music, love, and laughter, I quickly learned the value of a good story, a snappy comment, and the proper timing for a well-crafted punch line to a joke. May the fun stories never end!

—Laura S. Wharton
2015